GUNS OF THE VALPIAN

SURVIVAL WARS BOOK 6

ANTHONY JAMES

© 2018 Anthony James
All rights reserved

The right of Anthony James to be identified as the author of this work has been asserted by him in accordance with the Copyright, Designs and Patents Act, 1988

The characters and events portrayed in this book are fictitious. Any similarity to real persons, living or dead, is coincidental and not intended by the author

This book is sold subject to the condition that it shall not, by way of trade or otherwise, be lent, resold, hired out, or otherwise circulated without the publisher's prior consent in any form of binding or cover other than that in which it is published and without a similar condition including this condition being imposed upon the subsequent purchaser

Cover Design by Dan Van Oss www.covermint.design

Follow Anthony James on Facebook at facebook.com/anthonyjamesauthor.

CHAPTER ONE

FOR CAPTAIN JOHN NATHAN DUGGAN, his crew and soldiers, it was not a good day.

The ESS *Crimson* lay at an angle on the surface of Nistrun. One of its landing legs was gone – torn away by the savagery of its recent landing. Two more of the support legs groaned under the additional weight they were forced to bear. The exterior of the once beautiful spaceship was a ragged mess. Chunks of its armour plating had melted away, which, combined with the intolerable heat the hull had been subjected to, turned the clean lines into a smeared parody of the original. Aft, there were two enormous holes, irregular in shape, but easily identified as the result of plasma missile impacts.

It was daytime on Nistrun and the sun beat upon the barren surface of the planet, preventing the blisteringly hot metal of the spaceship from cooling down. The thin air shimmered, almost vibrating with the immense heat.

Inside, the bridge walls creaked and pinged as they responded to the effects of heat and stress. The warship had come down only thirty minutes before and the crew were already getting edgy. This deep into enemy space, there were numerous possibilities to worry about, not least of which was the alien base they'd identified on the way in.

Duggan had spoken to Lieutenant Ortiz in the troops' quarters shortly after the landing and was relieved when she reported nothing other than minor injuries. He didn't desire additional deaths on his conscience, particularly when he had so much else on his plate.

"Sounds like we're falling apart," said Lieutenant Frank Chainer.

Commander Lucy McGlashan looked up from her console on the other side of the bridge. "The ship is far too solid for that to happen."

"Come on!" said Duggan. "There's no time for small talk. I need you to give me information about the enemy installation. I can't make a decision without having a better idea of what we detected." He used the word *decision* as though he had some influence over their future. At the moment, he wasn't sure that was entirely the case.

"Sorry, sir," said Chainer. "My mouth talks independently of my brain sometimes."

"You don't say?" said Lieutenant Bill Breeze.

Breeze was in front of his own console, trying to figure out a way to divert power into the *Crimson*'s engines. At the moment, their output was close to zero and certainly insufficient for lift off.

"The drives aren't responding, sir," he said, providing his seventh or eighth repetition of the same bad news. "Without the main core, there's no hope of a quick repair."

"Is the core completely out of action? Permanently, I mean?" asked Duggan.

"I might be able to get a few cycles out of it eventually." Breeze didn't continue. It was quite obvious that even if the core flickered into life, it was too badly damaged to get them through the Helius Blackstar again. Unless something drastic changed, they were stuck here in Dreamer territory until the enemy located them.

"We can't wait," said Duggan.

"We have no choice!" Breeze responded loudly, the pressure of the situation getting to him. "I can get the backup mainframe working on the engines, but it's so slow there could be several years' worth of realignment to do. Even the Dreamer core might end up taking weeks and that's assuming we had it working at maximum output."

"Weeks isn't what I hoped to hear."

"It's the best I can offer, sir. We should be dead after what happened."

"Well we aren't, Lieutenant and I'm thankful for it."

"Small mercies," Breeze replied, trying to smile. The smile faded before it fully appeared and Breeze spoke again. "I think the AI is gone for good, sir. Gut instinct tells me I'm not going to get it to power up again."

Duggan patted him on the shoulder. "Not what I wanted, but I'm thankful for the honesty."

He crossed to the main console and studied it for a while, trying to find a ray of hope amongst the flood of damage reports. "The life support has stabilised at least," he said.

"The last jump to lightspeed was rough," said McGlashan. "I'd rather it showed some improvements instead of merely stabilising."

"I think I might have interpreted some of the sensor readings we got from the enemy base, sir," said Chainer. "It's nothing like as big as the other installations around the wormhole. I estimate it to be less than a thousand metres squared."

"That's enough room to house a lot of soldiers," said Duggan. "Can you see any structures which resemble their housing modules?"

"A few," Chainer admitted. "And there's this other thing here in the centre."

"I appreciate your technical terminology," said Duggan. "What *thing* are you referring to?"

"This." Chainer pointed at an area of his screen.

"An ellipsis?" Duggan frowned in puzzlement. The central building on the enemy base was more or less square, but with something oval-shaped on the roof. "A weapon?"

"It could be," said Chainer. "Or it could be entirely benign. We've probably not seen even a tiny fraction of their different emplacements."

"It uses a lot of power, whatever it is," said Breeze. "That doesn't help much, does it?"

"Not really," Duggan agreed. "The important question is whether or not they detected us when we came in to land."

"I'm not sure it's so important, sir," said Chainer. "If they saw us, we'll soon be dead. If they didn't see us, we can probably stay here as long as we want. The chance of an enemy warship stumbling upon us is remote."

"Not so remote," said McGlashan. "This area around the wormhole is soon going to be filled with their warships. They can't afford to stop looking until they've found us. We destroyed two major installations, Lieutenant. They will absolutely not sit back and wait!"

"If the base here on Nistrun didn't see us, the enemy forces may not know how badly damaged we are," said Breeze.

"Unless that wrecked cruiser which put these two holes in our tail was able to get a message out," said Chainer.

"What's your opinion, Lieutenant?" asked Duggan. "Did the base detect us?"

Chainer took on a pained expression. He was clearly reluctant to say one way or another, even though he knew how important it was. "It's almost certainly a military base," he began, "which makes me think there's a high chance they saw us. On the other hand, I have no idea what function it's meant to serve. It could sell ice cream and hot dogs to passing spaceships."

"I'd like a conclusion, without the jokes."

"They probably know we're here, sir."

Chainer's inconclusive response was better than no response at all, even if the difference was only marginal.

Duggan rubbed his chin. "Can we hit it with our Lambdas from here?"

"Yes," said McGlashan at once. "It won't be a precision strike though, since our sensor data is incomplete. If you want them destroyed, we can do it."

"It might be like cutting open the goose that lays the golden eggs," Duggan muttered to himself. "Can I have a moment's quiet, please? I need to think." He paced up and down, trying to pull an idea from thin air which would improve their position. The laboured groaning of the warship's damaged hull was a distraction and he tried his best to ignore it. He breathed in deeply. The pungent tang of hot metal which came in through the vents cleared his nostrils and the sharpness of it brought his mind back on track.

The *Crimson* wasn't going anywhere soon, he was convinced of that. *Weeks,* Lieutenant Breeze said and it sounded like an absolute best-case scenario. So, they could either sit here and try to get the core online, or they could do something to try and influence their destiny, such as leave the spaceship and see what they could find on the enemy base.

"Damnit!" he snapped. "My mind is telling me we should leave the ship and go see what's out there. I need someone to tell me it's a bad idea."

"It *is* a bad idea, sir," said McGlashan. "On the other hand, waiting here is also a bad idea." The message was unspoken, but clear: this was Duggan's decision to make.

"If we wait, there's a decent chance we'll be able to lift off eventually," said Breeze. "After that, I don't know what to suggest. We're unlikely to reach our maximum lightspeed without major repairs and I don't fancy trying to get home on the engines – that's a long way to go without using the Blackstar as a shortcut."

"We don't know the way, either," said Chainer. "Realistically, there's only one way home, and that's through the wormhole."

"Whatever happens, there's absolutely no way our existing core is going to be capable of a double lightspeed jump."

There was something in Breeze's use of the word *existing* which gave Duggan's brain the kick it needed.

"In that case, we need to find ourselves another core," he said. "Which means going to the enemy base."

"I can think of many potential pitfalls in that plan," said Breeze. "Not least of which is the near-impossibility of us being able to steal one of their cores *and* for it to fit neatly in the place of our existing one. On the other hand, I accept the need for us to remain optimistic in the circumstances, so I'm obliged to admit if we do nothing, we have a one hundred percent likelihood of dying out here. If there's a chance, however infinitesimally remote, we have no alternative other than to give it a go."

"We're carrying priceless intel," said McGlashan. "It could be worth billions of lives. Or it could be worth our entire species and that of the Ghasts."

"What is your opinion, Commander?"

"If we wait here, I believe there's a good chance we'll be able to get the *Crimson* off the ground again. It'll be way off its peak operational ability, but we'll still pack a punch."

"Do you think we should keep our heads down until we have a better idea of when we can get the *Crimson* on its way?"

She chewed her lower lip and then grimaced. "I have a strong feeling they'll find us before we get airborne. If the base saw us, they'll have alerted their warships to our presence. I think we wiped out all the ships they had in the vicinity when we destroyed Glisst with the Planet Breaker. If I'm right, it means they'll have plenty of replacements heading here at their fastest speed."

"If what you say is true, we could have hours, days or potentially weeks to act."

"Hours or days, sir," she said. "It's inconceivable they'll take weeks to get a warship here."

Duggan continued with his pacing, occasionally stopping in his tracks as if he'd reached a conclusion in whatever it was he was thinking. Then, he would start pacing again and with each step he became more aware of the passing time.

There were no good choices and no easy way to accurately evaluate the risks. His mind kept coming back to the thought that if they couldn't get through the wormhole, they were doomed. They might eventually get the *Crimson* flying, but the ship's offensive capabilities were crippled without the main core. They'd be reduced to looking for easy targets within Dreamer territory until they were eventually, inevitably, found and destroyed. They could do some damage on the way, but it didn't seem likely it would be extensive.

On the other hand, were they to escape to Confederation Space with the data they'd stolen, that would give humanity a significant boost in the coming war. He made his mind up.

"I'd rather die trying to accomplish something of significance than live out my days hiding amongst our enemies," he said.

"That's it decided?" asked McGlashan.

"Yes," he replied. "I promised I'd do everything to get us home and there's only one way that's going to happen. We're going to attack the base as soon as we can and see what we find."

"Sounds good," said Chainer.

"Our backs are to the wall. I can't see an alternative," said

Breeze. "I'll repeat my opinion that a successful theft of another Dreamer core isn't going to work for us, but we may discover other opportunities we are currently unaware of."

"We knew this mission was going to be a tough one, sir," said McGlashan. "I'll advise you of the options, but I'll do everything it takes to get home. I don't want to die here."

"Very well," said Duggan. He used the comms to reach Lieutenant Ortiz. "We're leaving the ship. I want everyone suited and ready in the cargo bay."

"Yes, sir," she said. After a short pause, she continued. "What's the plan?"

"I'm working on it, Lieutenant. This one might have to be figured out on the run. That's no hurdle for the Space Corps' finest, is it?"

"Hardly a bump in the road, sir," she said with traces of humour creeping into her voice. "We'll be ready in twenty minutes."

"You might need to wait for me."

"Take your time, sir."

The conversation with Ortiz was over and Duggan addressed the others on the bridge. "You three are staying with the *Crimson*. We can't leave it unoccupied and it needs a crew to deal with the repairs."

The order wasn't entirely unexpected and no one objected. Duggan saw from the set of McGlashan's face that she didn't like it.

"You've got a broken arm, sir," she said.

"It's halfway better already. By the time we get where we're going, it'll be good as new."

"You might jeopardise the others," she said, unwilling to let it go.

"I'm the only one trained for this," he said.

"Lieutenant Ortiz is well enough trained."

"Not in what technology we need to scavenge for the *Crimson*," he said. "And the Ghasts may still not follow her. I've made my decision, Commander."

He gave her what he hoped was a reassuring smile. She returned the smile though her eyes remained hard, like she felt he'd betrayed her in some way. It wasn't the time to deal with it, so he took a deep breath and pushed everything from his mind apart from the upcoming raid.

CHAPTER TWO

"LIEUTENANT CHAINER, I want you to download the sensor data into the spacesuits," said Duggan.

"What little we have, sir. It'll be waiting for you by the time you're ready to leave the *Crimson*. Routes, distances and which terrain you should try to avoid."

Duggan took a deep breath. "Two thousand klicks there and two thousand to get back. It's going to take us several days."

"I reckon it'll take between four and six days," said Chainer. "It's quite flat out there, but I don't know if you'll be able to maintain anything like full speed."

"I don't even know what transport we'll have," Duggan replied. "There are errors on three of the cargo bay clamps and they're designed to lock on failure."

"It's a long run on foot," said Breeze.

"I hope it won't come to that." Duggan headed towards the bridge exit. "Look after our spaceship."

He didn't wait around for an answer and made his way through the *Crimson*'s interior, until he reached the cargo bay. Considering the length of the vessel, the bay was cramped inside, with unreflective grey walls that exuded an air of timeless age. The *Crimson* itself was the oldest active warship in the Space Corps, yet the metals it was made from had been formed billions of years before. The thought of it caught Duggan unawares and his brain swam. He wasn't usually affected by such feelings and shrugged them off quickly.

The *Crimson* had been loaded with several armoured vehicles prior to the voyage. It was tight and the spaces between these units were filled with humans and Ghasts. They talked loudly amongst themselves, though it was easy to see their usual high spirits were muted by their predicament. Most of the soldiers were in spacesuits and going through the routine of checking out the gauss rifles, to see which one suited them best. It was little more than superstition – the rifles were made with utter precision and Duggan doubted if there was any measurable weight difference between them. Still, he wasn't going to criticise.

A figure approached, wending through the others. It was Ortiz, sporting a deep bruise on one of her high cheekbones. Her dark eyes were as sharp and dangerous as ever.

She was straight to business. "We've got three Gunthers and four light transports, sir. We've got a fail shut on all of the tanks. I've got Durham and Berg looking at the clamps."

"What about the transports?" asked Duggan. "Everything was red or amber when I looked from the bridge and there hasn't been time to check out the faults."

"Two of the transports will definitely release – I don't know about the others. Either way, we shouldn't need to do much walking. I got the bridge data – two thousand klicks would be a long way to go on foot."

"What about artillery?" he asked, indicating the two short-barrelled plasma turrets against one of the walls. The artillery pieces were dark grey in colour, triangular at the front and squared off at the back. Their muzzles were thick tubes with only a limited amount of rotational ability. The rockets they fired were semi-autonomous, so the barrel itself only needed to be pointed in the general direction of its target.

"We can attach those to the back of the transports, sir," Ortiz replied.

"Excellent - I don't want to rely on rifles and grenades. There'll be no air support this time."

"Shame."

The preparations took longer than expected, owing to numerous issues with the hardware release clamps. For a time, Duggan thought they were going to be reduced to using the transports only, so it was a bonus when Durham somehow managed to free up one of the Gunther mid-sized tanks. On this day of bad news, matters improved significantly when the second of the three tanks signalled its availability for launch at the very last minute.

"What the hell?" asked Durham. "I'd like to take the credit, but I have no idea why it's working now."

"Don't question it," said Duggan, his mood already much better. "Climb onboard and get it launched as soon as we're ready."

The unexpected availability of the second tank necessitated some shifting of personnel, which added a further short delay. The rearrangement left eleven soldiers in each of the Gunthers, with two to drive each transport.

Duggan sat in the cockpit of the first Gunther, his helmet on the floor between his feet. The cabin was cramped and already stiflingly hot. A dozen screens on the walls around him shone harshly and he turned the brightness of his own down until they glimmered only faintly. There were two others in the cockpit with him - Vaughan was driving and Kidd had got herself into the third seat at the weapons console. The place smelled of vulcanised rubber and the subdued chatter of the soldiers drifted in through the open door.

"Tank Two, Transporters One and Two are good to go," said Vaughan.

"We're in a hurry," said Duggan. "Let's not hang around."

The cargo bay entered a state of lockdown and the warning lights glowed a sullen red. The drivers of the other vehicles confirmed their state of readiness and Duggan gave the command to go, whilst keeping his fingers crossed there'd be no technical hitches.

The holding clamps disengaged without issue and the launch chutes positioned beneath each vehicle opened smoothly and cleanly. Duggan felt a slight jolt as the tank was ejected through several dozen metres of armour plating and then onto the ground beneath the *Crimson*.

"Tank Two and the transporters confirm successful launches, sir," said Vaughan.

"Initiate deployment of the artillery," said Duggan.

"Done. The plasma launchers are on their way."

Duggan focused one of the tank's sensors onto the underside of the spaceship and watched as the two launchers dropped onto the ground, where they remained stationary on their gravity drives.

"Transporters One and Two pick them up," said Duggan.

There was no requirement for a physical connection. The onboard computers on the transporters simply instructed the artillery pieces to follow at a distance of a few metres. The mobile guns slid into position behind the transporters. When he squinted at these vehicles, Duggan was reminded of children's building blocks – two rounded cuboids towing drab triangles. However, there was nothing innocent about the plasma launchers – they could do enormous damage to buildings, armour or enemy ground troops if given the opportunity.

"I've got our vector and we're moving out," said Vaughan.

"Make best speed," said Duggan. "We're in the shit here and the longer this takes us, the greater the chance we won't make it back."

"It doesn't take an expert to see the *Crimson* isn't going anywhere soon," said Kidd.

"Yeah."

As they moved off, Duggan saw the *Crimson* from a new angle. The extent of the damage nearly broke his heart and he realised he'd become more attached to the warship than any of the others he'd flown. He'd always done his best to keep emotionally detached – a spaceship was, after all, nothing more than a perfected weapon of mass destruction. In spite of it, there was something about the *Crimson* which had crept up on him and taken hold.

"It looks nothing like it did on the *Gargantua*," Vaughan remarked. "I can't believe we got out of there alive."

"They built that one solid," said Kidd. "I bet it could still fire half of its clusters."

"More than half," said Duggan. "It's a sitting duck without its engines and without its main core. If we don't do something about it and soon, the enemy will find it and destroy it from orbit. After that, they'll come for the rest of us."

"Are we hoping to snatch one of the enemy's cores?" asked Vaughan, his eyebrows raised.

"I'm told it isn't feasible," Duggan admitted. "We're just trying to do something – anything – that might tip the scales in our favour."

"Those are the missions I like," said Kidd, her expression making it hard to be sure whether or not she was joking.

"We either die on the *Crimson* from an orbital missile strike, or we risk our lives trying to find a way back home, soldier."

"You'll get no complaints from me, sir," said Kidd. "I love this job and even if I die, you won't be able to pull the rifle from my cold, stiff fingers."

Duggan smiled. "That's why you're here."

He turned his attention to the journey ahead. Chainer hadn't exaggerated when he said how little information they possessed on the terrain. The *Crimson* had landed almost blind and with the AI core burned out, the backup mainframe lacked the capability to take a detailed snapshot of the surface.

"It's over two hundred degrees out there," said Vaughan. "In about one hour when the sun's gone, it's going to be two hundred below zero. We're holding at sixty klicks per hour over this flat ground. I reckon we've got another couple of hours at this speed and then we hit those mountains up ahead. That'll slow us down, unless we get real lucky."

The mountains were part of the range which the *Crimson* smashed through when it landed. They stretched for several thousand kilometres around the planet, like the great, jagged spine of Nistrun. The scant data they had suggested the mountain range was anywhere between two hundred and six hundred kilometres in width. Duggan fervently wished this particular obstacle wasn't in the way.

"There's a strong wind here on Nistrun," Vaughan continued. "It's blowing constantly and bringing a lot of grit with it."

"It shouldn't be a problem," said Duggan. It wasn't unknown for delicate equipment to suffer gradual degradation under such conditions, but there was nothing exposed on a Space Corps tank. The artillery and transports were similarly resistant to erosion and could likely remain exposed to these conditions for a dozen years without issue.

"I was thinking about us, sir," said Vaughan. "If we have to fight in this, it's not going to be much fun."

"There might be no wind at all across the mountains."

"That's what I'm hoping."

Duggan checked in with the *Crimson*. He spoke briefly to McGlashan, who told him there was no change in the *Crimson's* situation.

"I wasn't expecting an improvement," he said. "It's only been an hour since we left."

"And you've got what you expected, sir."

He ended the connection and closed his eyes. McGlashan was angry he'd decided to lead this mission. He was aware he could be headstrong and he'd long ago given up pretending he wasn't stubborn. McGlashan knew him well enough realise this raid was something he had no choice to lead. He sighed, drawing covert glances from Vaughan and Kidd, though they were wise enough to hold off with their questions.

The armoured convoy forged on, leaving a shimmering trail through the disturbed air. The ground was pitted and undulating, though with few obstacles that necessitated a change in direction. Vaughan piloted them expertly, keeping as close to the pre-programmed path as he could manage. Tank Two remained directly behind, with the transports bringing up the rear.

Ahead, the mountains loomed, the highest summit in this part of the range reaching a shade over six thousand metres. The peaks were rounded and looked smooth. Duggan didn't know if this was an illusion, or if a hundred million years of wind-borne dust had stripped them of their edges.

"We're going up now," said Vaughan. "These are the foothills. Everything looks clear ahead – nothing we can't glide straight over."

Soon, they were deep in the mountains. The elevation climbed steadily until they entered a long, curved valley, at which point it levelled out at three thousand metres. The tank hummed along at fifty kilometres per hour, its gravity engine easily up to the task of pushing the vehicle's immense weight onwards.

"Look at this!" said Vaughan.

There was nothing in the man's voice which spoke of danger, but his tone got Duggan's interest.

"What is it?"

"Day is just about to become night," said Vaughan, his eyes fixed on the forward sensor.

Duggan peered across and saw the transition coming. A wall of darkness rushed over the top of a tall summit, several kilometres away. It advanced down the steep mountainside like a ragged line of a million charging warriors dressed in pure black armour. The darkness pushed the light back, inexorably sweeping it aside. In moments, the day was gone as if it had never existed. Duggan switched to one of the rear sensor arrays and stared quietly as night continued chasing the fleeing day.

"I can't remember how many of these crappy worlds I've been to, but it's nice to know I can still be surprised by something," said Kidd.

The sight had been majestic and, on another occasion, Duggan would have felt uplifted. On this occasion, he felt nothing and his mind switched back to the difficulties he was sure lay ahead.

CHAPTER THREE

TIME FLOWED by with its usual inevitability. Duggan was relieved when they encountered no significant obstacles. Once or twice, they were required to cut directly over the summits of some of the higher mountains. The tanks couldn't climb vertically, though they could ascend extremely steep gradients without difficulty. They were designed to handle rugged terrain and they more than proved their worth. Eventually, the armoured convey reached the far side of the mountain range after travelling at a reduced pace for a little more than six hours.

"One hundred and ninety klicks from the far side to here," said Vaughan. "I think we got lucky."

"We've lost contact with the *Crimson* at some point in the last few minutes," said Duggan. The comms on neither the tank nor the spaceship could penetrate directly through the rock of the mountains, nor could they travel around the curvature of the planet.

"Given how much reliance we have on comms, you'd think they'd have cracked the nut of how to get a signal through substances that are denser than cheese," said Kidd.

"Cheese?" asked Vaughan in puzzlement.

"I couldn't think of anything more appropriate, alright? Besides, I'm hungry."

"You'll get nothing that tastes much like cheese from the tank replicator," said Vaughan.

Even those ground-based vehicles on which it was deemed necessary to have replicator technology installed weren't provided with anything more than a basic model. The tank replicator produced a variety of different-coloured sludges, none of which performed an acceptable job of mimicking their intended product.

"I'd like to say you get used to the food when you've done this job long enough," said Kidd. "The truth is, it still tastes like crap."

"It's too early in the trip to live off the suit drugs," said Duggan. It wasn't strictly true, but for some reason he'd always felt it was wrong to rely on the sustenance provided by his suit. Not everyone agreed with him and Duggan found it a struggle to keep his views to himself.

"I suppose," said Kidd.

She rose to find the replicator, which was somewhere in the passenger compartment at the back. Soon, the sound of good-natured insults drifted into the cockpit as she joked on with the others.

"Sixty kilometres per hour, sir," said Vaughan. "That's about as fast as this baby will go."

"The guidance system predicts another forty hours until we reach the target," said Duggan.

"That sounds right. You don't look happy, sir."

"I'm not happy, soldier. I like being on the ground, but I also like knowing I'll be able to get into the air at the end of it. At the moment, I lack that reassurance."

"I take everything as it comes," Vaughan replied.

"That's the way to be," Duggan said. "I never learned how."

Vaughan laughed. "My old dad used to say I was too laid back for my own good." His smile faded and he took on a serious expression. "I had a look through the data we hold on the target, sir."

"What did it tell you?" asked Duggan. He was always happy to listen to the opinions of his squad.

"I notice the purpose of the central building is shown as *unknown*."

"We didn't get a good view of it when we came down. We don't understand the purpose of many things the enemy builds."

"If it's any help, I think it's a monitoring station," said Vaughan.

"What makes you say that?" asked Duggan, becoming interested. "It doesn't resemble one of ours."

"No, but it looks similar to an old observatory, sir. Like the ones we used to have centuries ago on Old Earth to look into space. They still keep a couple open for visitors."

"You could be right. What advantage can we take from the knowledge, if that's what it turns out to be?"

"I don't know about advantages, sir. It does mean they'll have definitely spotted us when we came down to land."

Duggan scratched his cheek in thought. He'd already become accustomed to the likelihood that the enemy was coming for them, so this new idea didn't give him additional reason to worry. "They could have some good kit in there," he mused. "We keep our own monitoring stations packed with the latest gear and it gets regularly updated."

"Yeah," said Vaughan. "Anyway, I thought I'd let you know what I guessed we might be heading into. I don't know how well-guarded it's going to be if I'm right."

"Thanks," Duggan replied, before lapsing into silence. He thought about Vaughan's words for a time and became gradually more convinced the soldier was on to something. Back on the

Crimson, Chainer hadn't identified it as a detection facility, though he'd clearly been uncertain. Whether it made any ultimate difference was another matter entirely.

The next few hours passed without incident and Duggan was undecided if he preferred the boredom or if it would have been better with some excitement. On balance, he decided that tedium was the preferable experience. The thinly-padded chairs on the tank could be made to recline slightly – it wasn't quite sufficient to ensure enough comfort to sleep soundly and Duggan occasionally wondered if this was a deliberate ploy, instigated for a reason he couldn't fathom. Therefore, he slept fitfully when it was his turn to take a break and when he awoke, he was not in any way refreshed.

Duggan stretched groggily after his nap. Vaughan and Kidd were at their stations, looking alert. The former kept his jaw clenched, which gave away the fact he was using one of the stimulants from his spacesuit to keep him going. Duggan tried his hardest not to judge and knew the failings were his. He was only a tool, sent here to do a job and it was incumbent upon him to do whatever was necessary to complete that job effectively. Whichever way he spun it, he couldn't convince himself.

At forty hours into the journey, the convoy came to an area which contained a series of deep, circular depressions in the ground, some over a kilometre across. They hadn't shown up on the *Crimson*'s scan and Duggan tried to figure out exactly what had caused them. After a time, he concluded there had been a number of meteorite strikes on this part of the surface, which had been slowly smoothed away by the grit carried in the wind. The tank's sensors weren't meant for geological analysis, but Duggan was able to ascertain that there were thick veins of magnetite running through the crust, presumably exposed by the impacts. They skirted around the craters with the steep sides and went straight across the others.

Day returned, dispersing the night in a mirror of the battle which had occurred at the beginning of the trip. One minute, the world was in darkness, which the tank's sensors interpreted as a collection of grainy image-enhanced greens. The next, everything was bathed in a yellow-white light that heated the ground and the thin atmosphere to a level which would have been fatal in moments for an unprotected visitor to this world.

"Six hours to go, if this estimation is correct," said Duggan. "We've made better time than expected."

"On the other hand, we have to fight in this," said Vaughan. "Call me old-fashioned, but I prefer the cover of darkness."

"Me too," Kidd agreed. "This damned wind hasn't let up either. It's blowing at an almost-constant thirty klicks an hour."

"We deal with what we're given," said Duggan.

"We've had it easy for too long," said Kidd, with a mock-grimace. "We don't want to be getting soft, do we?"

Not long after, Ortiz spoke to Duggan over a private comms channel. She was in the second tank and he hadn't conferred extensively with her up until this moment. She invited the Ghost Red-Gulos into the channel in order to plan for the coming battle.

"I've studied the terrain surrounding the enemy installation, sir," she said. "It's flat as can be. I can't see how we're going to surprise them."

"We'll get our surprise, Lieutenant, though it won't be because we sneaked up on them," Duggan replied. "There's no time for a cautious approach – we're in an all-or-nothing situation."

Red-Gulos laughed. The Ghasts were usually restrained and the sound was comforting, since it meant he was up for the fight. "Two tanks and two artillery launchers should be enough firepower to give our enemy a shock, Captain John Duggan. I am not sure how long we will survive once they realise how few we are."

"We have no time and no air support," said Duggan. "Worst of all, we have no choice. If either of you have a better plan, I'm happy to entertain it. Otherwise, we'll position the launchers one hundred klicks out and they'll commence bombardment as soon as the tanks reach the perimeter. We'll head directly for the central building, see what's inside and take it from there."

It was only a plan in the loosest sense of the word, though Duggan knew there were occasions when forceful, direct action was the best approach. These days, he preferred a meticulously-prepared assault, but he could remember half a dozen times from his past when an all-guns-blazing attack had worked for him.

"What if they know we're coming, sir?" asked Ortiz.

"I'm sure they know we're here on Nistrun," he replied. "Whether they are expecting us to attack them is another matter. If we arrive and find a dozen tanks arrayed against us, we'll beat a hasty retreat." He knew he was embracing madness, yet it made him feel better to shrug away the burden of caution.

Ortiz wasn't one to shy from a fight. She made one or two suggestions, without sounding negative about the whole affair. Red-Gulos was similarly pragmatic and between the three of them, they added a tiny amount of polish to a plan which Duggan could not deny was anything other than a turd.

"This is like being back in a Ghast ground assault unit," said Red-Gulos. The language modules hesitated fractionally at his words, conveying the impression there was no direct translation. Duggan had no idea if Red-Gulos was offering him a compliment or an insult. He let the Ghast have the benefit of the doubt.

At two hours distance from the target installation, Duggan got news that threw his most basic of plans into disarray.

"Sir?" It was Ortiz.

"What is it, Lieutenant?"

"Byers is on the comms here. She just saw a ghost at the extremes of detection range. It moved fast and now it's gone."

Duggan felt himself go cold at the words. "How sure is she?"

"She didn't want to commit one way or another, but I think it shook her up, sir."

Duggan cursed inwardly. A ghost on the sensors was a fleeting sight of a possible object, often so ephemeral that a poor comms operator would miss one entirely. The tanks weren't good at detecting orbiting spaceships, but they could still catch the occasional sight of one.

"I need a heading," he said. "Was it going to the base?"

"She isn't sure."

"I need something, damnit!"

He heard the sound of a short, heated conference, quickly resolved. "Byers doesn't believe it was heading towards either the base or the *Crimson*, sir," said Ortiz.

"Did she get a reading on the size of the ghost?" he asked, hoping to wring something useful out of the conversation.

"Nothing, sir. It could be a misread."

"You're amongst the Space Corps' finest," said Duggan bitterly. "It's not a misread. We have an enemy spaceship of an unknown size and type in orbit above us."

"What do we do now?"

"We pray, Lieutenant."

Duggan clenched his fists in helpless frustration. The fact the convoy was still intact meant they'd already experienced a minor miracle by avoiding detection. They were going to need a few more miracles to get out of this predicament.

CHAPTER FOUR

"WE'RE IN THE CRAP, HUH?" asked Kidd. There was little privacy on a tank and she'd overheard most of the details.

"That about sums it up," Duggan agreed. He didn't want to talk about it, since he needed some quiet time in order to think.

Kidd ploughed on regardless. "I was always told that if you worry about the stuff you can't change, you'll never accomplish anything. It's the fear, sir. That's what holds you back. Not, you personally, of course – it could mean anyone."

"Thank you, soldier," said Duggan. "I'd like some time to think."

There was little new or insightful in Kidd's words, but they somehow helped Duggan come to a decision. He couldn't pretend there was no enemy spaceship above them, yet there was nothing he could do to make it go away. It had certainly come to Nistrun in order to find them. Whatever action Duggan took, the enemy would eventually find the *Crimson* and the armoured convoy. There was a remote chance they might destroy the *Crimson* and assume their work was done. If it came to that, the soldiers who remained would be no more or less stranded than they currently were. Duggan swore under his breath.

When death was inevitable, the choice of how to experience it became the most important thing there was. On top of that, a new plan was beginning to form in his mind. There were no specifics as yet – he had far too little information to allow for certainty. It was going to be one of his most daring yet, such that he feared to picture it in his mind in case he started to believe it would work.

"Lieutenant Ortiz, there's a slight change," he said. "We're going to assault the main enemy structure, but we're leaving the artillery unmanned at the agreed distance of one hundred klicks."

"There's to be no bombardment, sir?"

"We're going to play it by ear – the guns will make an easy target for an orbiting craft and anyone with them will be killed, so we'll need to operate them remotely."

"You're up to something, sir."

"Maybe," he said, unwilling to give anything away. "I don't want to get your hopes up."

At the agreed location, the convoy drew to a halt. The troops in the two transports dashed out and clambered aboard the tanks. There was a considerable amount of mock-grumbling about the additional passengers, the presence of whom turned an already uncomfortable ride into a very uncomfortable one.

"You could fry eggs on the ground out there," said Cabrera from the passenger compartment. "As long as you don't mind breaking your teeth on the gravel when you eat them."

It was a throwaway remark which nevertheless produced a few laughs from the others. The troops were experienced professionals, but they knew about the ghost on the sensors. There was tension and the men and women were grateful for an opportunity to release even a fraction of it. The Ghasts didn't laugh – they sat impassively in their metal armour and waited for whatever would come.

The tanks moved off, the monumental thrust from their engines pressing the occupants hard into their seats. Duggan checked the rear sensors and stared for a moment at the motionless artillery. It would be easier if they remained unused, since it would mean his inchoate plan was working better than expected.

"Sixty klicks to go, sir," said Vaughan after a while.

"One hour of peaceful contemplation," said Kidd. "Then we can start shooting some alien bastards. As long as we don't get reduced to cinders by a surprise missile strike."

"Do you ever shut up?" asked Vaughan fondly.

"Only when I'm shooting at Ghasts. By which I mean Dreamers, of course. Some of my best friends are Ghasts."

At a different time, Duggan would have enjoyed listening to Kidd's dry sense of humour. While he was trying to figure out the best approach into the enemy base, it was somewhat distracting. Nevertheless, he let her talk and did his best to tune out the noise.

The images they had of the installation were rough and unclear. The greys of the alien structures blurred into the similarly-grey rock upon which they'd been placed, making it difficult to see where one ended and the other began. Duggan hoped he could discern something of use by staring hard enough. After fifteen minutes, he was left with eyestrain and conjecture. One thing was clear - the base was haphazardly arranged, or followed a pattern that made no sense to human eyes. Buildings sat at angles, some close enough that they almost touched, others several dozen metres from anything else. Finally, he reached a decision.

"We need to alter our approach by a few hundred metres," he said to Vaughan.

"Where to, sir?"

"I've overlaid a course onto the map of the installation. I'd like you to follow it."

"All the way?"

"Yes. All the way, without stopping."

"We're not going to fit through at least three of those gaps, sir."

"We'll fit," said Duggan grimly.

"Are we taking point?"

"I'd be no leader if I sat back. Make Tank Two aware of the new course."

"Right you are, sir. I'm sending them the details."

Duggan contacted Ortiz and Red-Gulos, to let them know what he hoped to achieve.

"We ignore everything until we reach the target?" Ortiz said.

"If we can. Once we're inside, we find their comms gear. That's now the primary objective."

"We're going to miss Lieutenant Chainer, sir."

"He's on the *Crimson*, Lieutenant and we'll have to deal with it. I have full confidence in Byers and McLeod."

"Do you really believe the enemy spaceship will fall for this?" asked Red-Gulos.

"If they don't, we're all going to die," said Duggan. "There are many possible outcomes, most of which will see us dead one way or another." He laughed. "Besides, you Estral are unfamiliar with the intricacies of human mistruths. I intend to take full advantage of our differences."

"You make many assumptions about the naivete of our enemies," said Red-Gulos.

"There's nothing else I can do," said Duggan.

When he finished talking, Duggan stood and attempted to relieve his muscles by stretching in the confines of the cockpit. The situation was no better than it had been since they crashed on Nistrun, but he felt much better for having a new set of goals which could give them a chance. It wasn't so much that success would allow them to return home to Confederation Space, but it would open up new opportunities. *The chance of a chance,* he thought. A thousand doors lay in front of him, with only one of them unlocked. If he could get everyone through to whatever lay beyond, he'd have far exceeded his expectations. In the circumstances, it was enough to give him renewed purpose and vigour. The tiniest of hopes was infinitely better than no hope at all.

"We should be able to get a view of the target shortly, sir," said Vaughan. "It'll be a poor image from this far away."

"Put it onto my screen as soon as you get a sight of it," said Duggan. "If the place is defended, it's going to get hot in here."

The reality was that the enemy base would try to communicate to the spaceship above and if the vessel had offensive capabilities, it would easily destroy the tanks. Likewise, even a couple of basic defensive emplacements would pick them off from afar. The tanks had countermeasures, but they wouldn't stave off a sustained attack. The only chance was for the base to be effectively undefended. It was unlikely, though not entirely beyond the bounds of probability. A monitoring station was designed to look upwards, rather than for a ground-based assault.

"Here you go, sir," said Vaughan. "There's too much dust to allow a clearer picture than this one."

An image appeared on Duggan's screen – it showed a wavering collection of metal structures, a good twenty kilometres away. Even though the ground was mostly flat, there were sufficient undulations for the installation to slip in and out of view.

"Doesn't look like much," said Kidd. "The same as the other places we destroyed, only smaller."

"Have you ever seen anything pretty way out in places like this?" asked Vaughan.

"I live in expectation," she replied.

"If you go on looks, this could be a Ghast base," said Duggan, finding himself drawn to make a response. "Hell, it could even be one of ours somewhere."

"If you don't like grey, you're in the wrong business," said Vaughan without turning. "I'm bringing us around a little."

Vaughan altered their course slightly, taking the tank in a direction which would cut to the right of the installation.

"Fifteen minutes to go if we maintain this pace," said Kidd, the humour gone from her voice with the approach of battle.

"I'm taking us into this depression," said Vaughan, altering course again to bring them into a wide, shallow bowl with smooth sides and a covering of grit. "It might buy us a few minutes."

"Good job the latest gravity engines don't kick up dust," said Kidd.

"They've not kicked up dust for decades," said Vaughan with a shake of his head. "You were born in the wrong century."

"Are you saying I'm old?"

Duggan recognized the talk as a sign of the soldiers' nervousness. Some people talked, while others sank within themselves.

"We'll leave the bowl shortly, sir," said Vaughan.

"Don't slow down," Duggan replied. "This is the critical time." He put on his suit helmet and the others in the cockpit did likewise. Once the seal about his neck had tightened, he patched into the internal comms of both tanks and instructed everyone to prepare. He gave them a couple of minutes and then repeated the mission objectives for the final time before arrival.

"This one is going to be tough," he said. "In addition, our goals might change at a moment's notice. We lack all the usual intel we'd have before a raid like this one, so everything is fluid. Once we've secured the objective, that's when the real fun begins."

"I think the fun is about to begin already," said Vaughan. "I think we've triggered an external perimeter alarm. Look!"

The secondary tactical screen to Duggan's left showed an

object arcing outwards from the base. It climbed to a height of twenty kilometres and then began its downward journey.

"That's a rocket," said Kidd. "Type unknown."

"Time to spray and pray," added Vaughan.

The Gunthers were equipped with two external Last Chance batteries – these were little more elaborate than a computer-targeted chain gun which could fire at a vast rate. In a world of technology, there were still few overtly better countermeasures than firing a quarter of a million rounds per minute in the direction of an inbound missile. The troops referred to the method as spray and pray, though there weren't many more effective ways to defend a vehicle. The hull of the tank grumbled under the recoil.

"Got it," said Kidd with unflustered satisfaction. "There're another four in the air."

Duggan checked the tank's speed and distance from the target. "Three more minutes until we're inside the perimeter."

It wasn't the ground-launched missiles he was worried about. Against those, the tanks stood a chance. The major concern remained the spaceship. Since the personnel on the base had detected the arrival of the tanks, they would have alerted the vessel. *Unless it's on the far side of the planet and out of comms sight, or so far out into space they won't get here in time.*

"Last Chance, don't fail us now. We got all four, with another five coming straight after." Kidd laughed – it was a sudden, infectious sound. "Makes you glad to be alive, doesn't it?"

"Always has and always will," said Duggan, the words wrenched from his mouth. "We're going to smash these bastards and show them what the Space Corps is all about."

In his seat up front, Vaughan tipped back his head and howled.

CHAPTER FIVE

THE NEXT FIVE missiles were destroyed by the Last Chance batteries. The chain guns smoked as they ejected their rapid-fire bursts of high-velocity rounds from the shoulders of the two Gunthers. Sharp fragments of a shredded missile rained down upon the ground, one or two pieces colliding harmlessly with the hull of the lead tank. The sound of the contact reached those within, producing a series of bravado-filled comments from soldiers who'd seen it all before.

Another wave of missiles rose and fell, once more failing to penetrate the hail of slugs directed towards them. Whatever weapons the Dreamers had on their base, they weren't the most appropriate ones to use against oncoming tanks.

"Here comes another round," said Kidd. "Whoops!"

Duggan didn't have time to consider her use of the word *whoops*, before a missile detonated off the Gunther's armour plating. The explosion tore a huge hole in the metal and ripped the main turret away. Plasma spilled across much of the upper section, softening the plating and pouring heat into the gravity engines. A siren started up in the cockpit.

"That's the main armament gone," said Vaughan. "The engines are running warm."

"Both Last Chance batteries fully functional," said Kidd, her voice raised above the peal of the interior alarm.

"Can we target those launchers?" asked Duggan.

"Negative, sir. Not without a clear line of sight." She paused. "Five more enemy missiles taken down."

They were now close enough to see the installation clearly on the sensors. The brightness of the sun highlighted the buildings in stark relief against the blackness of the sky. Shadows danced in the heat and the wind.

"They're going to have another three or four shots at us," said Duggan.

"Assuming they stop firing once we get amongst their buildings."

"They'll stop," he said, hoping his confidence wasn't misplaced.

"There's small-arms fire coming from somewhere," said Kidd.

In this instance, *small arms* turned out to be a type of gauss repeater, mounted on a roof. The low, cube-shaped emplacement had escaped notice until this moment, owing to the poor quality of the sensor feeds. The gun was also well-camouflaged and looked as though it was part of the building itself. A short barrel jutted through a dark slot and poured out metal at the Gunthers. Three more repeaters joined in, their bullets clattering as they deflected away from the front of the tank.

"Not what I'd call small arms," said Vaughan.

"Yeah well, it's not going to stop us, is it?"

The tanks were designed to repel this exact type of attack. There were many types of heavier gauss emplacements which could ruin tanks larger than a Gunther, but those on this base were little more than a distraction. Their sound filled the interior, drowning out the alarm. After a few seconds, Duggan ordered his helmet computer to attenuate the racket. He felt instant relief.

"Tank Two has taken one direct hit and we've just had a near miss," Kidd continued.

"What's the status of Tank Two?" asked Duggan.

"Still moving," she said.

"We'll cross the perimeter in twenty seconds," said Vaughan. "Sixty klicks per hour and holding."

Ahead, there was a wide gap between two of the enemy structures. The overhead scans from the *Crimson* showed the gap narrowing, before it opened up into what Duggan mentally referred to as a *plaza,* even if the word didn't seem appropriate in a place as barren as this. After that, there were a series of twists and turns until they reached their destination. Vaughan was going to have his work cut out.

They almost didn't make it to the perimeter. All bar one of the final volley of enemy missiles were destroyed close to their zeniths. The last missile plunged with inevitability towards Tank One. With only a few metres to spare, a slug from one of the Last Chance batteries tore through the missile's housing. The complex machinery within was destroyed, preventing detonation. However, the bulk of the heavy alloy propulsion section crunched into the Gunther's damaged upper plating. The noise was tremendous and Duggan thought the damage was surely terminal.

"Give me a damage report!" he shouted.

"Two burst ear drums!" shouted Vaughan in return. "They built these tanks to last!"

The ringing in Duggan's ears faded and he checked the status of the tank's hull. In spite of Vaughan's words, the final missile had nearly penetrated the interior of the Gunther and had knocked out ten percent of the gravity drive's output on its way through.

With its speed scarcely diminished, the lead tank entered the space between the two metal-walled structures. The clanking of enemy gauss rounds against the hull diminished at once, though it didn't stop entirely.

"They've stopped firing missiles," said Kidd.

"This going to be tight enough without having to dodge incoming explosives," said Vaughan.

The soldier was right – the gap between the two buildings closed up and when the tank burst through into the plaza, there was little more than a metre spare to each side.

"It's not going to get any easier," said Duggan.

Belying its size, the Gunther turned sharply to the left, scrubbing away a fraction of its speed in the process. The plaza was only a hundred metres across, with machine-levelled ground and five of the enemy structures crowding in from the sides. The tank was a bulky piece of kit, but the walls stretched high above its broken turret.

"There!" shouted Duggan.

"I see it," said Vaughan, guiding the tank into another opening, this one tighter than the last.

There were shapes ahead – Duggan saw a group of figures dressed in a mixture of flexible alloy and grey polymers.

"Grenades!" said Kidd.

The front sensor went fuzzy for a second when a plasma grenade exploded in the vicinity. To Duggan's relief, the feed steadied and continued to operate as normal. The tank didn't slow. Several of the enemy threw themselves to the ground and the tank sailed over them. Two of the Estral weren't quick enough and the front of the tank knocked them high into the air, their broken limbs flailing as they tumbled to the unyielding stone.

"Too tight," said Vaughan.

The passage narrowed to the point where the tank was wider

than the available space. Vaughan kept it pointed straight down the middle and the Gunther collided with the adjacent buildings. The alloy walls of the base structures screeched and ruptured, releasing their air into the near-vacuum. Tank Two followed a moment later, crushing the walls further with its unstoppable bulk.

"Left here!" shouted Duggan.

Vaughan did his best to turn the Gunther in the direction indicated. The impact with the buildings had knocked it slightly off course and it was difficult to correct at a speed in excess of fifty kilometres per hour. The tank's right flank connected with the flat wall of a building. The vehicle's life support struggled to keep the interior stable and Duggan had to grab the side of his seat to stop himself being hurled onto the floor. Pain flared and he realised he'd used his partially-healed broken arm by mistake. He gritted his teeth to stop from crying out. Kidd wasn't quick enough to grab a hold of something and she landed in an ungraceful heap on the floor, swearing loudly.

The Gunther's engines hauled it free of the wall and the tank continued on its course, leaving the structure behind crumpled and at a tilt. Something exploded ahead of them, flaring into white. The tank surged through the blast, leaving the plasma dissipating in its wake.

Kidd scrambled onto her seat. "More hostiles," she said, studying the console screens with her visor only centimetres away. Greens and blues reflected from the mirrored surface, giving the bizarre impression that her suit helmet was the source of the data.

Several grenades struck the tank and soon the top section was awash in flames. Something larger hit the Gunther's flank, cutting through the armour and blowing out a chunk of the plating. A second projectile hit close to the first.

"Shoulder launcher," said Duggan. "We don't want to take too many of those."

"Should I divert from our course?" asked Vaughan.

"Negative, soldier. Ignore them."

"Tank Two has fired its main armament," said Kidd. "Crap, would you look at that!"

The building to the right shook under the onslaught of high-calibre slugs. A line of enormous holes traced its way the length of the closest wall. The surrounding metal was buckled and crushed. Such was the power of the Gunther's main gun that the slugs travelled through several of the buildings beyond the first. A tank was a shitty opponent to face if you had no way to counter it quickly.

The flames which embraced Tank One faded, dwindling until they left patches of the hull a deep red colour. The Gunther collided with another building, shunting it to one side as it barrelled through. Duggan heard the renewed clattering of gauss rounds against the exterior and he did his best to ignore the sound.

"There!" he said.

"I see it," Vaughan replied. "I'm taking us straight towards it."

The target building was dead ahead, a short distance away. At eighty metres tall it was much higher than the surrounding structures. It was also longer, with sides close to one hundred and fifty metres in length. There was a cylinder protruding from the roof, which was capped with what looked like a fifty-metre, bulbous glass lens that had all-round vision. Duggan was sure it was made of something more advanced than glass, though he didn't know exactly what the material was.

In front of the building there were a few enemy soldiers visible, though nothing that resembled an organised response. Some chose to run, whilst others were foolish enough to stand and fire guns or throw grenades. These foolish or brave ones were knocked contemptuously aside by the tank as it headed towards the building.

"Down to thirty-five klicks per hour," said Vaughan. "Let's hope it's enough."

"Don't forget to knock!" Kidd said.

The Gunther smashed into the side of the main building. The alloys of the wall were exceptionally strong and designed to withstand harsh conditions on a hostile world. They were not, however, designed to withstand an intentional collision with one of the Space Corps' mid-sized tanks. In the blinking of an eye, the wall flexed, crumpled and then split. The Gunther tore through the gap, leaving a monstrous tear as evidence of its passing. A second later, Tank Two struck the building thirty metres to the right. The result was similar and a second enormous hole was ripped through the exterior.

Once the whole of the tank was inside, Vaughan brought it to a rapid halt, the deceleration inducing a fleeting nausea in many of the passengers.

"Tank Two, please report," said Duggan.

It was Ortiz who responded. "We're inside, sir and hidden from eyes in the sky."

"Excellent – if the enemy spacecraft knows we're in here, the plan won't work," he said.

With the first part of his plan a success, Duggan barked out an order for everyone on the tanks to disembark, leaving only a crew of two on each. The troops didn't need to be told twice and they scrambled out through the narrow doorways, their rifles held ready. Duggan followed, being one of the last to exit his vehicle.

He looked around him and discovered he was in a vast, open room which took up a large part of the building's ground floor. Pale blue light came from an unknown source, permitting excellent visibility of the carnage. The tank had caused immense damage on its way in and the escaping air made a low thrumming sound as it was sucked through the jagged hole.

Nearby, the second Gunther was at a standstill, its cargo of troops spreading out as they sought cover amongst the array of overturned consoles and metal cabinets. There were banks of screens on the far wall, some of them blank, while others continued to display whatever updates they'd been programmed to show. The turret of Tank Two was still in place and its additional height had opened a furrow through the ceiling.

Duggan heard a metallic ping from close by and he crouched low, keeping his shoulder pressed against the burning hot side of the tank. His suit duly informed him of the temperature extremes and he moved away, keeping a wary eye out for whoever had fired the shot. Elsewhere in the room, the other soldiers frantically searched for the sniper.

"Up there in the ceiling!" shouted Barron.

Five or six of the troops fired their gauss rifles. The delicate fizz of their projectiles was drowned out by a hammering roar when two of the Ghasts unleashed the ferocity of their hand-held repeaters through the gouge in the ceiling.

"More coming from outside!" shouted Chan.

Only a few moments had passed since they'd broken into the enemy building and they were already under pressure.

"Squad One, with me!" Duggan said loudly on the open channel. "Lieutenant Ortiz, ensure the enemy stays outside."

"Yes, sir!"

"Enemy sniper eliminated," said McLeod. "We're clear!"

The sound of repeater fire tailed off and Duggan waved his squad over. They broke from their places of cover and dashed towards him, where they stooped in the shadow of Tank One.

"Where will we find the comms gear?" Duggan asked, fervently hoping the tanks hadn't destroyed it when they broke through the wall of the building.

"It could be anywhere, sir," said Byers, one of the two comms experts he had with him.

"This isn't pieces of it on the floor around us, is it?" asked Duggan.

Byers' response was as a reassuring as it could be in the circumstances.

"I don't think so."

"If this is a monitoring station, the comms kit could be integrated with the main sensor panels," said McLeod. "I'll know it when I see it."

Duggan took the hint. "We need to move."

"Yes, sir," they responded.

The room was a mess, but it wasn't hard to locate an exit door. There was one about forty metres away from them, currently closed. There was text stamped on the door, visible even from this distance. Duggan was pleased to find it was something his Ghost language modules recognized. *KEEP CLOSED* it said. He shook his head at the mundanity and headed over, doing his best to keep low. Four humans and three Ghosts followed, quickly yet warily. In the vast expanse of the room, the pilots of the two Gunthers began the task of reversing the tanks close to the penetrations in the exterior walls, in order to make it hard for the enemy soldiers to enter.

Duggan reached the door, took a deep breath and made the swiping gesture necessary to open it.

CHAPTER SIX

THERE WAS a corridor on the other side of the door. Wide and with a high ceiling, it stretched away into the distance, before turning sharply to the right. There were other doorways to the sides, all sealed with slab-like alloy doors. The light in here was a more intense blue and it cycled smoothly through a variety of different shades. Duggan waited a few moments but there was no sign of movement or any sound which might indicate the presence of the enemy.

"Not much air coming through," said Bonner. "The building is depressurizing quickly."

"Good news for us," said Duggan. "Come on, let's move."

They entered the corridor cautiously, with McLeod and Bonner remaining in the doorway to provide cover. Without much in the way of a breathable atmosphere to carry the sounds, the squad's footsteps were dull on the metal floor.

As he advanced, Duggan half-expected the doors in the walls to open simultaneously and for enemy troops to pour out. It didn't happen and the six of them were able to reach the end of the corridor where it turned to the right. Duggan looked carefully around – the passage continued for another few metres and then it opened into another large room, which he guessed was exactly in the middle of the building. There were banks of screens and several complex-looking consoles visible, with bodies slumped across them.

"Byers have a look at this," he said.

He stepped a couple of paces back and Byers took his place. "This is what we're looking for," she said at once. "It's the main control room."

The certainty in her voice made Duggan breathe a sigh of relief. He'd already prepared himself for an extended and bloody scrap to capture this building. "Right, we go in," he said. "If anything moves, shoot it. McLeod, Bonner, get up here at the double."

The pair of them sprinted along the corridor, keeping their rifles at the ready. Duggan didn't waste time and made a quick run to the next doorway, where he chanced a look deeper into the comms room. It was forty metres to a side and with a ceiling twenty or more metres above. A thick, white column rose from the floor and joined with the ceiling above. The base of the column was circled by a single matte-green console which Duggan assumed went all the way around.

Everywhere he looked, there were bodies. Some of the Estral had died where they sat dutifully at their screens. Others had tried to extend their lives by running for the doors. They lay in twisted poses indicative of the agonising pain and fear they'd suffered as the vacuum took their lives. He didn't know how the room had depressurized so abruptly – it was a big building and it should have taken a minute or two before the oxygen had fled the room.

"Up there," said Red-Gulos.

Duggan looked upwards. There was a series of holes through

the wall, close to the ceiling. Each hole was nearly half a metre in diameter.

"Stray rounds from Tank Two's gun," whispered Rasmussen. "They came in at an angle and went through the ceiling."

"Their bad luck," said Braler, without emotion.

"It looks clear, get inside," said Duggan. "Find the doors and cover them. I don't want a squad of suited Estral taking us by surprise. McLeod, Byers, do your stuff. I want to know how this kit works and I want you to find that spaceship above us."

McLeod and Byers knew they were out of their depths the moment they laid eyes on the equipment and they said as much.

"I don't care if you don't like the look of it. You're the comms specialists, deal with it," Duggan said, kicking himself for not having the foresight to bring Lieutenant Chainer along on this mission.

They hurried off to get started. Duggan took the opportunity to check in with Lieutenant Ortiz.

"We're holding them, sir," she said. "We took them unawares and I don't think they've recovered yet. Either that or they only have a small garrison."

"It's a mixture of both, I suspect," he replied. "I reckon we're so deep into their territory they've forgotten how to respond to unexpected aggression."

"Have you found what you wanted, sir?" she asked. There was tentative expectation in her voice, reminding Duggan that even the hardest of his troops had no wish to perish out here.

"We've found what I believe is their main control room for the sensor array on the roof," he said. "There is definitely comms gear routing through it as well. We have to hope the kit they have in this building is their only way to speak to the spaceship above and also to anything further afield. It's going to take time to figure out how it works."

"McLeod and Byers are good, sir and I'm convinced they'll

do what you ask of them." She hesitated. "Do you think you'll be able to fool the crew of the enemy spaceship?"

"We're going to have to. Red-Gulos sounds up for the challenge. In truth, I think he's itching to prove his worth."

"He doesn't need to do that."

"We both know it. I'm not going to hold him back. I have no desire to speak with the enemy myself."

"There're several hundred years of language divergence to overcome." She laughed. "I wish I could be there to overhear the conversation."

"I'll let you know how it goes, Lieutenant. Over."

He couldn't stop himself from crossing to watch McLeod and Byers at work. It was plain to see they weren't comfortable with the arrangement of the console.

"The language modules are struggling, to cope," said Byers. "When the dictionary isn't clear on the translation, it makes guesses. I thought the guys behind the modules were cleverer than this."

Duggan recognized the frustration in her voice. "There's nothing much they can do when they lack the necessary examples of alien script needed to construct their programs. This is what we have to work with."

"I've got something," said McLeod. He leaned forward in an oversized metal-framed chair a few paces away.

"What is it?"

"The beginnings, sir. This is a record of their inbound and outbound communications over the last few days."

There was a list on one of the many screens. Duggan stared at it, trying to make sense. Some of the words were clear, but not enough for him to grasp the entirety of the messages. He called Red-Gulos over and the Ghast strode away from his position and joined the three of them at the console.

"Can you understand this?" asked Duggan.

The visors on the Ghost spacesuits were clear and Red-Gulos took on an expression which Duggan was beginning to recognize as a frown.

"Some. There are other words which are less familiar."

Red-Gulos fell silent for a while, though his eyes never left the screen of text. Duggan was impatient and found it hard to keep his mouth closed. After what seemed like an age, though was in reality less than two minutes, the Ghost spoke.

"They sent a series of messages approximately two days ago to an unknown receptor, stating they detected the presence of gamma radiation near the wormhole. Afterwards, there's another message describing the destruction of a planet – which we named Glisst - a short lightspeed hop away from here. Later, there's a communication to describe the arrival of an unidentified spaceship into the atmosphere of Nistrun."

"I didn't think our activities would go undetected," said Duggan. "What else was there?"

"There was a response, asking for confirmation on the location of the spaceship."

"That can only be the *Crimson* they're referring to. Did they give details of where we came down?"

"The installation controller advised that the *Crimson* was damaged, but they gathered insufficient data to state with confidence exactly how damaged."

"There's no mention that we crashed here on Nistrun?" asked Duggan with growing excitement.

"None – the installation simply states that we skimmed across the planet's atmosphere at an unexpectedly low altitude. They provided details of several likely destinations, none of which suggest we might have landed on the surface."

"Lieutenant Chainer is one of the best comms men and he only just caught sight of the base," mused Duggan. "Perhaps the enemy saw nothing more than a glimpse of us. It'll be damned good news if that's how it happened. What are the subsequent communications?"

"There is an inbound communication stating that many warships are heading to this sector. The first scheduled to arrive is named *Valpian* – the vessel our tank detected as a ghost. This installation received further orders to keep a watch out for the *Crimson*'s reappearance."

"Do they quantify the number of ships they've sent this way?" asked Duggan. "I'm curious to know what they think of us and how much of a threat they think we are."

Red-Gulos grunted with grim humour. "It's top secret, apparently."

"They don't want their own forces to know who we are?"

"Their high command is unlikely to know for themselves, Captain Duggan."

"True. What other messages are there on this audit list?"

"The *Valpian* made the controllers of this installation aware when it arrived. The installation responded with a standard acknowledgement. There are several similarly mundane communications, until we reach a period covering the few minutes since our arrival was detected on the perimeter of this base."

"Here's where it gets important," said Duggan. "What did they say to each other?"

"The installation controller attempted to advise the captain of the *Valpian* about our attack. The spaceship did not respond immediately."

Duggan spoke without daring to hope. "It must have been out of comms sight."

"The controller made several more attempts to send an urgent message to the *Valpian*, with a similar lack of response."

"Why didn't they speak to central command and control?" Duggan wondered aloud.

Red-Gulos uttered a barking, guttural laugh. "They tried,

Captain Duggan. They initiated a transmission a few minutes before our tanks broke through their outer wall. The transmission wasn't completed."

"The building must have depressurized at exactly the moment they tried to send their emergency broadcast!"

"That would be my conclusion," said Red-Gulos. "This installation hasn't received any further inbound communications since that moment."

"The *Valpian* doesn't even know we're here."

"I believe it does not," replied Red-Gulos.

Duggan could have shouted out with happiness. His plan had so many uncontrollable variables that he'd not even dared to think it might succeed. He wanted to capture this base and then use its comms systems to fool the captain of the enemy spaceship into thinking the *Crimson* was elsewhere. In the end, the Dreamers had already done the work for him. If the *Valpian* was far away, it bought Duggan and his troops time to search for the processing units which interpreted the sensor data gathered by the lens on the roof. Lieutenant Breeze had dismissed the chance that they'd be able to put a captured core to good use, but for Duggan this was a case of taking one step at a time, with each one a colossal victory in its own right. Even if the stolen core idea was a failure, they could still earn a chance for the *Crimson*'s backup mainframe to squeeze some life out of its damaged gravity drives. If they could take off, it would open a whole new raft of opportunities.

Duggan's good mood was soon to be swept away.

"Sir, I think I'm beginning to get to grips with this stuff," said McLeod. "Once you get past the differing arrangement, these consoles do much the same thing as ours." He pointed to a large screen in front of him. "I've managed to turn this on. It's a live feed of whatever is coming in through the lens. I think these symbols here relate to distance and if I turn this dial I can look further away or closer in."

Duggan peered at it. "That's as far out as it goes?"

"Yes, sir. The lens will only focus on a tiny area of the sky at maximum zoom out. It can't see much further than our own monitoring stations, but there's a big difference when it comes to the interpretation. This station makes sense of what it sees in only a few seconds and then it can look at a different area."

"They've got a big edge on us when it comes to processing grunt," said Duggan.

"We can see the effect right here, sir. Anyway, they have a series of satellites in orbit above, which gives them a way to see a target even when the planet's rotation would prevent a line-of-sight examination. The satellites aren't anything like as sophisticated as the main lens."

"Have they been watching anything in particular?" Duggan asked, already knowing the answer.

"The Helius Blackstar – that's what they've been looking at."

"How come they haven't been able to pinpoint the *Crimson*?"

"The satellites can only look in one direction, sir and that's at the wormhole. They'd have been better off with a custom-built spaceship to do their watching. It cuts out most of these limitations."

"What's that?" asked Duggan sharply. A blue circle appeared at the left-hand edge of the monitoring screen. It moved gradually to the right.

"Crap," said McLeod. "That's one of their spacecraft."

"The *Valpian*," said Duggan. "Keep your fingers crossed they're just passing through."

"I've got activity on this panel here, sir," said Byers. "It's one of the comms sections."

Duggan sighed wearily. "Is it what I think it is?"

"It's a message from the spaceship, sir. I think they're expecting an answer."

For just a brief moment, Duggan had been able to enjoy the feeling things were going right and that they'd avoided the need to speak to the *Valpian*. It wasn't to be. With trepidation, he indicated Red-Gulos should take his place at the console.

"Do your best," he said.

The Ghost gave another rumbling laugh. "Or we're all screwed," he said.

Duggan had no time to wonder whether the alien had learned the profanity from one of the human soldiers or if it was the language modules making a best guess. The Ghost sat and signalled for Byers to open a channel.

CHAPTER SEVEN

"I'M CONNECTING YOU," said Byers. "It'll be text only, no verbal. Let's hope they don't think it strange."

Duggan watched as Red-Gulos moved his fingers onto two areas of the screen and held them in place.

"This should provide a standard greeting," said Red-Gulos. "Assuming I've understood the writing correctly."

An adjacent screen lit up and displayed a series of characters in response. Something told Duggan it wasn't good news.

"They've asked if I'm shy," said Red-Gulos. He pressed another section of the first screen and then he spoke once more. "They are not happy. I will need to speak directly with them."

"Will your suit interface with their comms panel?" asked Duggan. His own suit had already identified a series of unrecognized open receptors in the vicinity, though that was no guarantee his computer would be able to pair with them.

"We are trouble if it will not."

"Do it," Duggan ordered. "I'm connected to your suit through our comms channels. I'll listen in."

The connection was made. There was an exchange of words

between Red-Gulos and whoever it was on the *Valpian*. The tone sounded hard and aggressive even to Duggan's untrained ear, and his language modules provided a patchy translation that didn't give away much. The conversation continued for a few sentences and then it ended abruptly.

"I think they are reassured," said the Ghast. "The man on the *Valpian* was curious about my origins and my unusual pronunciation. I told him I hailed from a place called Vempor."

"What?" asked Duggan in confusion.

"It is difficult for me to lie, so I gave the true name of the planet I originated from and let his mind perform the task of believing it was sufficient explanation for my peculiar speech."

"Is there a planet called Vempor in Estral Space?" said Duggan, his mind slower on the uptake than normal.

"I have no idea," said Red-Gulos. "I assumed there was no reason for a comms man to have a thorough knowledge of each planet that his species populates, especially since there are likely to be thousands of such planets."

"I see," said Duggan. He looked at the blue dot on the console which represented the spaceship. "The *Valpian* hasn't moved away."

"They are going to send down a shuttle."

Duggan was temporarily speechless. "I thought you said they were reassured?"

"They are reassured that we are not an invading squad of enemy soldiers, Captain John Duggan. However, in light of the recent events in the vicinity of the Helius Blackstar, they are dispatching a team of personnel to examine the data this monitoring station gathered in the last few days. They are convinced there is information to be unearthed on the *ESS Crimson* somewhere in our logs."

Duggan laughed bitterly. "They don't trust the people stationed here to do a good enough job."

"I think that sums it up."

Duggan knew he shouldn't be surprised – the same thing happened wherever you went. Not just in the Space Corps, but in every organisation. There'd be a person unable to trust the work of someone else and they'd need to stick their nose in. It was foolish to think other species didn't act in a similar manner.

"This could spoil everything we've achieved so far," he said.

He couldn't pretend it was anything other than an awful result. The raid on the Dreamer base had been conducted with minimal damage to the buildings, in order to make the signs of combat harder to detect. A transport shuttle was unlikely to be equipped with warship-grade sensors, but it couldn't fail to notice the activity on the ground when it got closer. Even if the shuttle's pilot was only a tiny bit suspicious, he might ask the *Valpian* to take a closer look. It wouldn't take a warship too long to realise the installation had been attacked.

His plan had been limited in scope – buy them some time and see what came from it. With the shuttle approaching, he was forced into taking a much bigger gamble.

"How big is the shuttle?" he asked.

"Twenty metres by forty," said Red-Gulos. "Perhaps a little larger. The parent ship is more than two thousand five hundred metres in length."

"Contact the *Valpian*," Duggan said. "Tell them our perimeter alarms have just sounded and we've detected hostiles in position for an attack on this central building. Make them believe this is a surprise to us."

"What will that achieve?" asked Red-Gulos. "It is difficult for me to speak mistruths."

"Then speak in riddles!" snapped Duggan. "Let me know what their response is."

"Very well. I'm opening a channel to the *Valpian*."

There was a further barked exchange of words between Red-

Gulos and the Dreamer warship. The anger was clear on both sides. After a few moments, the Ghast muted the connection in order to speak to Duggan.

"They are not happy about this sudden change of circumstance and have pressed me to provide specifics on the raiding forces."

"Keep them uncertain. Advise that the only reason for a ground attack on this particular building would be the theft of vital monitoring data. Make them believe this is an unfolding situation which we are struggling to adapt to."

There were more words, no less angry than those spoken earlier between Red-Gulos and the warship. "The captain of the *Valpian* wishes to speak to my superior officer."

"Tell them he's missing, or dead. Whatever is easiest for you. Request backup."

"There are insufficient armed troops on the incoming shuttle to repel a substantial attack on the base. They would like an estimation of the numbers we're facing. Their sensor scan of the installation suggests the attack is limited in nature and they can only detect their own soldiers outside."

"You're going to have to convince them," said Duggan. "I don't care how difficult it is, you'll need to lie through your teeth."

"Tell me what you hope to achieve. It will help me."

Before Duggan could respond, his eyes noticed the tiny circle which represented the inbound transport shuttle. The tiny vessel slowed and then came to a complete stop. It hovered in the middle of the display screen, as if it waited for more information before proceeding.

"Damnit, we need them to come here!" he said. "Advise of a breach in our external walls and that we're facing hostile forces who are attempting to gain entry to our central data room. Let the captain of the *Valpian* know that we've extracted the main AI core and the most recent data arrays. Request immediate evacuation from the roof. Make it clear we are facing superior numbers and we cannot hold out for long before the enemy captures or destroys this data."

Red-Gulos grunted in acknowledgement and began the task of convincing the Estral on the warship, high above the surface of Nistrun. The talking continued for a long time and Duggan's worries mounted. Then, he saw the transport vessel start moving again and it resumed its course towards the installation.

"It is done," said the Ghast.

"Yes!" Duggan growled. "Good work, soldier. Let's see what we can do from here." He spoke to Lieutenant Ortiz. "We have an inbound enemy shuttle which will attempt to land on the roof of this building. We need to capture it intact and before they alert their parent ship *Valpian*."

The briefing was only a few words, yet contained within those words were a thousand opportunities to fail, and difficulties beyond measure.

"Yes, sir," said Ortiz, as if he'd ordered her to do no more than run a hundred metres. "I've had a couple of the guys out scouting and we've already found a way to the roof."

"How much pressure are you under?"

"Some. I thought they'd have got their act together by now, but they're not well-organised."

Duggan had another idea - they were coming thick and fast. "I want our Ghost friends looking as much like Dreamers as possible."

Ortiz didn't reach her station because she was slow on the uptake. "There's a locker of enemy spacesuits here, sir. We can scavenge what we need. They won't be able to do a complete change of clothing without having air to breathe."

"I understand. As long as it fools the enemy for a second or two. See to it at once." He checked the speed of the transport shuttle. "I reckon there are less than seven minutes until they land. They'll be expecting to see a number of their brethren carrying data arrays and at least one AI core. We'll meet you up there as soon as we finish here."

"Roger."

No sooner had his conversation with Ortiz finished than Duggan became aware of a further development. The *Valpian* had launched two more vessels, these ones more than twice the size of the first.

"Those will carry the ground forces needed to repel our attack," said Red-Gulos. "They could contain several hundred soldiers, as well as some heavy weapons."

"They'll be here in twelve minutes, sir," said McLeod. "There's no room for those additional shuttles to land on the roof."

"They'll unload on the perimeter," said Duggan. "And I don't intend being here when they come knocking on our door."

"If we intend to steal their data arrays and processing core, we should begin the search at once," said Red-Gulos.

"Hold! We're going to try and land a much bigger fish now and I don't want to be slowed down by four hundred pounds of AI core and associated memory banks. We're going to have a hard time getting everyone to the roof in time as it is."

Byers spoke, as if she'd just that moment realised exactly what Duggan was planning and the reason they needed to capture the transport vessel. "Are we really going to storm the *Valpian*, sir?"

"We're going to give it our best shot, soldier. And for once, luck is on our side – the enemy has committed a substantial number of troops to reinforce this base. Except we're not going to be here when they arrive."

"We're going to be on their warship," Red-Gulos replied, sounding as close to happy as Duggan had ever heard from a Ghast.

Duggan hesitated before ordering his squad to move in the direction of the roof. "Is there anything we can do to disable this monitoring station?" he asked.

"Maybe," said Byers. "If so, I don't know how to do it. What about you, McLeod?"

"Sorry, sir. I can't help you with that."

"What if I got Rasmussen to blow this console up with his plasma launcher?"

"It won't destroy the data. They'll need to buy an expensive new piece of kit to replace this one, but the backups won't be here."

"Never mind," said Duggan. "I don't think it's of vital importance. They clearly don't know where the *Crimson* is. However, I don't want them recapturing this room and speaking to the *Valpian* while we're on the roof. Scatter grenades around it and leave them on a one-minute timer."

It didn't take long to leave plasma grenades at the edge of the main console. There was a lot of other equipment in the room which Duggan didn't recognize. They were going to have to leave it to chance and hope there was no backup comms gear elsewhere. Either that or rely on the enemy being slow to get here.

He ordered his squad to make haste and they doubled back to the huge room with the two tanks inside. The vehicles had been expertly positioned a few inches within the outer wall breaches to make it difficult for the enemy soldiers to get past. There was gunfire, which came in sporadic bursts and pinged against the Gunthers. Ortiz waited next to a distant doorway.

"This way!" she said. "The enemy have fallen back and they seem happy to wait us out."

"They have reinforcements coming, Lieutenant. Two big shuttles packed with their friends. They're probably congratulating themselves on their coming victory."

Ortiz laughed. "Follow me. There are a lot of steps."

"Is it clear?"

"As far as I know."

Duggan and his squad joined with Ortiz. They went through the doorway and into another passageway, which they jogged along two abreast. After forty or fifty metres, they passed something hanging from the wall, which Duggan realised with astonishment was a decorative picture. It consisted of a metal frame around a series of strong-coloured geometric shapes and was the first example of such he'd seen amongst either the Ghasts or the Dreamers. He felt an overwhelming temptation to take it with him, though it was not the time or the place to be carrying artwork. Aside from that, Duggan was an honourable man and he didn't think he'd be able to steal, even from his foes.

They reached a wide doorway on the right. A series of metal-grilled steps went upwards for a way, before doubling back on themselves and continuing. A light flickered on and off and something buzzed insistently.

"This leads all the way to the top floor," said Ortiz. "You can access the inside of the lens and there's a doorway onto the roof."

"Lead on," said Duggan, itching to see how this would play out.

CHAPTER EIGHT

THE STAIRS TOOK them into a comparatively small, square room, eight metres to a side. There was no decoration whatsoever and Duggan's suit helmet interpreted a smell in the air that was something akin to grease. It was unexpected, but not alarming. He listened for a moment, expecting sounds of pursuit. There was nothing.

"Over here," said Ortiz, setting off at once through another doorway. This was much narrower than the others and Duggan saw why. It led onto a staircase, wide enough for one human or Ghost to walk up comfortably, whilst ensuring there was hardly room for two to cross if someone was coming down while another came up. The staircase curved to the right, until it disappeared from view.

"Does this go around the lens housing?" asked Duggan.

"Yes. There's a whole load of technical stuff in a room above us. That's where the others are – it'll be a tight squeeze."

The staircase had no railing, but it was easy enough to climb. At the top, it was clear Ortiz had not been exaggerating about the lack of space. There was a small, circular room, so filled with suited humans and Ghosts that the last two of Duggan's squad had to remain on the steps. The walls were almost entirely covered in blue-lit screens, along with buttons and several banks of mechanical levers. It looked quite rudimentary.

There was a single exit door, constructed from thick-looking metal. It had a wheel in the middle to lock or unlock the door depending on how it was rotated. It was a long time since Duggan had seen such a mechanism. The Space Corps relied on electronics for nearly everything these days.

There were Ghosts at the door – Link-Tor, Glinter and Havon. Their hulking figures looked misshapen where they'd roughly clad themselves in the grey materials of the enemy space-suits. Even in the dull light of the room it looked unconvincing and Duggan doubted the makeshift disguises would fool the enemy for long enough.

He squeezed his way close to the front. Someone made a joke in the open channel describing how surprised they were to see him arrive on time. Duggan was a stickler for punctuality, though the troops hadn't forgotten the single time he'd kept them waiting.

"I think I've found my next volunteer," said Duggan, grunting with the effort of getting through the crowd. "When I need someone to throw a grenade into a repeater nest, I know McLeod is the man."

There was laughter, which quickly faded when the importance of the next few minutes reasserted its control over the mood.

"Sixty seconds until the shuttle lands," said Red-Gulos.

"Get the door open," said Duggan. "Don't make it obvious."

Glinter took hold of the locking wheel with one hand and give it a spin. The wheel turned easily. There was an associated handle which the Ghost pulled upwards. The seal made a quiet hiss as it was broken.

"We're going to need both skill and luck to win this one," said Duggan, speaking privately to Ortiz and Red-Gulos. "If the shuttle lands too far away or we're slow, it's game over for us."

"Nothing new," said Ortiz. She sounded on edge.

"Glinter, open that door a crack and stick your head out," Duggan ordered.

The Ghost didn't acknowledge and nor did he delay. He put his shoulder to the metal and pushed. Nothing happened and he tried again.

"It opens inwards, you stupid bastard," said Vaughan.

Far from being upset at the words, Glinter gave out a rumbling laugh and took a step back. He elbowed the other soldiers aside, and two more had to shuffle their way onto the steps. The Ghost pulled at the handle and the door let out a muffled clunk as it opened a fraction.

Duggan was close enough to see through the thirty-centimetre gap. There was a shape outside and the hint of flexible metal and an intricate helmet.

"Shit!" said Duggan. He tried to get his rifle free, but there was no room to bring it to bear. "Get back!" he shouted, pushing with his shoulders to try and clear some space.

Someone fired a gauss rifle. At the same time, Link-Tor thrust an enormously thick arm through the opening and pulled. An enemy soldier was dragged inside. There wasn't enough room to accommodate an additional body and Duggan heard shouts of alarm when several of his troops were forced tumbling into the stairwell. Fists rose and fell and a second gauss rifle fizzed three times in rapid succession.

"He is dead," said Link-Tor.

Duggan opened his mouth to order the attack. Another voice forestalled him - it was Jackson, the calmness in his voice a façade to cover the closeness of his death. "I've got a breach in my suit from that fall," he said.

"Someone patch him up!"

"No can do, sir," said Kidd. "His helmet is split open like a watermelon."

Duggan swore. It was too late to do anything other than continue with the attack. "We need to move!" he said urgently. "If the others on the shuttle saw what happened, they'll be halfway to the *Valpian* by now. Out! Go!"

Glinter tried to wrench the door open, only to discover the fallen enemy soldier was blocking the way. The Ghast kicked out a couple of times and hauled at the door again. This time, it opened much wider. Havon stooped and picked something up from by his feet, which Duggan hadn't seen until this moment. The Ghast lifted up a large pack, which was draped in the grey material of the Dreamer spacesuits. He carried this pack in such a manner that it concealed much of his head and shoulders from casual scrutiny.

Link-Tor and Glinter had their own packs, which they hoisted up, to make it appear as if they held a cargo of vital equipment rescued from the building below.

"Go!" said Duggan.

"We are not armed," said the Ghast.

"We'll follow."

Link-Tor stepped through the door, leading with his pack. "The enemy shuttle is to the left of the door and twenty metres away," he reported on the comms. "Two guards on the ramp with rifles. No sign of alarm."

The Ghast disappeared from view. Havon and Glinter followed a pace or two behind. Duggan took a deep breath – the shuttle was as close as he could have wanted, but there was still much that might go wrong. He found himself next in line to exit onto the roof.

"Don't put any holes in that shuttle," he said, stepping forwards. "It's Jackson's only chance."

Even as he emerged onto the roof, he knew the soldier was doomed. If Jackson held his breath, the air in his lungs would expand, killing him quickly. If he expelled as much air as he could, he'd pass out from a lack of oxygen in a few seconds. Duggan knew he couldn't afford to think about it and prepared himself for the coming attack.

He looked to the left and saw the shuttle parked nearby on the roof, resting on a dozen thin legs. The transport was rectangular at the bottom, with a curved roof. The cockpit was a streamlined wedge, with a silvery metal band running around the middle, which Duggan guessed might be a viewing window. The vessel was more elaborate than most of those in the Space Corps, but not exactly one to raise an eyebrow at the daringness of the design. The sun pierced the thin atmosphere and the temperature outside was searingly hot. The wind blew strongly and grit rattled off Duggan's helmet. The low thrum of an idling gravity engine reached his ears, along with indistinct sounds of activity on the ground below.

The shuttle's side door was down, creating a ramp. Havon and Glinter were halfway up and they grappled with two of the Dreamer guards as they attempted to wrest the weapons from the guards' hands. The Ghasts' packs were discarded on the roof nearby. Of Link-Tor there was no sign.

Duggan readied a shot and then thought better of it when he saw how risky it was. He sprinted over, his feet thumping hard onto the metal. He wasn't halfway to the shuttle when he saw other shapes inside, with more outside and to the front of the vessel. He estimated there might be ten or more in total.

The first of Duggan's squad dropped to their knees, firing shots in controlled bursts. Two of the Dreamers at the front of the shuttle were pitched onto their backs. There were others and they crouched behind the landing legs, preventing Duggan's men from getting a clear shot.

"Keep them pinned down!" shouted Ortiz. She fired three rapid shots into the interior of the shuttle.

"If you puncture that shuttle, Jackson's a dead man!" said Duggan.

"He's already gone, sir," she replied in the clipped tones she reserved for battlefield communications.

"Damnit!" Duggan fired two rounds from his own gun, anger making his aim poor. Nevertheless, he hit one of the Dreamers hiding at the front of the shuttle. It stumbled, clutching its leg, and was met by a hail of gauss slugs.

Duggan reached the bottom of the ramp. It seemed as if Havon was getting the best of his opponent, but Duggan didn't leave it to chance. He smashed the butt of his rifle into the side of the enemy's helmet. The Dreamer staggered to the side and Havon thundered a punch into its stomach. The enemy soldier tried to retreat into the passenger bay. A series of bullets hit it in the upper body, spilling its blood onto the hull of the shuttle.

Ahead, Duggan saw dark figures crouched in the depths of the shuttle's interior. His helmet sensor adjusted in a moment, highlighting the enemy soldiers in orange. He jumped to one side, away from the open doorway. A projectile clipped his shoulder on its way past – it was only a nick. There was blood, but no pain and the spacesuit did its business by sealing tightly over the wound.

"Sorry, sir," shouted Camacho.

"Shit, watch where the hell you're shooting!" bellowed Ortiz.

The last of the Dreamers outside the shuttle was killed by a series of well-aimed shots from Duggan's soldiers. There were five inside and they stayed in the cover of several bulky metallic objects near to the far wall. They kept low and fired randomly, making them difficult to flush out.

Suddenly, one of the enemy moved. He carried a metal plate awkwardly in front of him as a makeshift shield and walked with it, heading to the front of the shuttle. Dozens of shots pinged away, but the enemy soldier was protected by the metal. The shield jerked under the weight of the projectile impacts, yet it was strong enough to keep the soldier behind it safe.

"Shoot his damned fingers!" said Bonner.

"He's going for the bridge!" said Hendrix.

Duggan could scarcely believe it when the enemy soldier disappeared through an open doorway that led to the front of the shuttle. A moment later, he recognized the sound of the vessel's gravity drive building in preparation of a take-off.

"This is not going to happen," he said. He unclipped a grenade and threw it into the shuttle. It detonated, blowing a three-metre hole in the hull and spreading plasma across the interior. The enemy soldiers were killed instantly, torn apart by the blast before the heat of the aftermath could do the same.

Duggan was the first to react and he vaulted onto the boarding ramp. His broken arm buckled under the weight, letting him know it was still mending. With a snarl, he ordered the suit to inject him with a huge burst of pain blockers and rolled onto the ramp. He got to his feet, already aware it was far too late to stop the shuttle's pilot from either taking off or communicating news of the attack to the *Valpian* as it flew overhead.

A large figure stumbled from the cockpit and Duggan raised his gun to fire.

"Hold!" shouted Ortiz at the top of her voice.

"We need to move quickly," said Link-Tor, his voice weak.

Duggan pushed through the space between the Ghast and the cockpit door. There was a Dreamer there, its helmet ripped off. It thrashed and frothed. Duggan shot it and it lay still.

"Squad One, get those bodies out of sight!" he ordered. "The rest of you, get onboard!"

He looked around the cockpit. It was far too large for the amount of equipment it held. There was a two-person console at the front, with two padded chairs. He dropped onto one of them and scanned the layout. There were functions he recognized, whilst others were unfamiliar and labelled with script his language modules couldn't comprehend.

"Red-Gulos, get in here," he said, turning to find the Ghost already entering the cockpit.

"I will assist."

"Can you fly this?" Duggan asked.

"If it were one of ours, I could fly it," said the Ghost. "I would not like to risk piloting this one unless you order it."

Duggan was confident he could handle any kind of vehicle, as long as he knew what controlled what. "I'll do it," he said. "Tell me what these three panels do."

Red-Gulos struggled with the translation. After a pause, he made a few suggestions. Something clicked in Duggan's head and suddenly, the arrangement of the Dreamer controls made sense.

"If you can fly a warship, you can fly anything," he said to himself. He waved to the second seat. "Here's where we prove to the universe that impossible doesn't exist. In this instance, I've got it easy – all I have to do is fly. You, on the other hand, are going to work these comms and do everything you can to convince the *Valpian* to let us dock."

"I am glad we are no longer at war, Captain John Duggan," said the Ghost with another of his rumbling chuckles.

With that, Duggan checked everyone was onboard. Once he was satisfied, he closed the external boarding ramp, fully aware there was a big hole in the hull. He touched his fingers against two separate panels and the gravity engines climbed rapidly towards maximum output. With his brain remembering Lieutenant Chainer's hypothesis that there was a best way to do everything, no matter which species you belonged to, Duggan pulled on the control sticks. The shuttle lurched to one side until he steadied it. It rose into the air, slowly at first and then gaining momentum as Duggan's confidence grew.

The strip around the front of the shuttle wasn't a windscreen; rather it was a wraparound display, upon which Duggan was able to view the enemy base as it receded with distance. The lens of the monitoring station stared back as though it were judging him for his actions. He ignored the feeling and concentrated on keeping the shuttle heading where he wanted. By the time they were fifty kilometres up, he felt as if he'd been flying craft like this for a lifetime.

"Let's see if we can surprise the crew of the *Valpian*," he said, feeling light-headed from the adrenaline and the painkillers.

CHAPTER NINE

THE BEST DUGGAN was able to judge, it was a fifteen-minute ride up to the enemy warship. He didn't want to leave his seat to check the status of his troops personally, so he called Lieutenant Ortiz into the cockpit. She was still fully suited, to protect herself from the lack of pressure in the shuttle and Duggan felt momentarily foolish that he hadn't simply used the comms to speak with her.

"How are we doing?" he asked.

"Link-Tor is going to die," she said flatly. "Corporal Weiss is working on him, but he's taken a good few shots. I don't know how he managed to fool them long enough to get into the cockpit, but he did a good job."

"We owe him," said Duggan. "The Ghasts we have with us are everything Subjos Gol-Tur said they would be."

"That they are. We had to leave Jackson's body behind."

Duggan's anger returned. "What a pointless way to die," he spat. "Falling down a set of damned stairs."

"I should have ordered ten of us to wait in the room below," said Ortiz quietly. "I should have realised we were too bunched up."

"In that case the blame lies with me as well, Lieutenant."

"No, sir, it doesn't. You shouldn't need to micromanage everything. I'm meant to catch the little things."

"It happened and we can't change it. Grown men and women shouldn't need to be told that a steep staircase is dangerous. Besides, we needed to be out of that door as soon as it opened."

"Yes, sir."

She wasn't convinced. For his part, Duggan was deeply upset at the two deaths, but he knew when it was time to blame himself and when something was no more than a terrible accident.

"Are there any other injuries?" he asked.

"Only yours, sir. Want me to have Camacho flogged?" Duggan was relieved to hear the humour creep back. "There's a law from about fifteen hundred years ago that states an officer of lieutenant rank can order up to fifty lashes. They never saw fit to rescind that law."

"Oh?" said Duggan, unaware such a law existed. "How many lashes can a captain order?"

"Up to two thousand, I believe. The law stems from an ancient, barbaric period in the history of humanity."

Duggan looked at the place he'd been caught by Camacho's stray shot. There was a shallow graze over the material of his suit and it didn't take a medic to realise it wasn't going to be fatal. "Let him know I'll give the matter some thought. If he excels on the *Valpian* I might limit his punishment to a mere thousand lashes, administered by Red-Gulos here." There were times it was inappropriate to joke and others when it was all you had.

Ortiz laughed, the sound unable to completely hide her despair. "I'll send Corporal Weiss in to take a look."

"Don't," he warned. "Spend the time getting everyone

prepared. There's a good chance we're going to get blown out of the sky in the next fifteen minutes. If we manage to escape that fate, we've got an enemy warship to capture. It's two-point-five klicks in length."

"Size matters nothing if they've sent all their soldiers to reinforce their base. What happens if, I mean *when* we seize the *Valpian*, sir?"

"The honest answer is I don't know. I've been told on more than one occasion I overthink things. This time, I'm sitting back and taking it easy as far as the thinking aspect goes. We'll storm the bridge and see what happens from there."

"It sounds easy when you put it that way." She hesitated. "We've come a lot further than I thought we would."

"We're a quarter of the way up the ladder. There's a long way to the top."

"We'll make it."

"I'm trying not to look too far ahead. In case it brings us bad luck."

"I do the same, sir. I tell myself it's stupid, but I just can't help it."

Ortiz left the cockpit and returned to the personnel bay. Duggan asked Red-Gulos questions about various symbols on the shuttle's console that his suit computer didn't recognize. He knew the inevitable request from the *Valpian* was coming, though he tried not to think too hard about it.

"On a Space Corps vessel there'd have been an attempt at communication immediately after take-off," he said. "Is the Ghast navy as unconcerned as the Dreamers when it comes to the status of its units?"

"I would not expect to spend much time chatting with a comms man," the Ghast replied. "It is usually sufficient to speak a single time prior to landing."

"Is that what will happen here?"

"I think we will hear from them when we are within five thousand kilometres." Red-Gulos turned and Duggan saw cold, grey eyes through the clear visor. "These Estral have much in common with we who fled, but they have become soft with their power. Their advanced technology has been enough to overcome those who oppose them up until now. I am not certain they will enjoy meeting a foe as determined as humans or Ghasts."

Duggan thought the words well-spoken, even if he believed them over-confident. The Dreamers had the numbers and the resources to crush the Space Corps and the Ghast navies easily if they wished. The only hope was to play for time in order to prepare.

The two of them sat in silence for another few minutes. Duggan remained in the open comms channel and listened to Ortiz planning and organizing. Once they got onboard the *Valpian*, they'd need to move efficiently and act with ruthlessness in order to suppress the inevitable resistance. There could still be hundreds of enemy soldiers stationed within its hull, in which case defeat was inevitable.

They reached a point far above Nistrun and Duggan focused the shuttle's sensors on the *Valpian*. Operating the console was already second-nature and his hands were able to work without needing his brain to interpret the symbols on the screens. He'd always possessed an aptitude for flight. It wasn't something he bragged about – there were people who could produce wondrous works of art, whilst others could make music so beautiful it would bring tears to the eyes of the listener. Duggan couldn't do those things – he knew how to pilot vast machines of death and he could do it as well as anyone.

The image of the *Valpian* was muddy and wavering. Lieutenant Chainer had once speculated that the Dreamer sensor technology was hardly better than that used by the Space Corps.

Certainly the shuttle had a rudimentary sensor array and Duggan needed to peer closely in order to get an idea about the *Valpian*'s construction.

The enemy vessel was a long, slender cuboid with rounded edges. It was slimmer at the front and wider at the back. Its nose tapered into a wedge. Along the underside of the hull there were struts, holding what appeared to be landing skids, each one over two thousand metres in length. There was a single topside dome near to the front, with another to the rear. The rest of the hull bristled with square missile clusters, which protruded in groups of four. There was something else, which Duggan was unable to believe the first time he saw it - jagged blue lines of raw energy flickered at irregular intervals across the hull, as though the warship's physical form was incapable of containing the power within.

Had there been any doubts about the nature of the *Valpian*, they were dispelled as soon as its shape became clear. Duggan had up until now acted in the belief it was a warship, though without any proof he was correct. Here it was, with its sleek lines and brooding air of menace. The Space Corps' ships had the same threatening appearance, though theirs was that of a lean streetfighter. The *Valpian* looked as dangerous as an expert duellist.

"It looks new," said Red-Gulos.

"Yes. I've faced their cruisers before and this one looks like an evolution of the design. A big evolution."

"They will be surprised when we board them and shoot their captain," said Red-Gulos.

Duggan caught sight of an unnervingly white-toothed grin through the Ghast's visor and he couldn't help smiling himself. "They're too cocky for their own good. We'll show them what happens when they bite off more than they can chew."

The conversation was interrupted by a complex flashing

symbol on one of the comms screens. Duggan's helmet computer dutifully translated: *Inbound Message. Priority 5.*

"I will need to respond," said Red-Gulos.

"Are you clear what you will tell them?"

"We rescued the monitoring station crew and we are carrying one of the memory arrays. We suffered a grenade hit in the side and we have several injured personnel who require immediate medical attention."

"That covers it. Make them believe."

"There are ways to fool someone without lying," said Red-Gulos.

A deep blue panel lit up on the middle of the console and an alarm sounded, muted yet unmistakeably a warning.

"They've targeted us!" said Duggan.

"We're taking too long to respond."

"You'd better see what they want."

The Ghost activated the comms panel and spoke. Duggan was able to understand many of the words, but the nuances were lost, leading him to believe he was missing the underlying meaning. The Ghosts spoke in hints and suggestions, rather than outright lies. *Misdirection is the same as deception,* Duggan thought to himself. *We are closer to each other than anyone would like to believe.*

The conversation between Red-Gulos and the Dreamer on the *Valpian* continued for a time. The harshness in the two voices remained, as if all speech was conducted from a position of anger.

The *Valpian* was a thousand kilometres away and still there was no indication they'd been given clearance to land. There was a docking bay towards the rear of the hull, open and clearly-visible. Duggan aimed towards it and kept his speed down, so as not to cause alarm.

At five hundred kilometres, a series of purple lights flashed insistently to the left-hand side of the shuttle's control stick.

Duggan was sure it was the auto-dock function demanding to be activated. Red-Gulos didn't show any sign of finishing his conversation, so Duggan reached out, meaning to activate the autopilot.

"Don't!" said the Ghast urgently.

Duggan withdrew his hand and continued piloting the shuttle manually. The lights on the comms panel winked out, suggesting the conversation between transport and warship was concluded. Red-Gulos rolled his metal-clad shoulders as if he needed to release the tension in them.

"If this shuttle is anything like those in the Ghast navy, once you activate the autopilot you hand control to the parent ship, rather than activating a built-in routine on the transport itself. We would have no control over when we accept inbound comms, nor control over the outer doors. Everything would be in the hands of the *Valpian*, including access to the shuttle's internal monitoring cameras."

There wasn't any point in taking additional risks, so Duggan accepted the words without argument. "Are they happy with us landing manually?"

"I told them we have no choice, owing to the damage we sustained from the grenade blast. Their captain is very interested to hear about the so-called enemy soldiers we faced."

Duggan laughed. "I intend to meet him at the earliest opportunity." He brought Lieutenant Ortiz into the channel and told her it was nearly time. "There's no room for mercy here. We have to kill everything that gets in our way."

"I understand, sir. The troops are aware."

"Try not to shoot anything that looks as if we might need it later."

"You can't have it both ways, sir," she said in the perfectly-neutral tones of a junior officer politely telling her superior how unworkable his recent suggestion was.

"Fine. Shoot at will," he said. "Except on the bridge."

"Except on the bridge," she repeated.

The *Valpian* was flying in a high, tight circle over the installation below. Its course was predictable and so easy to match that Duggan did it without much effort. The landing bay was only a few kilometres ahead, a rectangular opening which spilled blue light into space. There was one additional shuttle inside, clamped in place to the side wall. It was much larger than their existing vessel.

"Room for four," Red-Gulos observed.

"The hangar is big – they must have plenty of spare power if they can afford to use all this space for shuttles instead of engines. And it's deserted," said Duggan. "So much for having the medical staff waiting. Do you know where we go to exit the bay once we've landed?"

"Your guess is as good as mine, Captain Duggan."

"I don't like guessing," Duggan muttered.

With that, he gave his utmost focus to the task of landing the shuttle into the bay of a fast-moving enemy warship. After a few minutes of careful manoeuvring, he set them down dead-centre and with barely a jolt. Behind, a thick alloy door rolled slowly up from its place between the walls of the warship's hull. It took a minute or two and once it was fully sealed, the lights in the landing bay vanished without warning, leaving the shuttle in absolute darkness.

"What's this?" asked Duggan, pointing to a request on the central display of the pilot's console.

"The *Valpian* is waiting for a code," said Red-Gulos.

"Why does it need a code? I don't have a damned code!" Duggan's heart sank when he realised he had no way to jump this security hurdle.

"I did not expect this," said the Ghast. "We may not be able to exit this bay until you provide a suitable authorisation code."

Duggan clenched his fists in impotent anger, while his brain struggled to think of a way out of the situation.

CHAPTER TEN

"INBOUND COMMS from the *Valpian*'s bridge," said Red-Gulos.

"They'll be wondering where their codes are. Can you tell them the person who knows them is incapacitated?"

"That is the logical next step. I will attempt to convince them."

The Ghast spoke only briefly and Duggan didn't need to understand the exchange in order to know there was a problem.

"What's wrong?" he asked.

Red-Gulos switched the comms onto mute. "I earlier convinced the bridge I am the shuttle's dedicated comms man. Apparently, I am one of the three people they expect to have the necessary codes to complete the landing process. The bay won't repressurize without them."

"They must know something is amiss," said Duggan.

"If they don't, it won't take long for them to realise. I believe their comms man is speaking to one of his superior officers."

"They'll recall the shuttles from the surface and this place will soon be crawling with their soldiers. We need to act."

Bonner was the explosives expert and Duggan spoke to her, looking for some guidance on whether or not they'd be able to blow their way through the internal bay doors to get into the other areas of the ship. The answer was not what he wanted.

"If the Dreamers build their warships remotely like ours, there's not a hope in hell I'll be able to get through any of the bay walls, sir. Not even if I had five packs of explosives. The two plasma tubes we're carrying won't get you any further."

"Damn," said Duggan.

He called up an external sensor feed and panned around the bay. The absence of light made the image particularly poor and he found it hard to locate what he was looking for.

"That looks like a door," he said, indicating a rectangular area on one wall, approximately two metres by three.

"A sturdy door," agreed Red-Gulos.

Duggan continued moving the sensor around, pausing when he noticed something at the front of the other shuttle. He jerked upright when he recognized it. "I need to get over there," he said.

"We have another comms request from the bridge," said Red-Gulos. "This time it's a Priority 2 message."

"Answer it," said Duggan. "Stall for time. We're losing our element of surprise and as soon as that happens, they'll recall the other two shuttles and they'll organise their internal defences."

"As you wish," said the Ghast.

Duggan didn't wait around to listen. He opened the cockpit door and went through to the passenger bay. The first thing he noticed was the pile of dead Dreamers. They'd been dragged onboard and dumped against the far wall.

"There was nowhere better to put them," said Barron.

The other members of his squad were mostly on their feet and they milled around nervously. A few lounged in the uncomfortable seats, presumably trying to affect an air of nonchalance.

Lieutenant Ortiz was there. "What's wrong, sir?" she asked.

Duggan didn't stop walking and headed towards the uneven grenade hole in the shuttle's double-skinned hull. "We're trapped in here. The crew are suspicious."

The edges of the hole were sharp, though it was easy enough to get through without damaging his spacesuit. It was two metres to the floor and he dropped down, landing more heavily than he wanted. There was movement and he saw Ortiz following, along with Rasmussen, the latter carrying a plasma tube.

"You need someone to cover you," she stated.

Duggan saw no need to disagree. "We need to get inside that shuttle," he said. "It's got a nose-mounted chain gun."

He broke into a run. The lack of an atmosphere combined with the denseness of the floor meant his footsteps made no sound. Usually the helmet microphone could register the presence of noise, even in a near-vacuum. This time, it picked up nothing.

There were no obstacles on the floor and it was a hundred-metre run to the second shuttle. The closer he came, the more detail his helmet sensor could resolve from the darkness. The vessel's purpose as a transport was obvious – it had an armoured hull and a single cannon to lay down suppressing fire during a troop drop. It was also sealed, with no way to get inside.

Duggan reached it first, with the others close behind. The shuttle was clamped in place, with its landing gear down – eight short legs rested on the floor of the bay. There were three doors in this side of the vessel and Duggan stopped at the nearest. The doors also acted as boarding ramps and with them closed, the floor of the shuttle was a good two metres up. Duggan cursed himself for not realising what a stretch it would be. There was a softly glowing panel adjacent to the door.

"That must be nearly four metres up," said Ortiz. "You can stand on my shoulders if you want."

Ortiz was strong but she likely weighed sixty pounds less than Duggan.

"Not a chance, Lieutenant."

"Your arm isn't better yet."

"Good point. Rasmussen, give the lieutenant a boost."

The soldier laid his plasma tube reverently onto the floor. He locked his fingers together in front of him and Ortiz planted her boot between his hands. With a grunt, Rasmussen lifted her upwards until she could get her palms against the side of the shuttle. Then, she stepped onto Rasmussen's shoulders. It was quick, if somewhat ungainly.

"Get it open," Duggan said.

She stretched up and pressed her fingers to the panel. "It's not responding, sir."

"Try again."

"I already did."

Time was running out. "Get down. Rasmussen, blow it open."

Ortiz jumped nimbly to the ground and Rasmussen retrieved his plasma launcher. The three of them ran directly away from the shuttle.

"I'm not sure I've got the firepower, sir. The armour looks pretty thick."

"Do it."

Rasmussen's doubts didn't stand in the way of him doing as he'd been ordered. He flipped the heavy tube neatly around until it was positioned on his shoulder. It was beeping even before it was in place and its projectile whooshed away within a split second. The rocket detonated with a grumbling thump against the side of the transport, obscuring a quarter of the vessel in white-hot plasma.

Rasmussen knew his stuff and didn't need to wait for the fires to recede in order to realise the first shot had failed. He fired again, the second rocket adding its heat to that of the first.

"Again," said Ortiz.

A third rocket followed and then a fourth. The alloys of the shuttle were turned into molten sludge, which dropped away in huge lumps. They splashed to the floor and splattered droplets of liquid metal in a wide area beneath the hole.

"That should do it," said Rasmussen.

"I need to get onboard," said Duggan, already running. "Sergeant Red-Gulos, get the troops out of the shuttle at the double. Cover the left-side bulkhead door. The *Valpian*'s internal monitoring will have alerted the crew about the plasma explosions in here. There's only one conclusion for them to draw."

"At once, Captain Duggan."

"You'll burn to a crisp if you get too close to that burning alloy, sir," said Ortiz, calling after Duggan. "Your suit won't help."

Duggan was willing to take risks. Even so, he wasn't suicidal and the blistering heat coming away from the breach in the shuttle's hull was enough to bring him to a halt.

"There's no damned time!" he growled in frustration.

"I don't think I'm strong enough to throw you through there, sir," said Rasmussen.

"Braler is," said Ortiz.

She called a command through to the first shuttle. The Ghast came, running with an oddly clumsy long-legged gait which reminded Duggan of his low-gravity training from many years ago.

"Get me up," said Duggan.

He knew the Ghast was strong but hadn't counted on just how strong. Braler put one hand beneath each of Duggan's arms and lifted him a metre off the ground without apparent effort. Then, he hurled Duggan forwards and away towards the hole in the armoured shuttle.

It wasn't perfect. Duggan's shins landed on the hot metal. The material of his suit melted at once and he kicked his legs frantically until he was inside. The pain returned from a combination of his partially-mended arm and the burns on his lower legs. His suit gave him a painkilling shot and the agony receded to a level where he no longer felt the need to grit his teeth.

He clambered to his feet, aware that four plasma explosions in the *Valpian*'s hull would have the troops onboard scrambling to investigate.

This second shuttle was much like the first and he found himself in a long, unlit room, with seating enough for three hundred or more troops. Towards the rear, there was a pair of evil-looking multi-barrelled heavy repeaters, mounted on what he assumed were compact gravity drives. The details were indistinct in the darkness. The cockpit door was to his left and it was open.

Grunting with the pain, he forced himself to run the twenty metres to the doorway. The cockpit was much as he'd expected it to be, with room for four to sit and an additional set of controls for the heavy gun mounted on the vessel's nose.

"Will it power up, sir?" asked Ortiz, concern in her voice. "They'll be coming soon."

Duggan sat himself on the central seat. There were no lights on the console, which was a bad sign – in the Space Corps it was usual to keep control equipment powered up at all times. He pressed one or two buttons, trying to activate anything that would respond, only to find the shuttle's control systems remained stubbornly offline. The nose cannon was the only weapon with the capability of getting through a four-metre thick bulkhead door, but if he couldn't get the shuttle working, there was no way to aim the gun where he needed it.

There was movement and a figure came through the door – it was Ortiz.

"Check out those mobile guns in the passenger bay," he said. "The shuttle's offline."

"I've looked, sir. Even if they're twice as powerful as the ones we use in the Space Corps, they'll burn out before they'll get us through the door."

Something caught Duggan's eye – there was a square slab of black metal propped up on top of the control console, which he'd missed because he was concentrating elsewhere. There were symbols on it, etched in white. His language modules translated them literally.

"*Operational misfit?*" he said. "What the hell does that mean?" He contacted Red-Gulos. "Patch into my suit camera and tell me what this says."

The familiar rumble of laughter reached his ears. "That is bad news for us, Captain Duggan. You have found a notice which says the shuttle is out of action."

The Ghost's words hit Duggan hard. They'd fought every step of the way, inch by inch bringing themselves closer to an improbable victory over their enemy. Now they were stuck, trapped in the bay of the *Valpian* with no choice other than to await the return of the other two shuttles, or for the troops already onboard to muster an organised response. The despair he felt wasn't for himself, it was for the people who'd followed him this far, drawn to his unspoken promises that he would eventually bring them home. He stood up, shaking with rage and the scarcely-masked pain of his injuries.

"I will not have this!" he shouted.

He kicked out with his foot, hitting the shuttle's console firmly at the base. Fresh pain shot through his toes. He didn't care and kicked out again and again. Suddenly, the console sprang into life, row upon row of lights and screens coming online in the blinking of an eye.

"Did that just happen?" asked Ortiz, sounding as utterly shocked as Duggan felt.

"Upon such tiny miracles does our existence rest," he said, quoting words the origin of which he no longer remembered.

The shuttle's gravity engines were cold and they responded sluggishly when he fed power into them. They'd likely need an hour before they could deliver anything like their full output. Fortunately, Duggan didn't need them to do much at all, other than rotate the vessel.

In the few moments it took to prepare the engines, he did a mental best guess about how long it would be until the other two shuttles returned – fifteen minutes, his mind told him. An insidious second voice whispered that it would be substantially less than fifteen minutes if the crew of the *Valpian* took active steps to close the gap between the warship and the returning transports.

"What would I do if I were the captain of a warship in this same position?" he asked himself.

He knew exactly what he'd do and he gritted his teeth in renewed anger. The only competent approach the Dreamer captain could take was to keep Duggan and his soldiers contained in the bay of the *Valpian*, recall the other two transports and then use their nose cannons to spray the hold with bullets. One versus two wasn't good odds and Duggan didn't fancy his chances of slugging it out with the enemy given the circumstances. They had to get out of the hold and they had to do it soon.

A flashing symbol brought him to back to the present, letting him know the engines had reached five percent of maximum output. After that, there was a brief moment when he thought the gravity clamps wouldn't disengage and he worried they might have been locked by someone on the bridge. He sighed with relief when they released and he fed a trickle of power through the engines. The landing feet scraped across the floor and the shuttle thumped twice as he moved it away from the side wall. When there was sufficient clearance, he turned the spacecraft until its nose pointed directly at the side bulkhead door.

"Lieutenant Ortiz, please do the honours," he said.

She sat at the weapons console. There was nothing complicated about it – a joystick controlled the movement of the gun and there was a button on top to begin firing. "With pleasure, sir," she said.

Ortiz aimed manually and pressed the button.

CHAPTER ELEVEN

THE WEAPON WASN'T STRICTLY a chain gun; however, most soldiers used the colloquial term as it was less of mouthful than 'rotating Gallenium-driven gauss repeater'. The model on this shuttle had ten barrels arranged in a circle and their bore was sufficiently large to put a hole in almost anything.

There was a short spool-up time, during which the chain gun rotated to its full speed. Then, the slugs poured out. In a vacuum there was little apparent drama – there was no muzzle flash and with no air to carry the sound, there was only a thrumming in the cabin to indicate the gun was firing.

Duggan found the sensor activation screen and brought up an external view. There was movement across the width of the hangar bay, like a thick, blurred line connecting the shuttle's nose to the far wall. Two thousand five hundred rounds spilled from the gun each second. They hammered into the opposite wall, pummelling the ultra-hard alloy with unstoppable velocity.

"Shit," said Ortiz in grudging admiration when she saw the damage inflicted on the hangar's interior door.

The metal heated, starting off as a red glow, which built into a deep orange. The hotter the metal, the softer it got, until eventually it would give way. That was the plan, at least.

"It's taking too long," said Duggan impatiently. Each passing second was a moment they couldn't afford to waste.

"This temperature gauge is climbing quicker than I'd like," said Ortiz, checking the gun's status display.

"Hendrix, Berg, Rasmussen, fire your tubes at that door."

"Those bullets will chew up the rockets before they explode, sir," protested Hendrix.

"Aim off-centre then!" Duggan snapped. "I need you to put as much heat as you can into that metal!"

"Yes, sir."

"And keep a couple of rounds in reserve. We might need them later."

The plasma tubes held six rounds each and they were disposable. Once the ammunition was gone, there was no point in hanging onto the launcher if you didn't need to. Duggan tried to calculate how many rounds they'd fired recently. He gave up quickly – Rasmussen's launcher was almost empty, but the others should have a few rockets left.

Plasma explosions joined the intense, torrential flood of gauss bullets. The door and surrounding metal became a mixture of orange and white, speckled with an ever-changing pattern of darker circles where the projectiles punched into it.

"Come on!" Duggan roared.

"The chain gun is going to shut down soon, sir."

"Don't let up!"

Two more plasma rockets detonated off the door and Duggan noticed a series of smaller explosions interspersed amongst the chaos. The soldiers knew their time was limited and they hurled grenades, darting out of cover in order to land their throws more accurately.

"Three of the barrels have shut off," said Ortiz. "Wait - make that six barrels."

"Keep firing! If we stop now we'll have nothing left to get us through."

The chain gun burned out a few seconds later and it stopped firing completely.

"Did we do it?" Ortiz asked.

"I don't know."

Duggan got out of his chair and ran through the passenger bay, with Ortiz following. The shuttle's doorway had cooled sufficiently and he was able to execute a quick hang-and-drop to the floor using only his good arm.

"Keep low," warned Ortiz. "In case we got through and there's someone waiting on the other side."

There was little in the way of cover and Duggan chose speed over caution. He dashed to the first shuttle, around which most of his troops were arranged. There were others who had taken the initiative and these five had their backs pressed to the bulkhead wall a few dozen metres away from the door.

"Two thousand Fahrenheit near the centre," said Cabrera. "I'm not going first."

Duggan crouched at one of the shuttle's landing legs and stared at the interior door. His helmet sensor struggled with the contrasts and he wasn't sure if there was a way through.

"Can you see?" he asked Red-Gulos, in case the Ghast sensors were stronger than their Space Corps equivalents.

"I can only guess."

Duggan lacked the patience to wait longer. He left the scant shelter beneath the shuttle and sprinted towards the five soldiers at the bulkhead wall. The temperature of the damaged metal had already dropped since Cabrera announced it at two thousand degrees and Duggan thought he could see through to the other side. His heart jumped at the possibility they might have broken into the ship. When he was fifteen metres away, his suit detected a faint breeze, as well as the presence of oxygen.

"We got through," he said. "The area on the other side of the door is depressurizing. I don't know how big the hole is."

It was inconceivable to think an entire warship would be vulnerable to something as simple as a breach into the vacuum. Sure enough, by the time Duggan reached the wall, the levels of escaping oxygen had already fallen, indicating the *Valpian*'s interior was compartmentalized.

Duggan shuffled his way along the smooth wall until he was only a few metres from the door. The alloy felt warm through the insulation of his suit and his HUD gave a warning about the temperature. There was no option other than to ignore it and he stepped ever closer to the doorway. The alloy had faded to a mixture of reds and oranges as it cooled.

"It's clear, sir! I can see through!" said Ortiz. She was standing opposite the hole, near to the first shuttle and with her rifle pointed forwards.

"Is there any movement?"

"Not on my sensors."

Duggan took a deep breath. The helmet sensors were good, but they could be fooled in a number of ways and extreme contrasts of temperature was one of them.

"Anyone else see movement?" he said across the open channel.

He heard a dozen negatives, which gave him some reassurance.

"They weren't expecting us to get through the hangar wall!" he said in realisation. "The stupid bastards thought they had us trapped."

It wasn't an entirely foolish notion to think the solid walls of a warship would be able to repel the attentions of a small band of soldiers, but it still took Duggan by surprise. He wondered if he'd become so used to the expectation of failure that he was becoming blinded to the chances of success. A wave of giddiness washed through him at the thought, insisting he grasp this opportunity with both hands and not let it go.

"We need to get through this door and take the ship while we still can!" he said.

"What about the shuttles, sir?" asked Ortiz. "If they land, we'll have hundreds of the enemy chasing us through the interior of the *Valpian*."

Duggan's mind churned through the options. There was no chance they'd be able to capture the entire ship, figure out how to operate it and then either destroy the incoming shuttles or simply fly away from them.

"Lieutenant Ortiz, I need you to get those gauss repeaters off the second shuttle and deploy them in preparation for an imminent attack from outside."

"Yes, sir," she replied at once.

Orders were given. Several humans and two of the Ghasts sprinted towards the second shuttle.

"What are your thoughts, Captain John Duggan?" asked Red-Gulos.

"I think we've caught them unawares, Sergeant. I think we've got our noses in front for the first time since we crashed here on Nistrun. If we don't take this ship, we've spurned our chances."

"They will know there's a breach through the internal hangar wall. We cannot let them pin us on the far side of this bottleneck."

The Ghast was right – they couldn't wait a moment longer before going through the gap in the blisteringly hot metal. If they could establish a strong position on the other side, it would give them the platform to push on.

"You can't go through, sir," said Ortiz.

"Stop reading my mind."

"None of us can fly a Space Corps warship, let alone a Dreamer one."

There was an excellent chance that the first person through would die if there were any enemy soldiers waiting in ambush. Unfortunately, there was no time to delay and they needed to know what lay beyond. "Who wants it?" he asked across the open channel.

"I've got this one, sir," said Camacho.

The man clearly hoped to repent for his stray shot into Duggan's shoulder.

"I don't hold a grudge, soldier."

"I didn't think so, sir."

Before a further word was spoken, the lights in the docking bay came back on. The sudden shift caused the sensor on Duggan's helmet to brighten almost unbearably before it adjusted. He looked around, seeing few new details of any importance. The only thing which concerned him was the light itself. It wasn't a static shade of blue like it had been when they came into land – this time the colour cycled from dark to light and back again.

"I know what that means," said Duggan with certainty. "It's an automated warning that the outer door is going to open." He called out to Ortiz. "We need those mobile guns in position, Lieutenant."

"We've just got here, sir. They're not the same as ours and we haven't figured out how to power them up yet."

"Does Braler know?"

"He's as much in the dark as we are, sir."

"That door is going to open soon. Get yourselves out of there and we'll get into the main part of the ship. We might be able to fortify."

"Negative, sir. We can get these guns working."

Ortiz wasn't *quite* disobeying orders but she was running it close. If Duggan hadn't trusted her so much he would have been angry. As it was, he left it to her judgement, instead of repeating his command for her to leave.

"It's in your hands, Lieutenant."

"We'll sort it, sir."

The conversation ended. Movement to his right caught Duggan's attention - it was Camacho. He was on the same wall as Duggan, a few paces further from the door. The soldier broke away and ran past. He hesitated only fractionally and then hurled himself at the gap in the red-hot metal, vanishing inside.

"Camacho, please report!" said Duggan.

"Damnit it's a sealed area!" was the response. "And my suit's smoking."

Before Duggan could request more details, he felt something clunk – he sensed it as a deep shudder within the wall behind him. He recognized it as the operation of something huge and mechanical. He jerked his head to the right, towards the vast, rounded external door of the hangar bay. A gap appeared at the top, through which the utter blackness of space was visible. The gap became steadily wider as the door slid smoothly downwards.

"Aw crap," said Barron.

Duggan couldn't have put it better himself.

CHAPTER TWELVE

DUGGAN'S BRAIN switched up a gear, into a mode where it grasped each possibility of the battlefield and evaluated each option swiftly and dispassionately. "Lieutenant Ortiz, get those guns working *now*," he said. "Bonner, go through this doorway and see what you can do. Check out what's blocking our progress - I want you to blow it open. Don't piss about."

"Yes, sir!" Bonner said. She was over by the first shuttle, fifty metres away. She covered the distance in less than ten seconds carrying her heavy pack of explosives. Without pause, she threw herself headlong into the gap in the hangar wall.

While Bonner ran, Ortiz spoke. "We've got both guns powering up now, sir," she said, relief evident in her voice.

"There's no time to position them nicely. You'll need to leave them on the shuttle and aim them through the side doors. Set them to auto and if we're lucky they should fire for a couple of seconds before the enemy craft realise what's happening. It might be enough."

Over at the second shuttle, he saw several figures jump through one of the side doors. They didn't stick around and they ran directly across the docking bay floor. There was other movement and the two gauss repeaters appeared, their muzzles aiming outwards and towards the opening hangar door.

"The rest of you, get to this wall!" Duggan ordered.

The few who remained around the first shuttle began to run. There was no sign of Ortiz and she remained in the second transport.

"Come on, Lieutenant, where are you?" he shouted. "You're running out of time!"

"There's no auto, sir. I'm staying here with Braler to fire the guns manually."

"Shit, get over here, Lieutenant."

"Negative, sir. This is the best chance we've got."

Duggan looked towards the outer door again - it was a third of the way open already. He couldn't see the enemy shuttles, even when he went to maximum zoom on his sensor. They were out there, he knew it with certainty. The only hope was they didn't have an angle to start shooting yet.

"How are you doing in there, Bonner?" he asked.

"There's a door, sir. It's going to take half of my charges to get it open. We'll have to come back into the hangar or we'll burn."

Duggan couldn't wrench his eyes from the main door. There was still nothing visible beyond it, but those nose cannons could likely target and fire from beyond the range of his helmet sensor.

"Negative, we're coming in!" he said.

He made the command over the open channel and one-by-one the soldiers dashed through the remains of the bulkhead door. It was a tight fit for the Ghasts and they had to turn sideways to manoeuvre their shoulder plates into the space.

Duggan took his turn. He faced the gap, his sensor able to make out more details now that the alloy had cooled somewhat. The combination of gauss rounds and plasma explosives was an ugly one, and they had punched an irregular opening in the door of about six feet high and four wide. The sides burned with dull anger, rather than the fury of before. It was more than hot enough to set off an alarm in his suit when he took the final step towards the threshold and he felt as if he were stepping through a gateway into the very depths of hell. Inside, the metal was rough-edged and he could see how treacherous it was – sharp pieces of partially-melted alloy intruded and he had to keep a careful watch to avoid them. Underfoot, it was similar and unseen objects slithered away when he trod on them. *We got through four metres of solid metal,* was the only thought he had time to form.

Then, he was on the other side, his HUD showing half a dozen blinking amber alerts. Here and there, the material of his suit was scorched black and he hoped it hadn't become brittle enough to split. He moved quickly away from the source of heat, to save his suit from further damage and to let the next person through.

His sensor adjusted quickly. This was a big room – fifteen or twenty metres to a side and with a single, simple control console on the right-hand wall. Red-Gulos was in front of it, pressing tentatively at one of the screens. Elsewhere in the room the soldiers had spread themselves around, with most of them looking straight towards Bonner. The squad's explosives expert had her pack on the floor and she was busy fixing pale-blue charges around the edges of another large door.

"How long?" Duggan asked her.

"I can be ready to blow it in less than a minute, sir." She hesitated. "It'll kill half of us if we stay in here. Really it will."

"We're not in the best of positions, soldier," he told her. "Let me know when you're ready."

The next voice was that of Ortiz, calm in spite of the perils. "I've got a target!" she said grimly. "Firing."

"Out of the way," said Duggan, pushing Vaughan and Cabrera to one side.

He crouched and looked through the hole into the hangar bay. He had a good view of the second shuttle and saw the two portable repeaters open up. As with the shuttle's nose cannon, they gave off no sound and no flash. The only indication of their activity was a distortion in the air, which traced a line across Duggan's vision.

"Come on!" he muttered, gripping the barrel of his own rifle until his knuckles ached and the bones in his forearm complained.

The two repeaters continued to fire for what seemed like an age and Duggan's hopes grew that it would be enough. Ten seconds passed during which Ortiz and Braler operated the guns without a response. Then, an answer came. Bullets raked into the hull of the shuttle. Its armour was sufficient to deflect the fusillade for a moment, but the attack didn't stop and the enemy slugs beat against the shuttle's metal plating. The vessel was gradually pushed away across the hangar bay floor, its outline becoming more distorted with each passing second. The repeaters operated by Ortiz and Braler vanished within a second of each other, smashed and broken into pieces.

The enemy stopped firing and everything was still. The second shuttle was a mess, filled with thousands of holes. Three of its landing legs had broken off and the hull was tilted to one side. Duggan swore.

"Lieutenant Ortiz, Braler, please report."

There was no answer.

"Lieutenant Ortiz. Report, damnit!"

"She is gone, Captain Duggan," said Red-Gulos. "And Braler."

"They can't be!" he shouted.

"Her vital signs are no longer registering on our close-range network."

Duggan punched the wall. He felt pain, without caring.

"We need to act," said the Ghast.

"What the hell can we do?" he asked, knowing at once how stupid the words sounded. He needed to take command and he did so. "Bonner, get those explosives ready! We're going to capture this ship if it's the last thing I do."

"Yes, sir. I'm placing the final two charges."

Duggan took another look into the hangar bay, wondering if he'd see Ortiz and Braler running to join with the rest of the squad. There was nothing – the ruined shuttle lay in its place, bathed in the ever-changing blue light.

He was about to turn away when his suit detected something that his unaided ear would have missed. It amplified and modified the vibration and transmitted it to him – it was more a sensation than an outright sound. There was a harshness that Duggan recognized at once – it was the labouring of a heavily-damaged gravity engine.

"Give me that launcher," he snapped at Rasmussen, holding out his hand. "Hendrix, Berg, follow me."

Rasmussen duly handed over the plasma launcher. Duggan waited only long enough to be sure Hendrix and Berg understood his order. When he saw them move towards him, he ducked his head and ran through the broken hangar bay door, producing a series of additional heat alerts from his suit.

It was more than a decade since Duggan had fired a plasma tube. Time hadn't made him rusty and he found his arms swinging the weapon up to his shoulder, smoothly and without conscious thought. His target was visible, three or four hundred metres away. The enemy shuttle hung in the vacuum outside the *Valpian*. It was badly damaged and Duggan had no idea how it was still in one piece.

With shame, Duggan realised he hated those onboard the shuttle. Anger was hard to avoid in the heat of battle and it was an asset if properly controlled. Hate, on the other hand, was an emotion which robbed him of his humanity.

The coils in the plasma tube hummed and the single remaining rocket sped away, leaving a tiny trail of grey-white particles in its wake. It hit the enemy shuttle where the cockpit joined the passenger area. The explosion seemed small from this distance. Hendrix and Berg were at his side and they fired their own tubes.

"That's me out," said Berg.

"I've got one more," said Hendrix. "Awaiting recharge."

As the two additional missiles crossed the intervening space, Duggan watched the front cannon turn in its housing, seeking out the two men and the woman standing below. Hendrix and Berg were experts with their chosen weapons and each scored a direct hit. The front end of the shuttle was engulfed and Duggan prayed it had suffered terminal damage.

The transport's chain gun opened up and a withering hail of bullets raked through the intervening space, smashing into the walls and floor behind the three who faced it. They stood, unwavering, as if their defiance would make them victorious against the raging metal. Duggan's gauss rifle was slung over his back. He shrugged it free and started shooting in controlled bursts, the faint thump of the recoil in his shoulder as fulfilling as it had ever been.

"They're firing blind. Must have burned out their front sensor array," said Berg, as if she were commenting on something entirely mundane and unimportant.

"Where's that last one, Hendrix?" asked Duggan.

"Coming."

A bullet tore a furrow in the floor less than a metre from

Duggan's left foot. He ignored it and fired again and again, with no idea if his efforts were in any way significant.

"There she goes," said Hendrix.

The final plasma round flew from its tube. From where Duggan was standing, the missile appeared to arc gracefully towards its destination. It struck the glowing nose of the shuttle close to where the others had impacted. This time there was no doubt – the transport was ripped apart, as though it had been held together by a web of threads, each of which were cut simultaneously by this last strike. The vessel fell away, the pieces separating and dropping out of sight, plasma still burning ferociously in half a dozen places.

"Gotcha," said Hendrix.

"Yeah," said Berg. There was no joy in her voice.

Duggan lowered his rifle and his anger faded. His treacherous mind recalled Ortiz's words that he was the only one who could fly the *Valpian* – he'd jeopardised the whole of the squad. He felt sorrow at his own weakness. *I'm as human as any of them.*

"Sergeant Red-Gulos. Get everyone out into the hangar bay. Tell them to prepare for whatever might be on the other side of that inner door."

While the soldiers emerged from the inner room, Duggan ran over towards the second shuttle. It was a mess and it was impossible to imagine anyone could have survived. The tilt on the shuttle allowed him to see easily inside the passenger bay. Braler was dead. He was only recognizable because pieces of his suit remained untouched. There was blood – seemingly gallons of it splashed on the floor and the walls.

Bonner spoke to him. "Sir, should I blow the door?"

"Yes. Blow it."

Duggan hauled himself into the shuttle. It was a mess of broken seats and metal containers, none of which had escaped damage of one sort or another.

"Heads down," said Bonner over the open channel. "This is going to get hot."

He was turning to leave when his suit highlighted the smallest of movements in a fleeting hint of orange. Ortiz was there, beneath a pile of crumpled metal boxes. He dragged the debris to one side until he could see her, prone and face down. She stirred, this time the movement was unmistakeable.

"Corporal Weiss, get here at once," he said. His voice croaked with the words and he repeated them in case they hadn't been clear.

Another voice spoke. "Hostiles. Squad Two into position," said Red-Gulos.

Duggan jumped out of the shuttle and ran to join the fray. The squad's medic sprinted to the shuttle as if her heavy pack was no burden at all and the two of them passed midway across the hangar bay floor.

It only took seconds for Duggan to reach the others. It was plenty of time for him to reflect on events which had taken him from the extremes of misery to the heights of exhilaration, with hardly anything in between.

CHAPTER THIRTEEN

BIT BY BIT they captured the enemy warship. It wasn't clear what the usual complement of soldiers was on a vessel such as this one, but it was soon apparent the majority of them had been killed on the two shuttles. Those few who remained lacked either training or motivation, both of which Duggan's soldiers had in handfuls.

There were one or two pockets of resistance as they advanced the length of the *Valpian*, most notably in a large mess room through which Duggan and his soldiers were required to pass in order to proceed. It took skill and bravery to flush out the enemy who were holed up in the room, but once their resolve crumbled it was easy to finish them off.

Lieutenant Ortiz was on her feet again, though her suit helmet was badly damaged. Her comms worked only sporadically and the suit's computer reported a variety of false messages to the rest of the squad. Weiss's opinion was that the lieutenant had suffered a serious concussion, leaving Duggan with no choice other than to temporarily relieve Ortiz of her of command. She didn't object and her injury meant Red-Gulos took over as Duggan's second.

A few minutes after leaving the hangar, Duggan felt the subtlest of dislocations. If he'd not served on a variety of spacecraft for so many years he would have missed it.

"We've gone to lightspeed," he said.

"I don't think we will enjoy the reception once we reach our destination," said Red-Gulos.

The longer he spent with the Ghasts, the more Duggan was able to pick up their dry sense of humour. They'd seemed dour and uncommunicative at first; now he could tell they were merely different.

The interior of the *Valpian* held no great surprises when compared to a Space Corps vessel. The Dreamer warship had more open space within, though that space didn't appear to serve much purpose. There were recreational areas, mess areas complete with elaborate-looking food replicators, and sleeping quarters which contained little in the way of recognizable home comforts.

Elsewhere, there was an unsecured armoury room, with most of its gun racks empty. There were three Dreamers inside, whom Duggan's troops surprised and killed. This area of the ship remained pressurized and the three aliens wore heavy uniforms of grey cloth, which Duggan assumed were their normal on-duty apparel.

Duggan was curious to see one of the enemy guns close-up. He pulled one of the few remaining rifles free from its rack and turned it over in his hand. It was a grey tube much like the one he carried and had four red buttons on the side. There was no way to tell if it was better or worse than the one he had and since this wasn't the time for experimentation he put it back in its place.

Deeper into the vessel, Duggan found two more wall pictures similar to the one he'd seen in the base on Nistrun. Later, he found something which might have been a cushion. He picked it up, looked at it for a moment and then discarded it, unsure what he should think.

Here and there, monitoring panels were embedded in the walls and, in what appeared to be the primary maintenance area, there was a vastly complex console which they had no time to study in detail. These areas were connected by wide, cold passages, which occasionally turned at right angles for no apparent reason. There were thick doors at intervals, invariably closed. They provided no barrier to the squad's progress, since each could be opened using a control panel in the wall nearby. It was as though the enemy never considered the possibility they might be boarded and had taken few precautions to defend against it. Everything was lit in a blue which exacerbated the impression of chill. Duggan had to resist the urge to shiver, even within his suit.

The spaceship was an evolution of the technology already possessed by the Space Corps and the Ghast navy. Duggan suspected the enemy engines were thirty or forty per more efficient than those built by the Confederation and he knew their AI tech was a good twenty or thirty years ahead. After that, it came down to the weapons and defensive modules they fitted onboard.

"They're not so far ahead," he said to Red-Gulos, wondering if he was trying to convince himself rather than the Ghast.

"Far enough, Captain Duggan. In terms of numbers, we will never catch them. Equal technology won't save us from extinction."

"We need a game changer."

"Easily said. Not so easily accomplished."

Eventually, they reached the bridge, with only three comparatively minor injuries amongst the squad. At a place where two main passages converged there was a short flight of metal steps.

At the top was a door. It was the same as many others on the ship, except this one displayed an easily-translated sign. *No Entry.*

"Secure the area," said Duggan. "Cover that doorway and these two corridors."

As the soldiers hurried to comply, Duggan moved cautiously up the steps towards the door. There was an activation panel adjacent. He crept down again, mindful he was the only one with a chance of flying the *Valpian*. He ordered his troops to withdraw until they were a good distance from the steps and around a right-angled corner. He didn't want to come all this way only to lose a dozen people to a plasma grenade thrown by someone on the bridge.

"McLeod, get up there and see if you can open the door," he said. "Cabrera, you provide cover."

The pair of them moved away at once.

"Bonner, have you got enough to blow that door?" he asked.

"Maybe," she hedged. "I'd need to take a proper look at it first."

They were stuck if they couldn't get the door open. The bridge on a Space Corps vessel was always behind a heavy blast door. If the *Valpian*'s bridge was similarly protected, they'd never be able to force a way through.

"I'm approaching the door," said McLeod in a hoarse whisper.

Several seconds passed, during which Duggan kept his fists tightly clenched.

"Please report," he said.

"We're clear, sir," said McLeod. "You need to come and see this."

Duggan ran from cover and towards the steps. He paused at the bottom and saw that the bridge door was open. McLeod was nowhere in sight, whilst Cabrera was standing at the top, looking inside. Duggan climbed to join her.

"The bridge," she said, indicating needlessly with a wave of her rifle.

Duggan stared into the room. It was blue-lit and compact, four metres long and six wide. The walls were plain and the floor was smooth. There was a single, curved console at the front which extended the full width of the bridge. A single glance was enough for Duggan to recognize both the differences and similarities to the equipment he was used to. There were eight seats arranged in pairs in front of the main console. These seats were large, with too many right-angles and no sign of padding.

There were bodies – seven of them in total and all male. They were in their seats, upright and with their arms by their sides.

"They're dead," said McLeod.

The Dreamers looked so naturally posed that Duggan couldn't bring himself to believe the words. He walked to the closest alien, keeping his rifle aimed towards it. McLeod wasn't mistaken. The crew of the ship stared ahead, their eyes open and their faces bereft of expression, as if they'd been frozen in time.

"Corporal Weiss, get in here," he said.

She didn't take long.

"Will your box of wonders tell us what killed these?" he asked.

"Probably," she said, already in the process of attaching wires.

"Well?" he asked. The answer wasn't necessarily important and he needed to get on.

"Poison, administered orally," she said. "Suicide."

"Are they safe to move?"

"I wouldn't like to kiss one, but there's no harm in touching them otherwise."

"Sergeant Red-Gulos, send Havon in here. We've got some bodies to move," said Duggan. "The enemy crew have killed themselves. The bridge is secure."

"Yes, sir," said the Ghost, referring to Duggan as *sir* for the first time.

"Keep the area secure. There are sure to be others still alive on the ship but we can't risk overstretching by trying to flush them out. It's going to take me a while to figure out how everything works."

"Do you need my assistance?"

"Yes. Come up here. Leave Corporal Gax in charge."

The former captain of the *Valpian* was easy enough to recognize. He wore red, where the others wore blue. There was an insignia on his chest and his cheeks were tattooed with blue symbols, their meaning unknown. Duggan looked into the open, grey eyes and wondered if he'd ever be able to feel so much shame that the only option left was to take his own life.

"They should not have given up," he said to Red-Gulos when the Ghost arrived.

"Perhaps they imagined the alternative was worse. The punishment for their failure might have been a thousand times harder than a quick death to poison."

Duggan was reluctant to dwell on it, though there was something about the suicides which took away from what should have felt like a great victory. *We haven't won anything yet,* his inner voice reminded him.

As soon as Havon dragged the dead captain away, Duggan sat. The captain's seat was cold and hard, without any side bolsters or support. He immediately wished he'd possessed the foresight to bring the cushion he'd found earlier. The seat was also designed to be occupied by a creature in excess of seven feet tall. Duggan wasn't a short man, but everything on the *Valpian*'s console was a little too much of a stretch. It irritated him immensely.

"Where're the engine controls?" he muttered to himself, trying to figure everything out. Exiting lightspeed before the

Valpian reached its pre-programmed destination was the main priority. They would also need someone to work the sensors as soon as they returned to normal space.

"McLeod, Byers, get to the bridge and see if you can assist Sergeant Red-Gulos," he said.

The two soldiers arrived, their suit helmets nowhere to be seen. "The interior is pressurized, sir," McLeod said. "The life support must keep things steady."

Duggan had been concentrating on other matters and McLeod's words reminded him that most of the *Valpian* had a breathable atmosphere. He'd left his helmet on simply because there was nowhere to put it down. With a feeling of relief, he unlatched it and put it on the floor beneath his seat.

"Check out the enemy comms gear," he said, pointing to his right. "I assume their comms and sensor arrays are closely tied in."

"A big assumption, sir," said Byers, taking a seat. She ended on a positive note. "I picked up one or two things on Nistrun. Maybe I can figure this out."

"Yeah, I think I can give it a go," said McLeod, sitting next to Byers.

There were screens, buttons, touchpads and four joysticks, none of which were labelled. Duggan pressed and pulled, with each action causing a response from one of the nearby monitors. Bit by bit, and with the assistance of Red-Gulos' superior knowledge of the Estral language, he built up a picture of how the *Valpian*'s controls worked. With a vast amount of learning still ahead, Duggan figured out how to disengage the warship's fission drive. He experienced the familiar sensation of a switch to gravity engines and it was done.

"What's out there?" he asked.

"We'll get back to you," said McLeod.

"There are several queued inbound messages, which arrived

as soon as we emerged from lightspeed," said Red-Gulos. "Each of them at Priority 1."

"The Dreamers will want to know what's happened to their valuable warship," said Duggan with a tight smile.

"Should I respond?"

"Not just yet. I need to think. How is the area scan coming along?"

"We're getting there, sir."

Duggan was on edge while he waited. He knew it wasn't the soldiers' fault they couldn't operate the *Valpian*'s sensors – their training was a mixture of combat and tech, whilst someone like Lieutenant Chainer was entirely focused on performing a single role. It needed someone at the absolute top of their game to take charge of totally unfamiliar equipment such as this.

"I think we're in the clear, sir," said Byers. "There's definitely nothing hostile close by."

"I'm still on the fars," said McLeod. "I need three pairs of hands to work this stuff and I'm a little rusty on the interpretation."

"We're right in the middle of nowhere," added Byers. "No planets, no stars."

"And no enemy spaceships," said McLeod, looking relieved at his conclusion.

"We've done it, sir," said Byers with an expression of dawning astonishment. "We've really done it."

Her words struck Duggan like a bolt of lightning. "Yes," he said. He cleared his throat. "Hell, yes!" He leaned across and clapped Byers on her shoulders. She grunted at the impact.

He accessed the open channel. The warship was ultra-dense and some of the troops were unreachable. "Pass the message on folks," he said. "We've done the impossible. We've stolen an enemy cruiser and got away with it."

There was a raucous cheer in response. The soldiers had

been under immense, unrelenting pressure for too long. The news of their success was just what they needed to give them some respite. Duggan's inner pessimist crept up to tell him there was plenty more to do. He ignored it and sat back to enjoy the moment, even if only briefly.

CHAPTER FOURTEEN

DUGGAN WAS MENTALLY and physically exhausted. Even so, he spent the following six hours familiarising himself with the controls of the *Valpian*. In a similar way to a Space Corps warship, the enemy vessel required only a small crew to operate. It was still too much for Duggan alone and he kept the other three with him and did his best to teach them the basics. He needed the support and these were the best placed to assist.

Reports came in from his men and he was pleased to learn that Corporal Gax had completed a careful sweep of the ship and reached a point where he was confident enough to advise Duggan that the interior was effectively clear of the enemy. Even if there were some left in hiding, there wasn't much they could do to wrest back control of the ship. Duggan was relieved, though he warned Gax to keep on full alert.

Corporal Weiss stayed close by and administered a variety of mild stimulants that would keep the warship's new crew alert, yet without filling them with bravado or making them overconfident. Duggan enquired after Lieutenant Ortiz and was told she would need a more in-depth medical assessment soon. She'd suffered an injury that the portable med-box could only partially diagnose and treat. The troops had found Ortiz a place to rest and she was in a closely-monitored sleep. The *Valpian* possessed medical facilities, but Weiss stated she wasn't sure whether any attempt to operate the alien equipment would end up doing more harm than good. Ortiz wasn't at immediate risk of death – at least as far as Weiss could tell – so Duggan suggested there was no need to push things just yet. He didn't like the situation, though with nothing he could do to make it better he got on with business.

"I can control the *Valpian* manually with these joysticks," he explained to Red-Gulos, Byers and McLeod. "It's not much different to what I'm used to, if a little nimbler than anything in the Space Corps. Some of the weapons are locked down and we don't have a code to work them. In fact, I can't even tell you what those ones are. Luckily, we can launch missiles and the energy shield comes on automatically when we power up any of the other weapons arrays. We have two particle beams as well and they're easy enough to lock on and target. The Space Corps and Ghast navies would give anything to learn how they keep the range and power so high."

"I think I can just about keep you informed of potential threats," said Byers. "McLeod can feed you the targeting information."

"It's the navigation I can't figure out entirely," said Duggan. "I can send us to lightspeed and back, I just can't work out how to tell the ship where to go. The arrangement is unusual."

"What is the plan?" asked Red-Gulos.

"I felt we'd done enough to return home before we crashed on Nistrun," said Duggan. "We've done more than enough now."

"So, we're going back?" asked Byers, not trying to hide her preference in the matter. "I think I'd like to see home again."

"We're going to *try* and go back," he replied. "There are a number of obstacles in the way."

"Will the *Valpian* make the transit?" asked McLeod.

Duggan's gut instinct told him the cruiser had been designed to do exactly that. He didn't know what gave him the feeling, other than the apparent newness of the design along with the evident eagerness of the Dreamers to plunder Confederation Space. "Maybe," he said. "I'd prefer to try it in the *Crimson* if at all possible."

"Isn't the *Crimson* a bit beat up?"

"It's not in good shape. It needs a new core to activate the double jump we use to get through the wormhole. Even if we could somehow extract one of the cores from the *Valpian*, the chances of getting a successful interface with the *Crimson*'s systems is vanishingly small."

"How many cores are on the *Valpian*?" asked Byers.

"Three. I have no idea where they are or how to get to them and I only know there are three because it tells me here on this display." He tapped a finger on one of the many screens. "They could weigh five hundred pounds each for all I know and operate at a thousand degrees Fahrenheit."

"Not straightforward, huh?"

"Too many unknowns." Duggan forced a smile. "We won't know until we try. One thing is for certain – we're heading back to Nistrun and we're going to see what we can do. If I can get my crew onto the *Valpian* I'm confident we'll be able to use it at a level much closer to its full potential. No offense meant."

"None taken, sir."

"A warship's navigational system must contain a comprehensive chart of known space. Once I can find it within all of these other systems here, I should be able to get us on our way to Nistrun. We were only at lightspeed for a couple of hours – a tiny step in the grand scheme of things, but far enough that we have no hope of guessing how to return."

"Anything we can do to help?" asked Byers.

Duggan chewed his lip. "I thought I'd be able to access the list of coordinates from here," he said. "Except there's no data."

"Could the enemy crew have stripped it clean?" asked McLeod. "That would be a good way to get revenge – send us on our way to one of their space ports and remove any way for us to go elsewhere."

"And stop us obtaining a map of their populated worlds," said Byers.

With a sinking feeling, Duggan believed they might be on to something. There was a single set of coordinates that he could locate easily and those were for the destination the *Valpian*'s crew had chosen. These coordinates were not linked to anywhere else within the ship's navigational system. Duggan had never flown on a vessel where the charts were difficult to access – they needed to be at the pilot's fingertips at every moment and it seemed unlikely the Dreamers would have significantly different methods.

Not one to give up easily, Duggan spent a further hour searching for a chart. There was nothing to be found. He swore and then swore again.

"The enemy captain must be laughing at us from his grave," he said.

Red-Gulos took on a puzzled expression and he turned to look over his shoulder. "I do not understand. The enemy captain is where Havon left him - in a pile with the other members of his crew at the bottom of these steps behind us."

"It's a figure of speech," said Duggan. He grimaced. "We have the freedom to go anywhere, but in reality, there's only one destination open to us."

The Ghost lowered his brow and looked at Duggan. "If we follow this one course, we will surely be destroyed upon our arrival. What do you expect to find? An undefended base with databanks of star charts, waiting for us to plunder them?"

"I don't know. I prefer to take direct action when I have the option. We may not know what we'll find but we are still doing *something*."

"There is always a choice. We could go anywhere we want and keep searching until we find an opportunity to improve our situation."

"If we lived to be a thousand years old, we might not come across anything more than deserted planets and dying suns."

"That is true. The point is, nobody can decide the course you take. Do not allow a dead man to defeat you."

Duggan pondered the words and realised he'd let himself be sucked into a position where the dead captain of the *Valpian* had dictated his actions. *There must be another way,* he told himself, trying desperately to believe it.

He put himself into the former captain's position, only this time he pretended the *Valpian* was a Space Corps vessel. He imagined himself having to strip out as much vital information from the databanks as possible before his spaceship fell into enemy hands.

"It couldn't be done," he said, shaking his head. If data was lost from one of a warship's primary systems, the ship's computer would assume it happened as a result of weapons damage and automatically restore the information from the backups. This process could happen repeatedly and it was unheard of for a warship to become permanently lost in known space.

"Could I delete the backups or prevent the restore?" he said, speaking his thoughts out loud. "Not without a great deal of time." He drummed his fingers on the console. "I could set the backups to restore their data to a secondary memory array. It would be still accessible to someone who knew what they were doing, but it wouldn't be visible on the primary systems."

He snapped his fingers. There was an old tale he'd once heard, possibly apocryphal, about a warship in the early days of the Space Corps. The tale described a rookie comms man accidentally deleting several of the primary databanks. In his panic, he'd tried to cover his tracks by restoring from the backups, only to create an endless loop of data swapping from one place to another. There were at least three different endings to the story which Duggan was aware of, none of which ended in disaster for the ship or its crew. The comms man was, however, dismissed from duty in each variation.

"The bastards have hidden it from us," Duggan announced. "I need to find out how and where."

"This reminds me why I'm just a lowly gun-toting grunt and he's captain," said Byers with mischief in her voice.

Duggan laughed and felt the pressure release as if he'd turned a valve. "I could be wrong and even if I'm not, I still have to find where the files are hidden."

"Some of the guys figured out how to operate one of these alien replicators," said McLeod. "It was the first thing they did once we got the ship secure. I can get you a coffee or something to eat if you want."

The words caused Duggan's stomach to growl loudly, alerting him to the fact that he was ravenous. The mesh accelerants attached to his broken arm stripped his body of nutrients. The spacesuit kept his body's reserves topped up, but an intravenous energy fluid was no substitute for proper food.

"If you can get me something that looks and tastes like five cheeseburgers and a cup of coffee, I'll treat you to something with a high alcohol content from the *Crimson*'s replicator when we get back onboard."

"You're on!" said McLeod, standing to leave.

Byers scrambled to follow. "Wait for me!" she said. "I know how to work a replicator better than anyone."

The two soldiers took fifteen minutes to return. Duggan used the time well. By assuming his answer about the hidden backups was correct, he was able to follow a series of logical steps which led him directly to the *Valpian*'s backup arrays. After that, he was able to track down two separate areas within the memory banks where a huge quantity of data was being shunted to and fro. The ship's AI moved the files to one of these places and then moved them immediately back to their starting point. There were user-added flags in each of these arrays, which made them appear to be the primary front-end. Thus, the process continued, with the backups moving endlessly between partitions. With a grim smile, Duggan deleted the flags.

Instantly, one of his screens filled with symbols representing Dreamer coordinates.

"Got it!" Duggan exclaimed triumphantly.

"You can take us back to Nistrun?" asked Byers.

"Yes. This is the place right here. This green symbol is Nistrun and the darker green one is the Helius Blackstar. We just need to work out how we're going to get through."

"It's a start though, isn't it?"

"Each step we take is heading in the right direction," he agreed. "I'm punching in the coordinates. I'll bring us out of light-speed a few hours away from Nistrun. That should minimise the risk we're detected by one of the enemy warships which are undoubtedly hunting in the area. If we can get the *Crimson* working, that's what we'll do. Otherwise, we'll play it by ear."

"What about the monitoring station? Won't that see us?" asked McLeod.

"I've already considered that. Its lens is focused on the wormhole, so they might not detect us if they aren't specifically looking. Also, we did some damage to their main console with plasma grenades. They're unlikely to be fully operational yet."

"Sounds good, sir."

"When the *Crimson* came down, I never thought we'd get a second chance," said Byers.

"Nor I," said Red-Gulos.

The *Valpian*'s three AI cores had a colossal amount of computational power and the warship entered lightspeed less than thirty seconds after Duggan began the warmup for the fission drive.

"How fast are we going?" asked McLeod.

"I'm not sure," said Duggan. "Faster than the *Crimson* and that's easily the fastest ship in the human or Ghast fleets."

"We should do our best to bring the *Valpian* with us and have our engineers strip it down," said Berg.

"We'll see," said Duggan. He just wanted to get home and didn't want to make any more promises. "There's no doubt both we and our allies could benefit from the technology onboard. We are in this together."

Red-Gulos nodded in acknowledgement at the words.

"How long have we got?" asked McLeod.

"Just shy of two hours. Get out there and make sure everyone in the squad is aware."

"Yes, sir." McLeod paused. "And sir?"

"What is it?"

"You've forgotten your cheeseburgers."

Duggan looked at the two plates which had been set down near him and which he'd entirely failed to notice. There were *things* on the plates, which he lacked the words to describe.

"I think I'll pass."

"What about that drink you promised, sir?"

Duggan grinned. "You'll need to do better than what you've brought me here."

"Not bad for a first effort, I thought."

McLeod left the bridge, while Duggan remained in his seat and worked through a series of possible future scenarios in his mind.

CHAPTER FIFTEEN

"WE'LL ENTER normal space in less than five minutes," said Duggan, speaking to his makeshift crew. "That is the time we're at the greatest risk - our fission signature will give any hostile warships advance notice of our arrival. We need to complete a near and far scan as soon as possible, and only then switch to the super-fars."

"Yes, sir," Byers and McLeod responded in unison.

"Sergeant Red-Gulos, I need you to figure out a way to communicate with the *Crimson*. I don't know exactly where we're going to appear in relation to Nistrun – there's a chance the crash site will be on the far side of the planet, in which case I'll pilot us around until we can speak to the crew."

"I am not convinced the Dreamer and human communication systems are compatible."

"A skilled comms man can pick out any kind of signal, as long as the sender isn't taking steps to hide it. I want you to send a tight-band transmission aimed directly at the *Crimson*. Lieutenant Chainer will hear – I guarantee it."

"Very well, I will do exactly as you ask."

"In the meantime, you have a second task, Sergeant, and this one will be much harder than the first."

"What task is that?"

"By this point, the *Valpian* will be flagged throughout the enemy fleet as a potential rogue. Their command and control will be exceptionally reluctant to entertain the idea that an entire ship has been hijacked, but they will most definitely inform others in the fleet to treat us with the utmost caution. If we encounter other spaceships, you'll need to confuse or distract them for long enough to allow us to escape or to destroy them."

"We're not trained for this, sir," said McLeod.

"I know that, soldier. Fighting is a last resort. We have energy shields, so we should have a bit of breathing room if combat is unavoidable."

"We'll do our best."

"As always," Duggan replied. "Get ready on those scanners - we're entering local space in ten seconds."

The *Valpian*'s AI switched off the fission drives and completed a smooth transition onto the secondary engines. On the bridge, there was tense silence for a time.

"I can't see anything in the vicinity," said Byers.

"I'm on the fars," muttered McLeod, his brows furrowed in concentration. "I can see Nistrun, but no hostiles."

"How long until we're at the planet?" asked Duggan.

"I don't know how fast the *Valpian* will go. Until I know that, I can't tell you."

Duggan found the course towards the planet and pushed two of the *Valpian*'s control sticks into position. The warship had a tremendous amount of thrust and after a period of brutal acceleration, it peaked at a fraction over two thousand three hundred kilometres per second. As far as gravity drive velocity went, it was tremendously quick.

"If that's as fast as we can go, we'll reach Nistrun in five hours, sir."

"That's fine," said Duggan. "I'd rather take it easy than rush in. We've come so far I don't want to lose it all because of impatience."

Five minutes went by, during which McLeod and Byers attempted to translate the reams of data from the warship's scanners. The further out you looked, the harder it became to make sense of the feeds. Chainer was a lot quicker, but even he couldn't provide an immediate response in cases such as this one. The real difference was in the way a trained comms man could skim over the unimportant details and rapidly identify the potential hazards. McLeod and Byers didn't have the knack.

"We're good, sir."

Duggan didn't have the heart to tell him they'd have likely been destroyed by now if the scans had come back with a different result.

"Do you know how to look for a fission signature?" he asked.

"Yes, sir. I think so," said Byers.

"Think or know?"

"I know," she replied.

"Watch out for incoming spaceships. You can't take your eyes off the console for a moment and you need to perform a full-circle sweep every two minutes. The rest of the time, keep a watch on Nistrun. The enemy know this area of space so they might well jump in closer than we expect."

"Yes, sir," she said with a distinct lack of relish.

"Do it exactly as I said and there'll be no blame if you miss something."

"I'm on it," she replied with forced enthusiasm.

"McLeod, you need to put the forward sensors into super-far mode and aim them directly at Nistrun. We're a good way out so the images will be grainy and you'll need to work hard. Look for the installation first, since it's bigger than the *Crimson*. From there, you can search for our spaceship. Do you remember the direction we came to get over the mountains?"

"Yes, sir. Enough to narrow it down."

Duggan found he'd been holding his breath and stifled the urge to empty his lungs in a loud sigh. The others were doing as well as could be expected and he needed to project calm over the bridge. He exhaled quietly and regulated his breathing to a steady in-out.

"I've found it!" said McLeod excitedly.

"Let me see," said Duggan, leaning across. He'd anticipated a much longer wait and the pessimist in him had also expected the base to be on the far side of the planet.

"There!"

McLeod had indeed located the base. It appeared on one of the screens looking much as Duggan remembered it – a collection of randomly-placed structures with a larger building in the centre.

"No sign of activity," said Byers. "It's night time. Maybe they're sleeping."

"We're too far out to see details," said Duggan. He put his finger close to the screen and traced a path away from the base. "Bring the sensors this way towards the mountain range," he said.

"Okay, sir. It's a bit hard to keep them steady."

"That's fine, just keep bringing them across."

Duggan remembered the enormity of the mountain range. From this distance, it looked like a collection of low, shadowed undulations on the ground.

"About here?" asked McLeod.

"Yes. I brought the *Crimson* down somewhere near there."

"I can't see it."

"Keep looking. The hull has light deflection properties even without the stealth modules running. It's made so that it's easy to overlook."

"Right, I'll keep on with it."

"Want me to help, sir?" asked Byers.

"Absolutely not. Keep watching for fission signatures."

"How are we planning to get on or off the *Valpian*?" she asked, her eyes still glued to her console. "Both the shuttles in the bay got chewed up by chain gun fire."

"Boarding ramps," said Duggan, tapping his fingertip gently on a tiny button at the top of his panel. "Front one here, back one here and these buttons are for the middle ones. I'd prefer it if we didn't need to land." He shrugged.

"Can't have everything our own way," said McLeod.

Duggan held the *Valpian* on its course for another thirty minutes. New technology excited him and he dearly wanted to spend some time with the vessel under less trying circumstances. It was fast, agile and he was sure it was superbly well-armed, if only he had full access to the weapons console. The sensors weren't a huge leap over the Space Corps versions, though Chainer would be the best-placed to conclude on that.

Most of all, he wished to have his usual crew sitting alongside him and his mind threw up a range of uses for a captured technologically advanced enemy cruiser. In reality, the *Crimson* remained their best shot at getting home since it was a known quantity. Even so, a little voice continued to whisper about the necessity of bringing the *Valpian* into the Space Corps' hands as a prize above all other prizes. *They'd strip it apart and take the pieces to a research lab,* he thought sourly, before chuckling at the pointlessness of the scenarios his brain conjured to keep itself occupied.

"Have you found the *Crimson*, yet?" he asked.

"I don't know." McLeod hesitated. "I found where we clipped the mountaintops on our way in," he said. "There's a clear furrow in the ground a hundred klicks further on and then a second after another fifty klicks."

"I didn't do any fancy turns in the air," said Duggan. "It was a straight line for the final approach."

"I remember you saying the same thing and I followed the line of the furrow way past its end."

"Take another look."

"I've been going backwards and forwards for the last twenty minutes, sir. I've covered this same area a dozen times."

"The *Crimson* shouldn't be *that* hard to find. It's only capable of avoiding casual attempts at detection."

"There's an area here that's covered in scrapes."

"Can you get a closer look?"

"No, sir. This is maximum zoom."

A warning began to chime in Duggan's head and he gave the matter his full attention. "That's the place we came to a stop," he said. "I'm sure of it."

"I'm not being stupid, am I?" McLeod asked. "There's really no spaceship."

"No, you're not being stupid." Duggan couldn't tear his eyes away from the sensor feed. "The *Crimson* is gone."

"What the hell? Could they have got it working and flown it somewhere?" asked Byers.

"I think not," said Red-Gulos.

"The sergeant is correct," said Duggan. "My engine man onboard said the *Crimson* wasn't going anywhere for weeks and that was with a replacement core. Using only the standard mainframe, he was talking about years before the ship would be at anything approaching a fully operational state."

"It's gone somewhere."

"If it hasn't lifted off and it hasn't been destroyed, there is only one conclusion," said Red-Gulos, as practical as ever.

"The enemy have discovered it and somehow managed to take it elsewhere," said Duggan with a grimace.

"It's practically impossible to capture an armed warship," said Byers. Her face fell. "Oh. We just managed it, didn't we?"

At that moment, a shadow fell over the *Crimson*'s landing site. The shadow appeared and then within the blinking of an eye it vanished.

"Quickly, zoom out!" said Duggan.

"Like this?"

"More. Track left. Keep going."

"Crap," said McLeod.

"What's that?" asked Byers, watching the shape as it sped over the surface of Nistrun at a height of only a few kilometres.

"It's one of their battleships," said Duggan.

"Why is it here?"

"Just to piss me off," Duggan replied, closing his eyes to calm his thoughts.

"What now?" asked Red-Gulos.

"Once again, we've been given no choice other than to risk everything."

Duggan already had a plan. It jumped fully-formed into his mind and waited brazenly for him to accept it. He spent the next ten minutes desperately seeking an alternative, before he succumbed to the inevitable.

CHAPTER SIXTEEN

"IS there another way we can find out where they've taken the *Crimson*?" asked Byers, once Duggan had outlined his intentions. "I thought in the Space Corps a warship captain could find out more or less anything he wanted."

"That's mostly true," said Duggan. "However, in order to do so, I need to jump through a variety of hoops, some of which are time consuming and all of which are designed to prevent imposters getting into highly sensitive military databases."

"On the *Valpian*, we can access most things we need in order to operate the ship, but anything else requires a code?" she asked.

"In a nutshell, yes. The code might be a biological one implanted in the bodies of the crew and used automatically to approve certain functions or it might be a combination of skin patterns and iris recognition. It's likely to be several different things, none of which involve the manual typing in of a ten-thousand-digit number."

"Can't we cut off the old captain's hand and press it against an activation plate somewhere in order to get access to what we need?" asked McLeod.

"You've been watching too many movies, soldier."

"A good idea is a good idea no matter where it came from, sir."

"In this case, we need something different," said Duggan, not entirely sure if McLeod truly believed the idea was a sound one. "Sergeant Red-Gulos, can you see any commonality between the methods employed by your navy and that of the Dreamers? I need anything that might help us."

"I am foremost a soldier, sir. I have some knowledge of our warships, but I have not commanded one. I have not seen a way in which I can help."

"Your time will come, don't worry," said Duggan.

He found his hand reaching out towards the control panel which gave access to the warship's encrypted data repositories. He withdrew the hand – his previous attempts to access the system had failed and he certainly wasn't going to succeed by guessing. It was possible to hack into a warship's backend though it wasn't feasible to do it without having a number of high-end AI cores working in tandem. In truth, he had no idea how the Dreamers guarded their military secrets and accepted there was no current way to gain entry by brute force.

"If at first you don't succeed, cheat," Byers announced.

"We need the battleship to leave before we can do anything," said Duggan. The *Valpian* was at a standstill, four hours away from the surface of Nistrun. It was mostly luck which had allowed them to spot the enemy warship from this distance and Duggan was confident the *Valpian* would remain undetected.

"They're doing thirty-minute laps," said McLeod. "I don't think they're in a hurry."

"We're in no rush, are we?" asked Byers.

"I don't want to hang around here for days," said Duggan. "If the battleship's crew is halfway competent, they'll perform a constant area scan. They'll find us eventually. Plus, I don't want the *Crimson* to remain in the hands of the enemy for a moment longer than necessary."

"It's got our secret data and our stealth modules on it."

The *Crimson* carried much that was precious to Duggan, though he wasn't going to spell it out. He was petrified something would happen to McGlashan and the others of his crew. The anguish beat against his resolve and insisted he act immediately instead of waiting for the best time. *She could be dead by now.*

"They're leaving!" said McLeod.

"Show me," said Duggan, springing across in a burst of movement.

"There – it's flying away from the surface at angle that will take it...nowhere?"

"It's preparing for lightspeed. Byers, please confirm."

"Uh, sorry sir, I was watching McLeod's screen. Yes, there's a fission signature."

"You can't let yourself get distracted, soldier. A warship's crew live or die by the speed of their reactions."

"Sorry," she repeated.

The battleship disappeared, leaving behind an invisible sphere of rapidly-fading energy.

"That's a fast one," said Duggan. "It took hardly any time between warmup and lightspeed. They must be sending their newer ships to the area around the wormhole since we destroyed their fleet."

"The *Valpian* is a new ship as well, isn't it?" asked McLeod.

"A cruiser is no match for a battleship," Duggan replied, returning to his seat. "We're not waiting any longer – I'm going to prepare a short lightspeed hop in towards Nistrun. It'll take too long on the gravity drives and there's nothing other than the monitoring station left to detect us."

"Will they report our presence to their superiors?"

"Maybe. Probably. It doesn't make much difference. If we

can't fool them, we'll know about it soon enough. We'll fly elsewhere and consider our next move."

The plan was a simple one and straight out of the beginner's handbook. Duggan was going to take the *Valpian* into comms range of the monitoring station. Then, Red-Gulos was going to try and convince the personnel on the base to divulge the location of the *Crimson*. The plan relied on two main assumptions – firstly, Duggan hoped the chaos from the earlier raid had left the place in disarray and perhaps killed a few of their senior officers. This would leave them vulnerable to bullying.

Secondly, there was a chance the monitoring station's personnel were not privy to top-level secrets such as the theft of a major warship. It was the kind of thing the brass tended to keep to themselves, owing to the limitless scope for embarrassment, sackings and, possibly, executions.

He looked at Red-Gulos, noticing for the first time the lines at the corner of the Ghost's eyes.

"Do you know what you're going to say?" Duggan asked.

The Ghost met his gaze. "I am confident in my dealings with anyone. However, it is not always possible to defeat someone in verbal combat."

"Of course. We're at war and we can't expect to win every battle." He smiled. "This is a big one."

The *Valpian* jumped in towards the planet. Duggan was a little bit rough-edged in his control over the engines and was still getting to grips with the coordinate system and distance counters the Dreamers used. Consequently, he brought them in somewhat closer than intended, at an altitude of seven thousand kilometres and directly above the installation.

"If they didn't know we were here before, they definitely do now," said Byers.

Duggan waved her to silence. He nodded at Red-Gulos. "Ready?"

The Ghost nodded in return. A row of symbols appeared on his comms screen. "They have initiated contact."

"They will be surprised to see us."

Red-Gulos stretched out a hand and accepted the inbound comms request.

The conversation went on for some time, during which Duggan kept the *Valpian* moving in a slow circle at a height of five thousand kilometres. His knuckles ached from clutching the control sticks too hard and he had to force himself to loosen his grip. The bridge suddenly felt colder than ever, though it didn't stop a sheen of sweat developing across his forehead.

He tried to listen in to gauge how Red-Gulos' attempts at persuasion were going. Unfortunately, much of the talk was in idioms and this foiled the language module's clumsy attempts at interpretation. One thing was clear – the Ghost was becoming increasingly competent at communicating in the Dreamer's version of the language. Duggan idly wondered if Red-Gulos had a side-line as a scholar of ancient scripts or if he was just a natural. Subjos Gol-Tur had promised the best and he hadn't exaggerated.

After a stressful ten minutes, Red-Gulos stopped talking. His comms screen went blank and he flexed his shoulders. His expression was inscrutable.

"Well?" Duggan demanded.

"I am not sure what to say," said the Ghost. "I have fooled them into providing us with something, but not what we need."

"Stop talking in riddles," said Duggan, already losing patience.

"I apologise – that was not my intent. I will explain what I have discovered. The commander of the monitoring station below was killed during our recent assault, leaving a more junior officer in charge. He has heard a series of rumours that the *Valpian* was somehow out of commission and he was especially curious to learn why we are in a low-altitude circuit over his station."

"Yes, yes," said Duggan, motioning for him to proceed.

"I assured him there is no problem with the *Valpian* and I told him we continue to look for a crashed enemy warship, sighted close to Nistrun. It seems that we missed the departure of what he described as a *Class 1 Neutraliser* by a matter of an hour or two."

"What the hell is a Class 1 Neutraliser?" asked Duggan.

"It doesn't sound like something we want to meet," said Byers quietly.

"Whatever it is, it picked up our warship and carried it elsewhere," said Red-Gulos.

"Where has it taken the *Crimson*?" asked Duggan, with a feeling he wasn't going to like the answer. He was correct.

"The information is one grading above the status of the monitoring station," said the Ghast. "I am not sure how the Dreamers tier the flow of their military information, but those on the base are not party to that which we require to know."

Duggan bit on his tongue to prevent a stream of expletives coming forth. "This the end of the road."

"Perhaps not, though you will not like to hear the alternative."

"Go on."

"The battleship we observed arrived as an escort for the Neutraliser vessel. The comms man on the battleship *Zansturm* was free with his tongue and he made it known his warship is taking up a position close to the wormhole, in preparation for an eventual journey through."

"This comms man told the base where the *Crimson* is?" asked Duggan with sudden hope.

Red-Gulos laughed without a trace of mockery and shook his

head. "Not at all. He told the base that he knows this information, yet without providing the location."

"Then there's nothing left," said Duggan.

"The way to proceed is clear!"

Duggan opened his mouth to insist the Ghost speak plainly. Then, it dawned on him exactly what Red-Gulos was suggesting. "You obtained the coordinates of the *Zansturm*'s destination?"

"I did."

"We need to speak to them and find out where the *Crimson*'s gone."

"Won't they shoot us down, sir?" asked McLeod.

"Maybe. Probably," he replied. "I've got a couple of ideas how we can get around that."

"There's more," said Red-Gulos, saving the best for last. "The *Zansturm* is joining with four other warships in the area. We'll have five enemy vessels to contend with."

For some reason the news didn't add anything extra to Duggan's burdens. "If we can deal with one, we can deal with five," he said. "The battleship is more than we can handle, so if it comes to shooting we've already lost."

The two human soldiers exchanged glances.

"Any objections?" Duggan asked.

"Without the *Crimson*, we're dead anyway," said Byers. "I always said I'd prefer a quick death over a slow, drawn-out one."

"I have a promise to keep," Duggan said. "And there's no room for further death."

"I have learned how to activate the internal comms," said Red-Gulos. "Would you like me to advise the others?"

"Yes. I'll speak directly to anyone who wishes to express their concerns."

"There will be no one."

"I know," Duggan replied.

Red-Gulos fed through the coordinates for their next destination. Duggan accepted them and instructed the *Valpian*'s cores to prepare the engines. The cruiser entered lightspeed on the short journey towards the wormhole. It didn't take long and soon the vessel emerged into local space. Immediately, a series of emergency warnings appeared across four of the screens in front of him.

"We've come in close to an unknown warship, sir," said Byers.

"I can tell," said Duggan. "It's locked on and is preparing to fire."

He didn't know how long they had left before the Dreamer warship launched its missiles – it was unlikely to be very long.

A couple of metres away to the right, Red-Gulos reached for his comms panel and attempted to open a channel to the other ship. They had only this one chance and they couldn't afford to squander it.

CHAPTER SEVENTEEN

SECONDS TICKED BY.

"No sign of a launch yet," said Duggan. "They still have us targeted." He noticed that one of the gauges on his console had climbed several million percent from its initial low value. "Our energy shield is up."

To his astonishment, there was no appreciable drain on any other part of the *Valpian*'s power output. He was sure Lieutenant Breeze would venture a few theories on the matter if he ever got the chance.

"I've got a comms channel through to the other warship," said Red-Gulos at last. The tone of his voice through the language module was unchanged, adding to the impression that Ghosts were immune to the effects of stress.

"Is it the *Zansturm*?"

"Negative. This is the cruiser *Soriol*."

"Find me the other warships, quickly," said Duggan to Byers and McLeod. His words were wasted, since they already had their heads down in concentration.

Red-Gulos talked, his harsh, alien voice uttering a steady flow of words without apparent concern.

"We came in almost on top of the *Soriol*, sir," said Byers. "It's thirty thousand klicks to starboard."

"Where are the other four?"

"I've located one," said McLeod. "It's half a million klicks in front of us. It *was* heading away, now it's coming about and heading towards us. It's a smaller ship – fifteen hundred metres. What's that make it? A light cruiser?"

"That's as good a term as any," said Duggan.

He tapped into three of the *Valpian*'s sensor feeds. The outline of the *Soriol* was sharply-etched on one. It was smaller than the *Valpian* and to Duggan's experienced eye, it looked much the older ship. *They're probably scared of us,* he thought.

In the background was the Helius Blackstar, many millions of kilometres away. The *Valpian*'s sensors automatically outlined the area in a pastel shade of blue. Other than that, there was little of interest – just an empty area of space with nowhere to hide and nothing which could be used for advantage. Duggan felt as if he were standing outside the door to freedom, without having the ability to turn the handle and escape. Even if he knew how to get through, there was unfinished business to deal with first.

"They're not happy," said Red-Gulos.

"No kidding. What's their main problem?"

"I don't think they know, sir. The *Valpian* has been flagged as missing and they want to know why we're here."

Duggan could have laughed. To use *missing* as an excuse for a captured warship reeked of panic amongst those in charge. It bore all the hallmarks of trying to cover up a vast, incomprehensible failing. The people behind it would be desperate to buy sufficient time to get their alibis coordinated. Even now, there'd be some poor, unfortunate Dreamer being lined up to take the blame.

"The crew of the *Soriol* don't want to fight us," Duggan said. "I'm certain we've got the superior warship and I'm equally certain they'd far rather there was an innocent explanation that will save them from having to open fire."

Red-Gulos grinned – it was a disconcerting sight. "Very well, I will provide them with an innocent explanation."

"If we can get the captain of this warship to believe us, there's an excellent chance we can convince the others."

"I think I've got the *Zansturm*, sir," said McLeod. "That's a long way off – over a million klicks."

"What's it doing?"

"Coming our way at two thousand three hundred klicks per second."

"There are two more out there," said Duggan. "They'll want to come for a look as well once they learn we've arrived."

"There's bad news," said Red-Gulos. "They intend to speak with their superiors."

"That's not what I wanted to hear. Even if their high command is trying cover things up, they'll ask the warships here to detain us."

He racked his brains to think of a way out. In Confederation Space, a warship's comms signal could travel from source to destination in a matter of seconds. He knew the Dreamers populated a far greater volume of space and he was reasonably sure their comms technology was little better than the Space Corps'. The aliens were likely to have numerous command and control stations. Even so, it might well be that a signal could take a number of minutes until it reached an officer capable of providing guidance on something of this magnitude.

"Tell them to speak to the monitoring station on Nistrun," he said in a flash of inspiration. "They can verify that our missing status no longer applies."

"The monitoring station only knows because we convinced them," said Red-Gulos.

"Your species is vulnerable to the machinations of those who can deliver outright lies," said Duggan.

"I am quickly learning how to speak them fluently," said Red-Gulos.

"Then take this as an opportunity to get more practise!" ordered Duggan. "Make the crew of the *Soriol* contact the monitoring station for corroboration of our mistruths."

It didn't take long for Red-Gulos to pass on the message. "I have advised them as such." He scratched his head in puzzlement. "So, we lied to the monitoring station and because they believed our words, they are able to pass them off as truth, even though the foundations of the facts do not exist. It is making my head spin."

"It probably won't work," said Duggan. "It wouldn't fool a human – any human – for more than a couple of seconds."

To Duggan's absolute amazement, the crew on the *Soriol* bought it. Or so it initially seemed.

"They've de-targeted us," he said with an unwillingness to believe.

"Their comms man has told me as much," said Red-Gulos. "They are standing down from full alert."

"The closest of their other warships – the light cruiser - is breaking off, sir," said McLeod. "It's back on its original course. No, wait! They can't make up their minds and they're turning again."

"This doesn't sound right. What's the *Zansturm* up to?"

"Coming our way."

Duggan frowned. "They aren't convinced."

"I have a Priority 1 message from the battleship," said Red-Gulos. "Am I to assume this isn't good news?"

"I don't see how it can be," Duggan replied. "I'm going to take us away from them as if we're establishing a pre-determined course. Continue speaking to the *Soriol* and find out what you can. They must know something is wrong. They'll get a response from their high command shortly."

"Should I answer the Priority 1?"

"Yes – try and buy us a few seconds. At the same time, press the comms man on the *Soriol* and find out where the *Crimson* is."

"I will try."

While Red-Gulos spoke, Duggan took the *Valpian* on a course heading away from the incoming battleship at a moderately high speed, hoping it wouldn't appear too obvious. The *Soriol* altered its own course, following a slightly divergent heading that was presumably meant to be surreptitious. Duggan wasn't fooled for an instant.

"I've got a name from the *Soriol*'s comms man – it's where they've taken the *foreign warship*."

Duggan's heart thumped in his chest. "Do you have enough information for us to get there?"

"I'm not sure, sir. Their comms man stopped himself midway through his sentence and then began talking about something else."

"That's how you Estral avoid lying, isn't it?"

"It's how we communicate," said Red-Gulos. "I also have the *Zansturm*'s captain on a separate comms channel. He asks if we are having a pleasant day."

Duggan shook his head in disbelief. "Tell him we're having a wonderful day. Ask him if his family is well."

"It is my strong belief they haven't been taken in by the ruse," said Red-Gulos. "I suspect they will fire as soon as they are in range."

"I know that, sergeant. In all my life, I have never heard a worse attempt to deceive than asking if I am having a pleasant day."

"The *Zansturm* is a big bastard, sir," said Byers. "Five thousand metres long and I can see four particle beam domes in the hull."

"How close are they?"

"Three quarters of a million klicks."

"I reckon it's got missiles that can travel that far," mused Duggan.

"Why aren't they firing?"

"Because they know we can get to lightspeed long before those missiles reach us."

"What about the *Soriol*?" asked Byers. "They could do some damage while we're trying to escape."

"It seems strange," said Duggan. "Unless, they also know we outgun them so much they won't be able to stop us. That would explain why they haven't locked on again – they realise it would be a provocation."

"Do you think they've already received a response from their high command to say we're a rogue ship?" asked McLeod.

"That's the only explanation for the way they're acting."

"The light cruiser is on a strange course," said McLeod. "It's sort of coming after us, but not very quickly. Like they're in no hurry to see what we can do to them."

Duggan thought fast. It was certain the Dreamers knew the *Valpian* had been hijacked. His first thought was to activate the fission drives and take them away in a random direction and hope they had sufficient information to locate the *Crimson*. The problem was, such action would force the *Soriol* to open fire. Even if he was correct in his assumption that the smaller cruiser wasn't a match for the *Valpian*, their crew were definitely better able to extract the maximum performance from what they had available to them. The enemy might cause enough damage to destroy the *Valpian* or prevent its escape, both of which were unacceptable.

"We have an energy shield," he muttered to himself. "From past experience, missiles won't penetrate. What happens to a particle beam directed at an energy shield? Does it extend through the shield or is it blocked?"

Time was running out and Duggan knew he had to act. Also, the crew on the *Soriol* had divulged the location of the *ESS Crimson*. If the *Zansturm* learned about it, they would surely know exactly what the *Valpian*'s planned destination was. Duggan didn't wish to have a battleship on his tail when he attempted to rescue his crew.

Surprise was one of the most powerful weapons available and he decided to utilise it. The *Valpian* was equipped with two particle beams, which were aimed by a simple method of selecting a target on the tactical display and then pressing a virtual button on a separate screen. Once he aimed the particle beams, it was certain the *Soriol* would recognize hostile intent.

Wishing he had his usual crew with him, Duggan targeted both particle beams and fired. A series of power bars jumped from zero to ninety percent, whereupon they began to fall gradually back towards zero. The cooldown time was exceptionally quick compared to anything Duggan had encountered on a human or Ghost ship, but the weapons couldn't exactly be fired rapidly.

As soon as he fired, he rotated in his seat until he was facing the navigational console. He entered a series of coordinates and gave the instruction to prepare the fission engines. *Less than thirty seconds until we're out of here.*

"I think the *Soriol* has fired at us, sir," said Byers, trying her best to help out. "A couple of these gauges have started to jump around."

It was immediately apparent how unprepared they were to engage in ship-to-ship combat. A series of alerts flashed across Duggan's screens, the symbols appearing and disappearing before he could make sense of them. He attempted to target the *Valpian*'s missiles, only to be diverted by a higher-priority prompt relating to the fission drives. Byers and McLeod stumbled over their words as they relayed the details on their own screens, without realising they weren't giving Duggan the information he needed.

It only took a few seconds for Duggan to realise he was in danger of being swamped. His experience saved him from the distraction and he was able to see through the operational haze. The particle beams had cooled down sufficiently and he aimed and fired them for a second time.

"The *Soriol* is gone, sir," said Byers.

"What do you mean *it's gone?*" asked Duggan. "Please confirm."

"We've destroyed it, sir. It's in pieces."

Duggan was dumbfounded by the ease with which they'd destroyed the enemy cruiser, but he had too much on his plate to think about it. The *Valpian*'s energy shield spiked once and then spiked again, this second time by nine million percent. To the left, the tactical display showed hundreds of inbound missiles, each with a distance and course overlay that convinced Duggan they'd been launched from separate places.

The Dreamer missiles didn't reach the *Valpian*. The cruiser entered lightspeed many seconds before its shield could be tested. As soon as Duggan confirmed they were travelling at the warship's frankly incredible maximum speed, he blew out his pent-up breath. Their randomly-selected location was several hours away, so there was time to think and talk.

"That went better than expected," he said.

The other three stared at him, a dozen emotions writ large across their features.

CHAPTER EIGHTEEN

SOMEHOW, the *Valpian*'s sensors had captured a recording of the recent engagement with the *Soriol* and Duggan watched the replay for the third time. The first two particle beams raked through the smaller vessel's hull, leaving several hundred metres in a patchy orange colour. The *Soriol* replied with missiles and its own particle beam, none of which had any apparent effect other than to produce a colossal energy surge in the *Valpian*'s shields. The following two particle beam strikes split the *Soriol* into three brightly-burning pieces, effectively destroying the vessel.

"Their energy shields didn't help them against our particle beams," Duggan said. "Yet their beams were unable to penetrate our own shield."

He cast his mind back to the first appearance of the Dreamer mothership and he remembered how easily its particle beams had destroyed the human and Ghost fleets which were in the vicinity of the Helius Blackstar. It appeared as if the *Valpian* was equipped with a similarly-powerful weapon.

"We've got newer and better," said Byers. As a way of explanation, it was surely correct, yet completely unsatisfying.

"We must make every effort to bring this vessel through the wormhole," said Red-Gulos. "If it carries the enemy's most cutting-edge technology it is imperative our own navies are given the opportunity to copy it."

Privately, Duggan agreed. He wasn't in a position to commit to anything he couldn't fulfil. He'd made only one promise and that was to get them home. If he could get more out of the situation, so much the better. He simply didn't wish to risk his word by chasing the unattainable.

"Does the location you got from the *Soriol*'s comms man tie in with anything on the *Valpian*'s charts?" asked Duggan.

Red-Gulos was still searching. "He only provided partial details before evidently realising we were imposters," said the Ghost. "We have a name, rather than a set of coordinates. Luckily for us, the name is an unusual one and there is little repetition of it, even amongst the vastness of the enemy's holdings."

"Have you narrowed it down to something we can use?"

"Yes. The name *Antrajis* occurs only three times on the *Valpian*'s charts. The first is a planet, which might be a logical destination, except that it is approximately eighty-nine days away from here."

"I'm not sure we can dismiss it so easily," said Duggan.

Red-Gulos raised a hand to indicate he wished to continue. "The next mention of the word *Antrajis* relates to an ancient satellite which again is located far from here."

"They're probably not on a satellite," Duggan agreed. "What's the last option?"

"Here," said Red-Gulos, indicating an image on his screen.

"What is that?" asked Duggan, looking at the object in question.

The *Valpian*'s memory banks held a three-dimensional image of the *Antrajis*. It was comprised of two tori. A cylinder ran through the middle hole of each ring and was connected to them by a series of evenly-spaced struts. Red-Gulos zoomed in and rotated the object so that Duggan got an idea of what it was.

"An orbital," said the Ghast.

"How close are we to it?"

"Three days at our current speed."

"That's got to be the place," said Duggan.

"My thoughts exactly."

Duggan returned to his seat and called up the *Antrajis* on his own screen. The computerised model was exceptionally detailed, showing three vast external hangar bay doors, countless viewing ports and even the thousands of sensor arrays mounted on the orbital's hull. The bay doors were part of the main cylinder, with the upper and lower ones being above the tori and the middle doors being between them.

"It's twenty klicks long and twelve wide across each ring," he said. "The central cylinder has got a three thousand metre diameter."

"It's quite big, then?" asked Byers.

"You could say," Duggan agreed. "It's not the size that worries me so much as these particle beam domes here and these missile batteries here, here, here and here."

"We fly in, shoot the place up, jump onto the *Crimson* and then fly out," said McLeod. "I was always told to keep it simple."

"Thank you for the advice," said Duggan drily. "If we shoot the place up, we might end up killing the crew and that's assuming the orbital isn't protected by the biggest energy shield we've ever seen."

"It was just an outline," said McLeod, unrepentant. "Something to build on, you know?"

"We'll see," said Duggan. "There's no doubt in my mind about our destination. I'm altering our current course to take us there."

Changing course was easier said than done and it took him

fifteen minutes to figure out how to alter the *Valpian*'s course while it was already at lightspeed. It drove home how much he had to learn before he could captain the vessel efficiently.

"I think that's it," he said. "Seventy hours until we're at the *Antrajis*."

"It's going to be frustrating, sir," said Byers. "Every time we jump one hurdle, there's another. Now I just want to face all the hurdles at once and have done with it so we can go home."

"You and me both," he replied. "On the bright side, you're not going to have much time for frustration."

"Why's that?" she asked suspiciously.

"Because I'm going to teach you three the basics of how to operate a warship in combat. Seventy hours isn't nearly enough, of course, but I want to show you what's important and what isn't. Something as big as the *Antrajis* is likely to be heavily defended and I can't pilot the *Valpian* at the same time as I'm doing everything else."

"Suits me fine," she said.

"Hell yeah!" said McLeod.

Duggan was pleased he'd been given soldiers who were both excellent in combat and also had exactly the right attitude. He spent the following eight hours showing them what he expected should they begin an engagement with an enemy warship. There was plenty more to do, but Duggan decided to give them a break, conscious of the human brain's need to rest. He would have dearly liked some time to sleep, though with no one to properly cover the bridge he had to content himself with some stimulant drugs from Corporal Weiss. She assured him they had no side-effects, which was something he'd heard before and never quite believed.

Weiss checked his arm before announcing it to be healing well, which was a surprise given how poorly Duggan had treated it. In truth, he had to keep reminding himself it was broken since it gave him no pain when he used it for light duties. His shoulder injury wasn't a concern. It had scabbed over and needed no further attention.

The condition of Lieutenant Ortiz was unchanged since the last time he'd enquired – she slept and the diagnosis of her injury was incomplete. He asked Weiss to keep him informed and then dismissed her to whatever else she needed to do.

An hour later, Corporal Gax arrived to report. The soldiers had completed a final, thorough sweep of the *Valpian*'s interior and they were confident it was clear. Duggan was pleased at the news – on a vessel as large as this one there were sure to be hiding places for an enemy if they were determined to cause mischief.

In addition to completing the sweep of the ship, Gax had also produced a rough inventory of the hardware onboard. There were no great surprises. The *Valpian* carried a few hundred assorted rifles, handheld repeaters, grenades and explosives. It also had a secondary holding bay in which there were four mobile plasma launchers, four fast-firing heavy gauss guns and two armoured vehicles, exact type unknown.

"It looks more advanced than the equipment we have in our own navy," said Gax. "Yet it appears to perform the same function."

"It shoots stuff where you point it," said Duggan. "There's only so much you can realistically develop ground weaponry, given that a single spaceship can target and destroy it from thousands of kilometres above."

There was one surprise, saved for last. Gax led Duggan to an area deep within the hull of the ship and stopped at a thick metal hatch embedded in the floor. There was an access panel nearby and the Ghast activated it with a sweep of his fingertips. The hatch swung outwards until it was resting against the adjacent wall. There was a shaft with a ladder leading down.

Taking care with his arm Duggan descended to the bottom,

where he found himself in a high-ceilinged room, four metres by eight and lit in a blue so pure it was nearly white. When he removed his helmet, his breath steamed in the air and what he thought was moisture on the walls turned out to be a thin coating of ice.

There was a cylinder, as long as the room itself. It filled most of the available space and rested on a long metal plinth designed specifically to accommodate it. The cylinder was perfectly smooth, its surface the deepest of blacks. Each end disappeared into the walls, making it impossible to know its precise dimensions.

Duggan knew what it was – he'd seen this same material within the pyramids deployed in Confederation Space.

"This must be how they generate their energy shields," he said, wondering if the obsidian-like material also contributed its power to other areas of the ship.

Gax shrugged, as if it were something for other people to worry about.

"Let's go," said Duggan, resisting the urge to put his gloved hand on the surface of the cylinder. "Best keep the others out of here."

Gax returned to his duties, leaving Duggan wondering about the Dreamers. They were quite clearly warlike in nature and he knew they were fighting against at least one other enemy besides humans and Ghasts. However, the *Valpian* was equipped to carry a comparatively large number of troops and it also had a reasonable quantity of ground weaponry. It implied they still engaged in surface combat to some extent, though his own experience suggested they were not the best-trained soldiers. On the other hand, here in the middle of their territory he might have only encountered some of their weaker ground units.

Then there was the mysterious black material that could generate more power than any other known substance. Duggan wanted to know if it was part of every Dreamer warship or if it was only installed on the newer, more advanced models such as the *Valpian*.

"So much we don't know," he said, not for the first time.

The remainder of the time before their arrival at the *Antrajis* orbital was spent in a continuation of basic training, during which Duggan also learned much about the *Valpian*'s operation. Many of the vessel's operational capabilities remained locked down, though he became increasingly convinced there were other parts of the weaponry in particular he should be able to use if only he had the time to figure it out. There was at least one disruptor, access to which was buried deep inside the warship's weapons console and showing as unavailable for use.

As it was, Duggan had to content himself with missiles, particle beams and a reliance on the energy shield to keep them safe. He worried the enemy could have a way of disabling the shield remotely. The *Soriol* had given no sign it was able to, but something more advanced like the *Zansturm* might have the ability. Eventually, he realised he was worrying needlessly about something he couldn't change.

His stand-in crew proved themselves eager students and they were soon able to use the *Valpian*'s sensors to detect incoming enemy fire, as well as target and use the onboard weapons. In truth, much of it had been designed for easy use – in the same way as it was on a Space Corps vessel. The difficulties would come if events ever took a turn for the worse and the damage reports started rolling in. Duggan knew he'd be effectively on his own if things ever got really tough. He didn't blame the others one little bit. This was the hand they'd been dealt and he had no complaints about how they were playing it.

During the final twelve hours, Duggan finally felt able to take himself off to sleep. One of the soldiers directed him to what could only have been the officers' quarters for the *Valpian*. There was an area separated from the rest of the ship by a single door, behind which were ten cramped, individual rooms. Duggan found one which was unoccupied. It smelled of chilled meat and cool metal. There was an Estral-sized alcove in the wall for sleeping, as well as a wall-mounted screen and a chair.

Unable to resist, Duggan turned on the screen, only to find himself presented with a menu of different choices. He selected one and a video started playing. It depicted seven Dreamer ships flying in a way that had clearly been doctored to make it appear as though they were in tight formation. A rough-edged voice talked over the action and, using his suit helmet for interpretation purposes, Duggan was able to understand bits and pieces of a Dreamer propaganda video. He turned it off.

The bed itself had no blanket and the stiff, miserly mattress on top was less than an inch thick. It was as uncomfortable as it appeared, while the room was several degrees too cold for sleeping. All-in-all, Duggan was thankful he was wearing his suit and he managed to snatch three welcome hours sleep. He woke up with a pain in his hip, making him question if he was getting too old. A last glance at the mattress allowed him to assign blame to the bed instead of his body.

On his way back to the bridge, he exchanged jokes with a few of the soldiers, both human and Ghast. He stopped at a bells-and-whistles replicator in the mess room and tentatively pressed a few of the symbols on its screen. The machine gurgled alarmingly and then a tray appeared in the wide, dark slot underneath the selection panel. He withdrew the tray and stared with distaste at four green mounds of something-or-other. Wrinkling his nose, he pushed his fingertip into one of the lumps and found it to be slightly warmer than the surrounding air. He tasted it and discovered a product with a flavour somewhere between smoked fish and mushrooms, with the texture of coarsely-ground peanuts. Figuring it would be something to tell the grandchildren he might one day have, he sampled each of the four foodstuffs, before dropping the tray on the floor and kicking it away.

"Maybe that's why the Dreamers are so angry," said Bonner, who'd been close enough to watch the whole affair with amusement. "I'd be pretty pissed off if I signed up for service and they fed me this crap."

Duggan grunted his wholehearted agreement and left the room. He spent the remainder of the pre-arrival time helping his crew with their questions about the warship's operation, and also in thought about how he was going to deal with the upcoming hostilities. He didn't take long to decide that out here in hostile territory, faced by an enemy who knew the *Valpian* was a rogue ship, the best approach was going to be a forthright one. He gave orders to Corporal Gax and the soldiers and then modified those orders twice more until he was finally satisfied.

"Five minutes until we exit lightspeed," said Byers, now assigned mostly to engines and status updates.

"Does everyone know what's expected of them?" asked Duggan, more for his own reassurance than for anyone else's.

McLeod was assigned to a 'fill in' role and would try and catch whatever the others missed. It wasn't a perfect arrangement by any stretch of the imagination. The soldier grinned broadly. "Yes, sir. We fly in, shoot the place up, jump onto the *Crimson* and then fly out."

Duggan couldn't help but laugh to hear a repeat of the words he'd earlier dismissed. "Sometimes that's what it comes down to," he said. "We're going to arrive right on top of them. They'll have an energy shield and we need to find out its radius before anything else. If we can, we'll lightspeed jump through the shield and take it from there."

They entered local space half a second late, not that Duggan was counting. Red-Gulos had proved reasonably adept at learning the intricacies of the sensors and he brought up an image of the *Antrajis* station on a huge bulkhead screen they hadn't even realised existed until Duggan had accidentally turned it on a few hours previously.

"It looks bigger in real life," said Byers.

"Yeah. A lot bigger," said McLeod.

"We don't have enough soldiers to storm that place if they've taken the crew off the *Crimson* and quartered them elsewhere."

"We're going to try," said Duggan. "We can't leave our people or our technology in the hands of these murderous bastards."

The station looked exactly like the computerised model, except it was a much darker grey. It orbited a red-hued gas giant and from the angle of their approach, the *Antrajis* stood out in sharp contrast against the roiling, toxic surface below. The exterior metal also had a strange, shimmering appearance, as though it was covered in an early morning dew that refracted the sharp light of the nearby sun. Stars glinted like the eyes of creatures in a night-darkened forest and for the briefest of moments, Duggan remembered how the infinite beauty of nature and its contrast with technology had captivated him as a young boy.

"What's our distance?" he asked.

"Sixty thousand klicks. A good landing," said Red-Gulos.

"I'm reading a power surge from the station," said Byers. "I don't know a number big enough to tell you what it is."

"There are three smaller vessels in our vicinity," said Red-Gulos. "I am gathering more details."

Duggan put the gravity drives to full output and felt a rush of exhilaration at the power coursing through the *Valpian*. It surged through his veins and he knew that he could grow to love this warship, should he get the chance.

"Let the fun and games begin," he said.

CHAPTER NINETEEN

"I AM ATTEMPTING communication with the *ESS Crimson*," said Red-Gulos. "I have aimed three narrow transmissions – one towards each of the exterior doors on the *Antrajis*. If it's in one of the hangars, we should soon find out."

"I'm firing a single missile at the space station," said Duggan. "Missile away. Let's see where they've got their shield."

"The *Crimson* is here," said Red-Gulos. "I have a response."

"That was quick," said Duggan sharply.

"It's an automated reply and it's asking for a code." said the Ghast.

The *Crimson* was a military vessel and shouldn't have acknowledged any inbound communications without being specifically instructed to do so. It definitely shouldn't have asked for a code and Duggan was mystified at what information it was expecting. He asked himself if this was some sort of emergency protocol initiated by Lieutenant Chainer. There was too much happening elsewhere for him to give it his full consideration.

"Our missile has detonated off the orbital's energy shield," said McLeod.

"Shit," said Duggan. "Their shield only projects five or six klicks outside their walls. There's no way I can jump us through that – not without colliding with the station."

"The *Crimson* is behind the central of the three doors," said Red-Gulos.

Duggan glanced at the image of the space station. The upper and lower bay doors were huge and the middle ones larger yet – they were fifteen hundred metres wide and four hundred high. There was plenty of room to fit a *Crimson*-sized ship inside. The *Valpian* would be rather more of a squeeze.

"We're not going to fit this cruiser in the bay. Not easily," he said. "Even if we can get through their energy shield."

"Our own energy shield has come up," said Byers. "We just took a hit. A particle beam, I think."

"I'm detecting multiple launches from the station," said Red-Gulos. "Five hundred missiles."

The lights on the bridge dimmed and then returned. "We've had a wobble," said Byers.

"Disruptors," said Duggan. "They've got some in the space station."

"Two of the smaller vessels are preparing for lightspeed," she said.

"The third vessel is also firing at us," said Red-Gulos. "One hundred missiles from a range of ninety-six thousand klicks."

Almost without thinking, Duggan set the *Valpian* on a course that would circle the space station at high speed. Then, he targeted the hostile vessel and sent two waves of fifty back at it. The *Valpian*'s missiles travelled at incredible speed – faster than any Duggan had used or faced in the past.

"Our shields dropped for a fraction of a second when we launched, sir," said Byers. "The *Antrajis* tried to get us with a particle beam while they were down."

"I've got plenty to learn," said Duggan.

"The enemy missiles will impact in five seconds."

"Pray that our shield is strong enough," said McLeod.

"Impact."

The *Valpian*'s energy shield was struck by five hundred high-yield missiles from the *Antrajis* station, followed a moment later by a further hundred lower-yield plasma warheads from the patrolling vessel. The external sensor feeds went completely white and a series of gauges went crazy, their needles bouncing up and down, before rapidly stabilising. One gauge – this one more prominently displayed than the others – dropped by fifteen percent and remained there for a moment before recovering much slower than the rest. This gauge was unlabelled.

"This one's something to do with our ability to maintain the shield," Duggan said. "I always thought they could keep their shields up indefinitely, but it appears there are limits."

The lights on the bridge dimmed again.

"The enemy patrol vessel was not destroyed by our attack," said Red-Gulos. "It has launched a hundred more missiles."

"The other two have entered lightspeed, sir," said Byers.

Red-Gulos brought up an image of the remaining vessel on a secondary screen. It wasn't necessary for a warship captain to see his foe, but Duggan preferred to know who he faced. The vessel was fifteen hundred metres long - not exactly an insignificant opponent.

"I think they've fired a particle beam at us," said McLeod. "To go with those missiles."

"The orbital has launched again," said Red-Gulos. "Five hundred."

"There's another big spike on our power charts," said Byers.

The *Valpian* was under sustained attack and Duggan knew he was being too passive. With a series of quick gestures, he targeted the light cruiser with two hundred missiles and the rear particle beam. As soon as that was done, he launched the remainder of the *Valpian*'s available missile clusters towards the space station – a total of four hundred additional missiles.

"That light cruiser is on fire," said McLeod. "Like, *really* on fire."

"Our shield has taken another wave of a hundred," announced Byers. "Correction, make that six hundred."

The gauges did their dance and once again stabilised. All except the main gauge, which hadn't yet recovered from the first wave of missiles.

The bridge lights dimmed for a third time.

"Two more particle beams on us," said Byers.

"They're trying to synchronise," said Duggan. "To hit us when our shields are down."

"The enemy light cruiser is breaking up," said Red-Gulos. "The energy reading from the main section is eighty percent below its earlier peak."

"They're gone," said Duggan. It wasn't unknown for the Gallenium in a warship's engines to continue reacting at half of its maximum output even when the hull was in pieces. The Dreamer vessel was way below that. Unwilling to take risks with warship debris after what happened to the *Crimson* near the Helius Blackstar, Duggan launched another hundred missiles towards the wreckage.

"Our four hundred missiles have not penetrated the *Antrajis*' energy shield," said McLeod. "They made a big cloud, though."

"Keep it relevant," said Duggan, his irritation compounded by another flicker of the lights. The space station evidently had several disruptors, though they weren't proving too effective against the three AI cores on the *Valpian*.

The *Antrajis* launched a third wave of five hundred missiles and kept up its particle beam and disruptor attacks. The *Valpian* remained undamaged, though the central gauge had dropped below the halfway mark. It seemed likely the orbital had plenty of power in reserve to keep its shield going against any number of the cruiser's own missiles, so Duggan gave the front particle beam a try. He aimed at the central hangar bay door and fired.

"That one got through," said Byers. "They've got a big patch of orange to show for it."

"What if our crew aren't sitting nicely in the *Crimson* behind those hangar doors and waiting to be rescued?" asked McLeod. "That's a big place if we have to start looking for them on foot."

"In that case, we've lost!" said Duggan. He was angry – not at McLeod for asking the question, rather in worry that the soldier might be right.

"There's something building on the orbital, sir. It's some kind of massive reading coming from the two rings. It's different to anything else I've seen."

Duggan would have preferred specifics, though he couldn't blame Byers for not knowing.

He fired the second particle beam, again aiming at the central hangar doors. The beam was invisible to the human eye, though its effects were not. It heated the alloy of the door until it was glowing. The first beam hadn't recharged and Duggan had to circle the orbital for a few additional seconds until the weapon was ready. A fourth wave of missiles crashed against the energy shield, pushing the main gauge slowly towards zero. If the power bar was fully depleted it seemed certain the shield would fail and the *Valpian* would be vulnerable to missile fire.

After a third particle beam hit, the central doors on the *Antrajis* turned to sludge and then sagged away from the orbital's hull, leaving a vast hole through to its interior.

The reason for the orbital's power spike soon became apparent. Firstly, came the sweeping nausea of a life support system struggling to cope with massive, instant deceleration. Then came Duggan's realisation that the *Valpian* had stopped moving. Something was holding it in place, fifty thousand kilometres away from the *Antrajis*.

"What the hell?" said Byers. "They've got us with something."

Duggan had seen this before when he'd witnessed a Dreamer mining vessel bring a colossal chunk of rock to a standstill. It appeared the same technology could be used offensively as well.

"Whatever they're using it must be housed in the tori if that's where the power readings are coming from," he said.

"Can we destroy them?" asked McLeod.

"They're big," said Duggan. "I'll fire when able."

"I can see the *Crimson*," said McLeod.

"Yes, it is there," said Red-Gulos.

"Try communicating with it again," said Duggan. "I need to know if the crew is onboard."

With a rising dread, Duggan realised they were running out of options. Before their arrival, he'd pinned his hopes on being able to lightspeed hop through the outer energy shield, from where he'd expected to launch some kind of assault on the orbital.

Since the lightspeed jump wasn't feasible, they were reduced to firing missiles and particle beams at the space station. It didn't seem likely its shield was about to crumble and while the particle beams worked well enough, the *Antrajis* was too big to disable quickly with only two of the weapons.

Finally, while *Crimson* was in the middle hangar they had no way to get to it. If the crew were onboard, they were certainly unable to take action. They may be in cells somewhere deep within the *Antrajis* and far out of reach of a quick incursion from the soldiers on the *Valpian*. A thought appeared before he could stop it. *If they're still alive.*

He swore in frustration. There were times when you just had to give something a go and hope to find a way. This time it hadn't worked and they were trapped by some kind of new weapon. In truth, he was confident they could execute an escape at lightspeed, but he wasn't ready to give up quite yet. Angrily, he launched from every one of the *Valpian*'s clusters, sending six hundred missiles to collide fruitlessly with the orbital's energy shield.

"The *Crimson* is still asking for a code," said Red-Gulos.

"The orbital is no longer firing missiles," said McLeod.

"We should think about getting out of here, sir, assuming we can," said Byers. "They must have trapped us for a reason."

"What damned code is it after?" asked Duggan.

"You're the captain, sir," said McLeod.

The words sparked recognition in Duggan's brain. "Of course! It wants my personal codes. It must be something Lieutenant Chainer has set up."

He took two quick strides to bring him alongside Red-Gulos.

"Do you want to sit?" asked the Ghast, an absurdly mundane question in the circumstances.

Duggan didn't answer, since he was too busy studying the comms panel. To his relief, he saw there was a facility to transmit biological data. He instructed his suit to provide his encrypted biological codes to the *Valpian*'s comms panel. The *Valpian* then relayed the codes onwards to the *Crimson*.

"I'm receiving data from the *Crimson*," said Red-Gulos.

"What does it say?"

"It's a video file. I will play it."

Duggan wasn't surprised when Lieutenant Chainer's face appeared on his screen. He was wearing a spacesuit without a helmet. The man looked tired and he was even scruffier than usual, with his hair tangled and his stubble overgrown. It was difficult to tell where the video had been recorded, since the angle and lighting were poor. Duggan suspected it was on the *Crimson* somewhere, though he couldn't be sure.

"Hello, sir," the image of Chainer said.

"Get on with it," muttered Duggan.

"Things have not gone well since you left the *Crimson*." The image took an exaggerated look over its shoulder as though it was expecting hostiles to appear at any moment.

"Frank, I'm going to wring your neck when I see you, if you don't speed things up."

Chainer turned his face towards the screen once more and opened his mouth. At that moment, Byers interrupted, her words loud enough to drown out the recording.

"There's an incoming fission signature, sir. It's close and it's a big one."

"Ten to one that's the *Zansturm*," said McLeod.

"When – or if – you receive this message, rest assured we will no longer be on the *Crimson*," said Chainer.

"They're not here?" asked McLeod.

"I don't know!" said Duggan. "Listen!"

Chainer's mouth opened with glacial slowness as he began his next sentence. "A large spaceship appeared two days after you left for the enemy base on Nistrum."

Duggan felt like putting his head in his hands. "Please, Frank, keep it short," he begged.

"The *Zansturm* has appeared in local space," said Red-Gulos.

Duggan swore.

CHAPTER TWENTY

THE BATTLESHIP DIDN'T MAKE any overtly hostile moves. It held fire and started moving in a wide arc around the *Antrajis* station, maintaining a constant distance of three hundred thousand kilometres.

"What are they up to?" Duggan asked himself.

"We're trapped, sir," said Byers. "What are we going to do? Should we keep firing missiles at the space station's shield?"

"Hold for a moment!" said Duggan. He realised why the *Zansturm* had chosen to stay so far away. "They're keeping out of particle beam range. They don't want us to land a couple of lucky shots on one of their critical systems."

"Why don't they finish us off?" asked McLeod. "If it was me, I'd be firing missiles at us as quickly as they'd reload."

The answer came to Duggan. "They want their warship back," he said. "This must be the best they've got in its class. Perhaps it's carrying new weapons, defences or just plain information that they can't afford to lose."

"Didn't stop the space station firing plenty of missiles at us."

"What else were they going to do?" asked Duggan. "They must have received instructions to hold us a couple of minutes after we engaged, so they've stopped the missiles."

"Shouldn't we take this opportunity to try and destroy the *Antrajis*?" asked McLeod.

"I don't think we can destroy it with just particle beams – it's too big," said Duggan. "That wouldn't usually stop me firing, it's just that our crew may still be onboard."

"Haven't we lost, sir?" asked Byers. "Maybe it's time to go down shooting."

Duggan preferred to use the time to think of a way out of their situation, if indeed such a way existed. If they started unloading on the *Antrajis*, it might push the enemy into a position where they decided to destroy the *Valpian* anyway. The orbital looked significantly more valuable than the cruiser to Duggan's eyes. Besides, the energy shields on the cruiser were almost depleted. The gauge was slowly recovering, but the shield would take a good few minutes before it reached anything like full strength.

A voice intruded on the brief silence. It had been talking in the background, but some of the words forced their way into Duggan's consciousness.

"They used a new kind of disruptor on us," said Chainer, as though he were having a gentle chat on a Sunday afternoon. "Not before we'd fired a couple of nukes at them from where we were on the surface. They didn't like that one little bit."

"Is he going to tell us his whole life story?" asked Red-Gulos.

Chainer continued talking, with Duggan keeping one ear on the monologue in case the lieutenant decided to divulge anything of importance to their current situation.

"The translation modules are a little flaky on these things, sir," Chainer continued. "However, I managed to pick up some details of where they're taking us. I've encoded the information into this video."

That was more like it. "Sergeant, find the place Lieutenant Chainer refers to," said Duggan.

"They're not here," said Red-Gulos after a few seconds. "I don't have details of where they've been taken – I can only tell you it's not the *Antrajis* station."

"Good enough," replied Duggan. "It's time to go elsewhere and I don't like to leave people behind. The shields look as though they can withstand another short bombardment. I'll point us somewhere and we'll take this chance to regroup. Let's see what the bastards do when they see our fission signature."

"This might be our only chance to destroy the *Crimson* and prevent its technology falling into the hands of the enemy," said Red-Gulos. "They lack the stealth modules you have installed onboard."

The Ghost was right – if they ever returned to the orbital, it would be protected by a dozen warships. Not that the *Antrajis* needed a great deal of assistance when it came to defence.

"We have no choice," said Duggan. "This one we can't win."

With those words, he loaded up the fission engines and punched in the code for a random location. A countdown started, the strange alien symbols updating smoothly as they headed towards zero.

"The *Zansturm* is still not firing, sir," said Byers. "I'd have expected some kind of farewell salute."

"We'll be out of here in ten seconds," Duggan said. Something about Byers' words bothered him, though he couldn't quite put his finger on what it was.

"The *Antrajis* must be conserving its ammunition," said McLeod. "Maybe they know we're going to piss off – maybe they don't care."

It dawned on Duggan why the enemy wasn't firing at them. "Damn," he said in resignation.

His hunch was correct – the fission engines didn't activate properly. They gave their usual vast energy reading for a nanosecond and then simply shut down as if they'd been purposely taken offline.

"Well, that's us screwed," said McLeod.

Byers proved to be more pragmatic. "Can we try again, sir? Perhaps we could load up the engines and fire a couple of last-moment particle beams at the space station and hope it shuts down whatever weapon they're using to hold us."

"It's a long shot," Duggan said. "I need a moment to think."

"This is a stalemate," said Red-Gulos. "How do they intend to board us? We will shoot down any troop transport vessels they send to recapture us."

Before Duggan could decide one way or another there was more bad news, which also answered Red-Gulos' most recent question.

"Here comes another fission signature," said Byers. "If the last one was big, this one is a word that's much bigger than that."

A vessel appeared near to the orbital – very, very near. Red-Gulos focused the sensors on it and the four of them stared.

"Big..." repeated Byers, her mouth hanging open.

Duggan had never seen the like before. The enemy vessel was close to the *Antrajis* space station in size and volume. It was eighteen thousand metres long, with two vast spheres at the front and back. These spheres were attached to a comparatively narrow hull beam which joined with a large, central superstructure which was the shape of a round-edged trapezoid. The vessel was almost black in colour, such that it would have been difficult to see without enhancement from the *Valpian*'s sensors.

"What is that?" asked Byers.

Duggan had no answer and could only shake his head in

disbelief. Jagged flashes of white-blue skittered across each of the spheres in random places and at irregular intervals, like a storm of lightning held in place by a black hole. It was similar to the effect on the *Valpian*'s hull and much more intense. The only explanation was that the enemy vessel generated more power than it could contain and had to discharge the excess through its walls.

Chainer hadn't stopped speaking for one moment, most of his words being easy to ignore. Then came a sentence which answered more than one question and asked many more.

"Then this warship – I've heard them call it a Class 1 Neutraliser - picked us and there was nothing we could do about it."

"There's the Class 1 Neutraliser," said Duggan.

"I think it's called the *Excoliar* or something," Chainer continued. "If you see it, you're probably screwed. It shut us down in moments, what little we had to shut down. Commander McGlashan wanted to initiate the *Crimson*'s self-destruct, but we were taken by surprise and then it was too late."

The lights on the bridge went out, leaving the crew in complete and utter darkness. Duggan waited a few seconds to see if the emergency lighting would come on. It didn't.

Duggan kept his suit helmet close by. It was an encumbrance to wear it constantly, so he was reluctant to keep it on except when he needed its sensor to translate Estral symbols for him. He could fly the *Valpian* easily enough now and the helmet's external speaker acted as an interpreter for Red-Gulos. Duggan patted around beneath his chair.

"That probably means no life support as well," he said. "Get your helmets on."

He put his own over his head and realised immediately something was wrong – the HUD was off and there were no other signs it was operational.

"Shit," he said, ripping the helmet off over his head. "The suits are affected as well."

He remembered that each suit was equipped with a battery-powered torch, clipped to the belt. It was ancient technology, but when he fumbled his torch out of its fastenings he felt immense relief when its yellow-tinged beam cut through the darkness. He swung the torch left and right, illuminating the concerned faces of Byers and McLeod. They didn't need to be told and they took out their own torches.

The beams lit up the face of Red-Gulos. He remained in his seat, his expression impassive. The Ghast opened his mouth and uttered a series of harsh phrases. With the suit helmets disabled, there was no way to understand his words.

Duggan swore again. "Let's hope we can get by with sign language," he said.

"How long do the batteries last on these torches?" asked Byers.

"I have no idea," said Duggan truthfully. He couldn't recall the last time he'd needed to use a suit's hand-held torch.

With the assistance of torchlight, Duggan tapped at certain areas on his console a few times to reassure himself what he already knew – the *Valpian* had been comprehensively disabled.

"We're dead in the water," he said. "This is how they intend to resolve the stalemate."

Corporal Gax appeared, his looming, metal-clad shape looking like a cross between something living and something mechanical. He had his own torch, obtained from an unknown place. It gave off an extensive light and he pointed it straight at Duggan. Gax spoke and Red-Gulos responded.

"This isn't good," said Byers.

"Great use of understatement," McLeod congratulated her.

"Is there a plan, sir?" asked Byers.

"I'm working on it," said Duggan.

Whatever had passed between Red-Gulos and Gax was a mystery, However, Gax left the bridge immediately, turning and hurrying away with a faint clatter of sound-deadened shoulder plates.

"How are we getting out of this?" asked McLeod. For some reason, he didn't sound especially concerned, as if he'd been in worse situations than this one on many occasions.

"At least Lieutenant Chainer's stopped talking," said Byers with a mischievous laugh.

There'd been a time when Duggan had lived for moments like these – the camaraderie of others as they faced insurmountable odds. The flame within him hadn't died, but he wanted only to get everyone home as quickly as possible, rather than having to fight tooth and nail for each tiny step of progress. He didn't know if they were any further forward than when they were sitting on the crash-damaged *ESS Crimson*.

"We've still got a chance to shoot a few of those bastards when they attempt to storm the ship," said McLeod. "Unless you want us to surrender?"

"We're not giving up are we, sir?" asked Byers.

The fight was still strong within the soldiers and Duggan took strength from it. "Not while I'm still breathing!" he said. "Grab your weapons!"

As the others scrambled to pick up their kit Red-Gulos got to his feet, evidently aware he was going to have to follow until they found a way to communicate again. Duggan nodded at the Ghost by way of encouragement.

During this very short period of activity, Duggan conceived his plan. The potential of it roared through him like a vicious animal and he laughed at the lasting damage they might cause to the enemy if they managed to pull it off. There was only one potential stumbling block.

"Something funny?" asked McLeod in confusion.

Duggan ignored the question. "What do your field comms packs run off?" he asked.

"It's a type of mega low-drain battery," said Byers. "I can give you specifics if you're interested."

"Check it for me, please. Does it work?"

Byers and McLeod kept their field kit against the back wall of the bridge. They went across and looked to see if their comms gear was affected by the *Excoliar*'s power drain.

"Mine's working," said Byers. "There are lights on my rifle as well. They run off the same batteries as the comms gear."

"Mine too, sir."

"Look after those packs – we're going to need them," Duggan replied. "Does anyone remember how far away the *Excoliar* was parked from the orbital? I need corroboration of what I remember."

"Forty-one klicks," said Byers without hesitation. "Far closer than necessary."

"To the contrary, soldier. They are at a near-perfect distance from the *Antrajis* station. Now come on!" he shouted. "Quickly!"

The faster they acted, the easier it would be to pull off an audacious move that would give them a fighting chance to rescue the *Crimson*'s missing crew and return home. Duggan's feet practically flew across the metal floor and carried him to the forward mess room. As expected, there were others of his squad there. They had their torches out and talked amongst themselves, clearly undecided on what they should do. Duggan provided guidance.

"Find everyone and get back here. Do it fast."

"Yes, sir!" they responded, already heading for the exit.

The troops were professionals and kept themselves within a limited area of the ship in order to watch over each other. Consequently, Duggan wasn't waiting long. Soldiers – human and Ghast alike arrived at the double and stood before him in the room to hear what he had to say. Torch beams jumped around, their sudden movements a reflection of nervousness amongst the troops. The Ghasts stood amongst the others, though they surely didn't understand a word of what was said.

Duggan explained the situation for those who hadn't already worked it out. "We've been shut down by a vessel called *Excoliar*. Our suits aren't working, nor is anything else on the *Valpian*. If the life support is offline, we'll run out of air in a few days, assuming we don't freeze to death first. Fortunately, I have a plan that will ensure we don't freeze or suffocate, as long as it works. Firstly, we'll need to get to the external hangar bay door. It's still open and has been since we first stormed the ship."

Someone tutted in comedic judgement of his carelessness.

"Yes, it's like leaving your shoelaces undone," said Duggan with unexplainable high spirits. "Just be thankful I had my hands full learning how to fly this thing, else closing an external door would have been the first thing on my to-do list."

In truth, he'd forgotten all about the open hangar until a few minutes ago. There'd been no alarms on the bridge consoles – the Dreamers appeared to deal with safety matters in an entirely different way to how they did it in the Space Corps.

"Can someone tell me how many sealed doors there are between here and the rear hangar?" he asked.

"Just one, sir," said Lieutenant Ortiz, her voice heavy and slurred. Her eyes were distant and remote. "The rest of the *Valpian* is fully pressurised and able to sustain life."

"How far away is the door from the breach into the hangar?"

"One hundred and ten metres. A straight run, sir," she said, the words sounding like they cost her a great effort.

The demonstration of Ortiz's injury knocked the levity from Duggan's mood, though it only increased his determination to succeed.

"Bonner, do you have enough explosives to get through that door?" he asked.

"I'm not sure, sir. I used up most of my pack on the way in."

"Is there anything you could use in the ship's armoury?"

"There are explosives, sir. I've left them well alone."

"No professional curiosity?"

"Curiosity gets you killed when you're handling explosives, whether it's *professional* curiosity or not."

"I understand your reluctance; however, we need to get into the hangar and we need to do it soon. Get what you think will do the job. Take Durham with you in case it's heavy. Meet us at the sealed door as soon as you can."

Bonner went, pulling Durham with her. Duggan continued.

"Does anyone know if there is any way to take one of those mobile plasma launchers from the hold and get it through the ship to the hangar bay?"

"No," said Rasmussen. "The artillery will not fit."

"Shame. It means rifles, repeaters and grenades only."

"We're low on grenades, sir," said Hendrix. "I've had a little play with the ones in the armoury – they're different to the ones we carry. I recommend we do not attempt to use them."

Duggan accepted the recommendation and finished his briefing. "If I were the enemy, I'd have a troop transport coming our way immediately, so we'll encounter hostiles if we don't act quickly enough. The *Antrajis* station is holding us stationary and unluckily for them, the *Valpian*'s open hangar door is facing the breach we made in their hull. The range is extreme, but once we're in the hangar, I can use the squad's portable comms gear to activate the *ESS Crimson*'s self-destruct sequence. It's carrying many conventional missiles as well as a large store of huge-yield nuclear warheads. The results of a detonation within the hull of the *Antrajis* should be spectacular."

The troops greeted this with enthusiasm. Duggan waved

them to silence and ordered them to run for the sealed door that separated the open hangar from the rest of the *Valpian*. The Ghasts didn't need to understand the words and they followed at once. Duggan joined his troops in the sprint. While he ran, he thought about the possibilities that could lead his plan to failure. There were many such possibilities and for once he pretended they didn't exist. This was a final throw of the dice – not an unusual situation for him, Duggan reflected – and he wouldn't countenance failure.

CHAPTER TWENTY-ONE

THEY GATHERED at the door which sealed off the rest of the ship from the vacuum in the hangar. The torches lit the corridor well enough to see, but Duggan found himself wishing for the interior lights to come back on. There were soldiers who liked to fight in the dark. He wasn't one of them.

He took a look at the door. It was fairly standard-looking and designed as proof against escaping air and accidental explosions. The metal was featureless, sullen and probably several feet thick. Any hope Duggan had that the door possessed its own, separate power system which was somehow shielded from the effects of the Class 1 Neutraliser, were dispelled immediately.

"The panel's completely dead, sir," said Barron. He made a couple of redundant swiping gestures to demonstrate his words.

"Where's Bonner?" asked Duggan.

"Not here yet."

"Come on," Duggan muttered to himself. He shifted his weight from foot to foot, aware his fidgeting gave a bad impression. The air seemed colder already, a feeling he put down to imagination.

Bonner arrived, dragging a wheeled trolley behind her, upon which was a metal box with an open lid. "It doesn't look as if these Dreamers do subtle," she said. "There must be enough explosives in this box to blow a hole through ten metres of alloy."

"Can't you use half?" asked Duggan drily.

"I don't know what the exact yield is, sir. I've got a few Space Corps charges left." She cast a glance towards the door. "I'm not sure if they'll get us through."

"*Not sure* isn't good enough," said Duggan. "We can't spare the time for a second attempt. Rig up these additional charges and we'll retreat through the ship until we're far enough away."

"It'll be quicker to let me try a smaller series of charges first, sir," she said, not afraid to stand up for herself. "You'll have to run halfway through the ship before you're safe from these Dreamer explosives."

"I thought you didn't know what the yield was?" he asked.

"I don't," she replied. "That's why it'll be safest to get a distance that errs on the side of caution. That means a *lot* of distance."

"Very well, try your standard-issue explosives," said Duggan. He turned to the others and spoke in a loud voice so that everyone could hear. "As soon as this door is open, the air in the ship will begin to escape through the hole leading into the hangar. You will be aware that your suits contain an emergency supply of oxygen and you will be equally aware that your suit cannot dispense that oxygen without a power source."

"Yeah, we're pretty badly screwed," said Camacho.

"It gets better," said Duggan. "There is a chance we will find enemy soldiers coming to meet us. If you put your suit helmets in place, you'll be protected from the vacuum and there should be enough oxygen inside to keep you going for a couple of minutes."

A few of the soldiers gave resigned laughter.

"We need to run more than a hundred metres and fight with the enemy, all on two minutes' oxygen?" asked Berg.

"That's what you signed up for," Duggan agreed with a smile. "Even if the enemy is right on the other side of this blast door, you'll still need to come with me to provide cover while I send the signal. If it goes to plan, we should get power back immediately."

"Maybe their soldiers will be deprived of power like we are," said Kidd hopefully. "They might just have to wait us out."

"For some reason, that's not what I'm expecting," said Duggan.

Kidd snorted. "Nor I, sir."

"Won't we still be in a vacuum once you're done, sir?" asked Vaughan.

"Yes, we will," Duggan replied. "I'm hoping the suits will start working again. If not, we'll need to get deeper into the ship and reach an area that's pressurized. The doors should work by that point, so anyone who makes it will be able to reach an area of safety."

"The closest door is sixty metres back the way we've come," said Cabrera, looking over her shoulder. "That's a lot of extra running."

"If the suits stay powered off, we're dead anyway," said Duggan. "Is everyone clear on what we're doing?"

"Not them, sir," said McLeod, thumbing over his shoulder towards the Ghasts.

"They're quick learners," said Duggan. "I'm sure they'll see what we're up to."

Nevertheless, he spent a few seconds in front of Red-Gulos, waving his arms and acting out what he thought was an obvious description of the plan. The Ghast stared at Duggan as if he were mad.

"He thinks you're asking for his hand in marriage, sir," said Byers.

"That'll have to do," said Duggan, doing his best to ignore the quip. "We can't wait any longer. Bonner, I assume you're ready?"

"I'm always ready, sir," she said, pointing at a series of charges arrayed along the edges of the door. She waved them towards a branch in the corridor fifty metres away. "Everyone get around that corner."

The squad moved quickly back.

"What if you only blow a small hole in the door?" asked Chan. "We'll get the vacuum without being able to reach the hangar."

"Won't happen," said Bonner.

"Yeah, but what if it does?" Chan persisted.

"They're going off in ten seconds anyway."

"Everyone get your helmets on!" said Duggan. He took two deep breaths and then put his in place, before manually tightening the neck seal with his fingers.

A spacesuit was very good at excluding sound from outside. Consequently, Duggan didn't hear the angry crackling of the shaped charges when they detonated. He did, however, see the blue light reflecting off the walls.

Bonner poked her head around the corner. Evidently satisfied, she made a beckoning sign with her arm and then ducked into the passageway. Kidd and Havon followed, the Ghost having evidently decided he wasn't going to miss out on potential action.

Duggan came next, with Byers and McLeod close behind. They carried their comms gear over their shoulders and knew it was imperative they stay close. Without the internal comms on the helmets and without the movement or heat sensors, they had to rely on skill and discipline. Most of all, they were relying on luck.

The passageway was lit by torchlight and by the glowing metal of the blast door. Bonner had done her work well and the door had fallen neatly away onto the floor, where it continued to smoke and burn. Duggan ignored the furious heat and leapt onto the alloy slab, idly noting it had been much less than a metre thick. He did his best to breathe evenly, not wanting to burn up his precious supply of oxygen too quickly.

Lieutenant Ortiz's description of what lay beyond the door wasn't quite accurate. The corridor went straight, before cutting left at a right-angle and then turning immediate right. Duggan found himself in the room which lay just beyond the breach into the hangar bay. The light from several torches danced over the ragged opening. The metal was completely cool now, though it was black in colour and heavily scarred.

Duggan glanced behind to check if Byers and McLeod were still with him. One of the two raised a hand in mock-salute and ushered him onwards. Duggan walked quickly to the hole in the wall and stepped into the gap, his gauss rifle clutched awkwardly in one hand and his torch in the other. The rifles weren't made for one-handed use and Duggan told himself that if he ever got out of this, he'd put in a recommendation for the weapons to have clips fitted which could hold a torch to free up a soldier's second hand.

The hole in the metal was deeper than he remembered it, and the bullet-torn edges sharper and more eager to cut into his flesh. He saw it then – there was an enemy troop transporter in the hangar bay, thirty metres above the floor. He wasn't sure if it was hovering or if, for that brief moment, his mind worked so quickly that time itself appeared to stand still, giving the impression the vessel was suspended in the air.

His torchlight flickered over the transport's nose, where a chain gun was mounted. To the right, the external hangar door was open in the position he'd left it, a yawning gap into eternal distances and the absolute certainty of death. He knew his thoughts were drifting and he tried to focus them, aware the shortage of oxygen was making him light-headed.

That gun is pointing entirely the wrong way, he thought. *If we run to towards the hangar doors, they won't have time to stop us.*

He sensed movement behind and turned awkwardly. Byers and McLeod were there, with others edging into the hole afterwards. A voice, dispassionate and separate, warned Duggan he had only this one chance. Retreat wasn't an option – it hadn't been ever since the *Excoliar* arrived. The only way was forward, ever forward. He asked himself if he were being tested by a vengeful god he'd somehow, unknowingly insulted. It seemed that every time he thought he'd beaten the odds, he was given another trial each more difficult than the last, until he'd eventually meet an obstacle he couldn't overcome. *Or perhaps the final test has only a single available outcome – one in which I lose whatever happens, and everyone else dies with me.*

With a growl of anger heard only by himself, Duggan took the final strides into the hangar bay. The transport hung in the air, somehow protected from the *Excoliar*'s power drain. It didn't move and Duggan wondered if the pilot was incompetent or if he were simply laughing at the pathetic efforts of the soldiers below. The thought made Duggan even angrier. He tried to put the fury aside, aware it was making him burn his irreplaceable oxygen at an uncontrollable rate.

In the hangar, Duggan found the beam of his torch jumping from place to place, like it had a mind of its own. The light wasn't nearly enough to illuminate the whole bay and it cast elongated shadows against the floor and the nearby walls. He caught glimpses of the ruined shuttle in the distance, a broken shell of metal and spent ammunition.

He ran to the right, not caring if he depleted his oxygen supplies too soon. There was a single task for him and he was determined to finish it. The opening in the *Valpian*'s hull was vast and the closer he came to it, the less significant he felt. He reached the edge and stood there, fearlessly, looking out into the void of space. Distant stars, the names of which he would never learn, twinkled and once again, Duggan felt like a boy dumbfounded and awestruck by the magnitude of everything.

Someone tapped him hard on the shoulder and Duggan stepped back from the precipice. *Byers,* he thought. *She's a little shorter than McLeod.* Beyond, the transport vessel descended until it was only a few metres above the surface and it executed a half-turn, bringing its nose cannon closer to where Duggan and the others were standing.

Byers and McLeod shrugged their cloth packs from their shoulders and placed them on the floor. There was a flap which could be pulled away to reveal the workings of the units within and the soldiers took only a few seconds to prepare for a transmission. Byers knelt beside hers and she beckoned Duggan to crouch next to her. She tried to nod to let him know everything was ready. The movement was clumsy, but Duggan got the idea. He pulled his glove off with a violent tugging action and felt his skin tightening immediately in the freezing air. He pressed his palm against the transmission pad on the comms unit for a split second, to send his authorisation codes to the *Crimson*. He withdrew his hand and looked at Byers for confirmation. Once his codes were accepted it would be time to send the self-destruct command.

Byers looked at him, her reflective visor giving nothing away. She raised a hand to her throat and made an obvious cutting motion. There was no way to misinterpret the signal – something had gone wrong. Duggan tried desperately to think what it could be and then he guessed. The *Antrajis* station was holding the *Valpian* at a slight angle. Duggan had been confident there was a clear line across the fifty thousand kilometres between the open docking bay and the *ESS Crimson*. With the failure of the signal to reach the *Crimson*, he was sure the walls of the *Valpian* were impeding the transmission.

There was only one solution. Duggan picked up the comms

unit and took a step towards the edge, meaning to jump out in the hope he would be able to send his command to the *Crimson*. Before he could finish, he felt a hand grab his shoulder. It pulled him backwards with great force. He tried to resist but found his limbs weak and unwilling to respond. Byers pulled the comms unit from his hand and ran past him. She took three quick steps and leapt into the blackness.

Duggan stumbled away and half fell onto his haunches. He felt exhausted and the pain in his hand was indescribable.

McLeod pointed angrily at Duggan and then at the second comms unit. The words were unspoken but the meaning was clear. *Don't waste the gift of her sacrifice.*

Duggan fought hard against the effects of oxygen deprivation. He looked outwards, the enemy transport forgotten. He saw Byers, drifting and spinning slowly, with the comms gear clutched to her chest. The red lights on the unit were visible. They blinked slowly and accusingly at Duggan for his weakness.

With a monumental effort, Duggan pressed his hand on the second comms unit and sent his codes to Byers' pack for it to relay onwards to the *Crimson*. He had no idea how to tell if he'd met with success or failure. He looked to McLeod for help. The soldier lifted his hand to his neck and made the same cutting motion that Byers had made only a few seconds before. *No connection.*

Duggan had never once in his life given up. He snarled and pressed his palm to the comms unit again. Without knowing what made him look up, he turned his head once more towards Byers. She'd drifted far away, though she was easy enough to see if you knew where you were looking. There was something different on her comms unit. Where before there had been a blinking red light, now there was a solid green one, from this distance no larger than a full stop on the page of a book seen across a room. McLeod raised his fist with the thumb pointing upwards.

Duggan sent the command. He knew the *Crimson*'s mainframe wouldn't accept something so calamitous at the first instruction, so he sent the command again, three more times in quick succession. He closed his eyes tightly and begged for victory or forgiveness.

Nothing happened.

CHAPTER TWENTY-TWO

DUGGAN KNEW HE WAS DYING. He felt detached from his body and imagined his consciousness floating somewhere a few inches above his corporeal form. He was able to see – he observed the enemy transport as it touched down on the floor of the docking bay. He watched as its landing gear flexed under the gentle impact. The chain gun remained quiet and Duggan asked himself if the enemy were so confident of success they'd chosen to minimise any additional damage to the *Valpian*.

The mistake was theirs to make. Duggan saw three objects sail one after each other from the breach in the hangar wall. They travelled far and fast. *Thrown by a Ghost,* he realised. The objects clunked against the far side of the transport's hull. Seconds passed. Then, one-by-one, they exploded. The small craft was lost in the whiteness of the blast and Duggan was forced to squint against the intense light.

He closed his eyes, his oxygen-starved brain neither knowing nor caring if he'd ever open them again.

John Duggan didn't die. Time went by and a sound reached his ears. It was the distant chime of an alarm. His fragmented thoughts coalesced and he realised the alarm was coming from a place much closer than he'd first thought. With an effort, he opened his eyes. The HUD on his spacesuit was active and he tried to make sense of the words. There were many alerts relating to heat damage on the suit's exterior. It had been in a bad way before the explosion and it was close to critical failure now. Amongst the sea of red was a single amber warning relating to the oxygen levels in his blood. Before his eyes, the alert changed to green.

Duggan struggled to his feet. His hand hurt in a strange, remote way, as if it no longer belonged to his body. His glove was back on somehow. He couldn't remember replacing it though it could have been no one else.

Voices reached him. They were sporadic and filled with uncertainty.

"Who's left?"

"Fall back! Get out of the hangar!"

"Did we make it?"

A violent hammering in his chest told Duggan the spacesuit had injected him with a cocktail of drugs to try and revive him. They reached into every corner of his body and mind, bringing clarity to his thoughts and adding strength to his limbs.

The enemy transport was destroyed. It was a crumpled heap of metal, knocked many metres away by the force of the explosions. From the direction the vessel had been thrown, Duggan could see that its hull had protected him from incineration. Whoever hurled the explosive packs had done a good job, either by accident or design. There was no sign of enemy soldiers.

Movement caught his eye. A figure next to him on the floor stirred weakly. Duggan reached down and hauled the soldier upright. It was McLeod and the man swayed unsteadily.

"Get your comms pack," ordered Duggan. "We have to reach the bridge."

McLeod said something nonsensical, but he stooped to collect the pack anyway. "Byers?" he said at last.

"Gone," snapped Duggan. "She saved us."

"We won?"

"No, we damn well haven't won," said Duggan, setting off and dragging the soldier by one arm. "The *Zansturm* is still out there."

"Shit."

The urgency was driven home before they'd taken a dozen steps. The hangar bay was suddenly illuminated in a light which seemed as intense as that from the hottest of suns. The image from the helmet sensor fizzed and spluttered in distress. There was no sound, yet Duggan's earpiece shrieked like it was overloaded.

Duggan ran. There were members of his squad positioned defensively inside the room beyond the hangar. They carried rifles or repeaters and kept a watchful eye on the remnants of the enemy shuttle. Duggan ignored them and kept going.

"Sergeant Red-Gulos, this is Duggan," he said while he ran. "Can you provide an update on our situation?"

"Power is restored throughout the vessel. I have handed over responsibility for troop organisation to Corporal Gax. I am on my way to the bridge."

The Ghost had done exactly what Duggan wanted. "Excellent. I'm coming there myself. The *Zansturm* has fired upon us."

The corridors seemed longer on the return journey and it felt to Duggan as if he were experiencing a nightmare where his best efforts to make headway were ineffective, like thick mud clung to his arms and legs. His mind worked at double-speed, adding to the frustration, since it evaluated each possibility a dozen times yet without the ability to act upon his decisions.

Hanging above everything was the knowledge that the *Valpian*'s shields were already heavily depleted, whilst the

Zansturm had only been three hundred thousand kilometres away. That wasn't much over two minutes travel time for the battleship to reach them – and far less for its weapons.

In spite of the illusion he was travelling at a crawl, Duggan managed to overhaul Red-Gulos a few yards from the bridge. Even if the Ghosts were big, they were clumsy runners and Duggan sprinted up the few steps and jumped into his seat. The two remaining members of his crew piled in behind him.

"We're moving at more than half speed," said Duggan in surprise. "The *Valpian*'s engines must have resumed where they left off from before the *Antrajis* froze us in place."

He increased their speed to maximum. The tactical display showed the direction of the *Zansturm*'s approach and Duggan adjusted the cruiser's course to ensure the distance between the two vessels remained as large as possible.

"More missiles," said McLeod.

The second wave of plasma warheads crashed into the *Valpian*'s shields.

"We can't take many more like that," said Duggan. "The shield gauge hasn't recovered from the last time."

"They've launched a third wave, sir."

"I'm activating the fission engines. We're going somewhere that isn't here."

"We should be away before the third wave reaches us," said McLeod.

"The *Excoliar* isn't destroyed," said Red-Gulos.

A chill ran through Duggan. "What do you mean it isn't destroyed?"

"I have located it on the fars. It is close to the surface of the gas giant, almost one million kilometres from us. It is definitely intact."

Duggan set the lightspeed sequence away and a number

started its countdown. "What readings are you getting from the *Excoliar*? We should be safe at a million klicks."

"Its engine output is predictably huge and it is currently focused on providing thrust to bring the vessel away from the planet."

"Have they seen us?" Duggan knew the answer.

"By their heading, they know we're here. Their speed is approximately two thousand kilometres per second."

Duggan tipped his head back and closed his eyes. "We're quicker than they are."

"There is a power surge from both the front and rear spheres," said Red-Gulos. "They have vanished."

This was something Duggan had witnessed before from the Dreamer mothership and he'd hoped never to see it again. "Check again!" he said with urgency.

"The *Excoliar* is now only two hundred thousand kilometres distant," said the Ghast, betraying the faintest surprise.

Duggan fired every available missile from the *Valpian*'s launchers. He didn't know if they'd have any effect on the Neutraliser but he had to try.

"What's the range on its lockdown?" asked McLeod.

"I have no idea," Duggan replied. "Less than two hundred thousand klicks from the looks of it."

"There is a second power surge from the *Excoliar*," said Red-Gulos.

"That's us done," said McLeod.

The enemy Neutraliser completed a second short-range jump towards the *Valpian*. By an amount of time too small to easily measure, it was too late. The cruiser's fission drive activated and the warship vanished, leaving the *Excoliar* and the *Zansturm* behind.

"Close," said Duggan. He unlatched his helmet and put it

under his seat. The cold air on the bridge struck his skin like a welcome shock.

"Is it always this way?" asked Red-Gulos.

Duggan laughed. "Not always. More often than I would like."

"Where are we going?"

"Nowhere in particular. We'll find out where Lieutenant Chainer and the others have gone to once I've confirmed the *Valpian* is secure. I'll change course when we're ready."

He didn't need to make use of the internal comms. Corporal Gax appeared at the door to the bridge, his suit helmet in one hand.

"The enemy soldiers did not survive the three explosions," he said. "There are no hostile forces on the *Valpian*."

"What of our men and women?"

"Five became unconscious through oxygen starvation. Corporal Weiss has seen to them and they will recover quickly."

"Only one loss," said Duggan.

"One is too many," said Gax.

"Always. We are here because of her actions."

Gax nodded his head and turned to leave. He stopped himself. "I have closed the outer hangar bay door. There was a control panel near to it."

"Thank you," said Duggan. For some reason it seemed important – as if a loose end had finally been tied up. "Keep me updated."

When Gax was gone, Duggan asked to see the recent sensor recordings. The *Valpian*'s front arrays had been pointing towards the *Antrajis* station when he issued the self-destruct command to the *Crimson*'s mainframe.

Red-Gulos displayed the video on the main screen and the three of them watched in silence. For a time, there was no change – the orbital appeared motionless whilst the gas giant in the background slowly rotated. The damage to the space station's central hangar doors was clear and the burned metal slowly cooled. Inside, the *Crimson* waited, sitting on its twisted landing gear. The missile craters were easily seen. The longer he watched, the greater was Duggan's sorrow. He felt as if he'd somehow betrayed the warship, even though he knew the idea was nonsense. The *Crimson* was a tool of war and he'd used it as best he could. The thought didn't make him feel any better.

Shortly after, another sensor showed the arrival of the *Excoliar* and then everything went blank.

"Show me the resumption," said Duggan.

When the recording started again, the view was a different one. The gas giant was where it had been, but now the *Antrajis* was gone, torn into a million pieces that scattered across the sky. Much of the wreckage glowed white-hot and, where the pieces travelled quickly enough, they left fading lines in their wake to describe the course they had taken.

At first, the *Excoliar* looked unaffected. Then, several huge pieces of burning debris struck the vessel. They travelled at such speed they sent the Neutraliser spinning towards the planet below.

"Their shield didn't work?" asked McLeod.

"The *Crimson*'s nukes would have shut it down," said Duggan. "That and probably several others of their major systems."

"They know what it feels like."

"It didn't destroy them."

"I'll bet they took a lot of damage," said McLeod enthusiastically. "Look at the size of those pieces they got hit by!"

"I'd rather not see it again. Not without a greater knowledge of its weaknesses."

"Do we have a copy of the data we stole from the hub planet?" asked Red-Gulos.

"No, Sergeant. It's gone, along with our only Planet Breaker. In its place, we have something of potentially far greater value." Duggan leaned forward and tapped the console. "All that remains is for us to rescue the missing crew and to figure out a way to return to Confederation Space."

The words were easily spoken, but Duggan wasn't foolish enough to think the result would be easily won.

CHAPTER TWENTY-THREE

"THEY'VE BEEN TAKEN to this planet here," said Duggan, pointing to a complex chart he called up on the main display. "The Dreamers call it Invarol."

It had taken him an hour to extract the map data from the *Valpian*'s memory banks and he believed it showed the enemy's significant holdings in this particular sector. Mostly there were planets, not all of which he believed were populated. There were bases, space stations and mobile shipyards amongst others. It would have Fleet Admiral Teron apoplectic when he saw the strength of their foes.

"Anywhere specific?" asked McLeod. "An entire planet is a lot to search for three people."

"Very well observed," said Duggan wryly. "Fortunately, Lieutenant Chainer mentioned the name of a military base, which is listed in the *Valpian*'s arrays. Their captors were evidently not too concerned about a possible rescue."

"Do we have to watch the Lieutenant's video message again, sir?" joked McLeod. "There're only twenty hours remaining until we get to this planet."

"I think he was trying to provide as much information as possible, soldier. Perhaps he didn't know we'd be under so much pressure when we received it."

"What are we going to find on Invarol?"

"I have no idea," Duggan confessed. "There's more unencrypted chart data in the *Valpian*'s memory arrays, but I lack the knowledge to organise it in the time we have available. Commander McGlashan is good at this sort of thing. Otherwise, the Space Corps has hundreds of personnel who'll be able to look at it once we land."

"We will only have one chance," said Red-Gulos. "After that, our surprise will be gone."

"I know. I feel naked without the stealth modules. They are both a crutch and a game-changer. I'd give anything to have them installed on the *Valpian*. As it is, there're are plenty of things I still don't know about this cruiser. The enemy's eagerness to recover, rather than destroy it, makes me exceptionally curious."

While he talked, he stared at his heavily-bandaged hand. Weiss had injected it with something to restore the dead tissue and she'd used a brutal device to debride the outer layers of dead, cold-blackened skin. The treatment was unpleasant and high doses of painkillers had been necessary to ensure the pain was no worse than a moderate discomfort. It would get better in time, though the colour of the new skin wouldn't match that on his other hand for a good number of months. For the moment, he could use the hand well enough to operate the spaceship. When it came down to it, there wasn't really an alternative.

"Does this mean we're going to come out punching?" asked McLeod.

"We'll have to."

Red-Gulos said something, which the language modules interpreted as a question about a hippopotamus in the vicinity.

Duggan scratched at his stubble in puzzlement before he understood.

"What elephant in the room?" he asked.

"The battleship *Zansturm*," said the Ghost. "It has a habit of arriving when we do not wish to see it. What if her captain guesses where we will go? What if he transmits that information ahead and we find others waiting for us?"

"We've come this far. It's an acceptable risk in the circumstances. The journey is only twenty hours, so it may be the enemy are incapable of getting reinforcements to Invarol before we get there. They have plenty of ships, but a lot of territory to cover. They can't be everywhere at once."

"Which leaves only the *Zansturm*."

"They're no quicker than we are on gravity drives. They may be no quicker on fission engines. If we assume their captain needed some time to collate information, plus some additional time to connect the dots, it may be that we have a head start."

"We get there, kick the shit out of the alien scumbags and then off we go to the wormhole. Easy," said McLeod.

Duggan studied the soldier's face and saw that he genuinely believed it would be as straightforward as he described. "I have to admire your optimism," he said.

"It's served me well, sir."

There were times when a direct approach was best and Duggan was already convinced this was to be one of them. With things more or less under control on the bridge, he called a meeting with the soldiers. They were as laconic as usual, which he took to be a good sign. Certainly, they looked as up for the fight as ever.

"We've got one last place to go," he told them. "The *Crimson*'s crew have been taken to a military facility on a nearby planet. I need them on the bridge if we're to have any hope of getting through the wormhole again. Even if that wasn't the case, I don't abandon anyone."

"A bit more shooting and then back home? Sounds good," said Kidd.

"I somehow doubt it'll be that easy," said Duggan. "The *Valpian* might not have the capability to make it through the Blackstar."

"Anyone can see it's a new ship, sir," said Hendrix.

Duggan smiled. "I didn't want you getting your hopes up prematurely. If this ship is designed for the transit, I have no doubt my crew will be able to get us through."

Afterwards, he said a few words for Byers and hoped the others would be uplifted by her sacrifice rather than becoming melancholy at her death.

When he was done, he set off to find the one person whose absence was easily noticed. He found Lieutenant Ortiz alone in one of the officer's rooms. She was sitting on the bed with her knees drawn up to her chest. She had her spacesuit on, with the helmet placed on the floor. Her dark eyes stared into nothingness for a few moments before she looked across at Duggan. There was hardly any recognition.

"Jess?" he asked.

"Hello, sir," she said with a half-smile.

"We'll be going home soon," he said.

"Will we? That would be nice."

"You've just got to hold it together for a few more days," he said. "The *Valpian*'s fast – real fast. We'll get you fixed up again."

Corporal Weiss entered the room. "I tried to have a word with you after the meeting, sir," she said. "You left before I could catch you."

"Is it about Lieutenant Ortiz?" He'd stripped her rank temporarily but it was hard to refer to her as simply *Ortiz*.

"Yes, sir. I wanted to let you know I've relieved her of all duties."

"I understand."

Ortiz had lost interest in the conversation and she closed her eyes. Duggan led Weiss away.

"Will she get better? If we get her to a base hospital, I mean."

Weiss looked upset. "She's getting worse. The specialists can do wonderful things, but I don't know if they can bring her back from this."

"They had damn well better bring her back," said Duggan. "Thank you, Corporal. Keep an eye on her and let me know if she deteriorates."

"Yes, sir."

The sight of Ortiz reduced to the state she was in left Duggan in a foul mood. This mission through the Helius Blackstar had been one of incredible highs and indescribable lows. He wondered if Admiral Teron had any idea what he was going to put everyone through when he conceived the mission.

Of course he knew and I'll bet he hates himself for it, he thought. Teron was a man who shared in the pain every time he sent someone out to fight. It had taken a while for Duggan to realise it.

He reached the bridge and took his seat. Red-Gulos was nowhere to be seen, though McLeod was at his console.

"Made me feel like a real Space Corps captain for a few minutes there, sir. Being all alone on the bridge. The sergeant said he wanted a couple of hours rest before we arrive. He mentioned something about needing a lot of energy to fire a repeater."

"I need to set up a rota," said Duggan. A Space Corps warship did the administration stuff automatically. The *Valpian* had no such facility Duggan was aware of.

"Not much time left now, sir. We'll be home before you know it."

"I've heard that one before."

The remaining hours passed quickly. Duggan didn't bother to draft in a replacement for Byers – there wasn't the time to train anyone and uncertain hands just slowed things down. He allocated himself five hours for sleep and managed to doze for about half of that. His body was still awash with miraculous cures and stimulants administered by his suit and Corporal Weiss, which made sleep difficult even though his body quite obviously required it. His hand hurt and his forearm ached. In a way, he was grateful for the distraction. The mission was coming to a head and he didn't want to dwell on his worries.

It had taken him long enough to realise he had feelings for Lucy McGlashan and he didn't want to lose an opportunity to change his life and his future by letting her die on an enemy facility. He didn't want to die either, for that matter. The only acceptable outcome from here was to get everyone home without further casualties. It was a long shot and he knew it.

A few hours before their estimated arrival at Invarol, the under-strength crew of three took their posts with the intention of remaining there until they entered local space. Without advance intel, there was little planning to be done and they did their best to learn more about the operation of the *Valpian*. There was no instruction manual and there were some things it was impossible to figure out without formal training – or something to target and shoot at. Duggan noticed Red-Gulos getting frustrated.

"This equipment has been designed so that it is as hard to operate as possible!" the Ghast growled.

"Leave it for the moment, sergeant," said Duggan. "You have done admirably so far, but you can't expect to learn the intricacies of a warship like this one in a day or two. Especially when you lack the background training."

"It is infuriating."

"Do you fellers drink?" asked McLeod. "That's what we do when we get pissed off with something. We get shitfaced."

Duggan had no idea how the language modules coped with that particular delivery. Red-Gulos seemed to get the message.

"We have a variety of poisons to make life easier," the Ghast said with a smile. "And competitions to see who can consume the most."

McLeod shook his head in mock anguish. "We've been fighting for thirty-odd years when really we're exactly the same. Except for you being grey and tall."

"Perhaps we're the same as all Estral?" asked Duggan.

"No," said Red-Gulos. "We are not. You are not."

There was no further elaboration and Duggan didn't push. The Ghasts couldn't possibly have any memories of their parent species, yet the hatred was clearly strong. Whatever the reason for the schism, it had brought about a lasting enmity.

Twenty minutes from Invarol, Duggan checked they were comfortable with the plan. There wasn't much to it.

"The cores on the *Valpian* are fast enough that I feel confident in taking us out of lightspeed very close to the planet. The military facility is known as Dantsvar and if we're lucky, it'll be straight below us when we enter local space. More likely, it'll be someway off around the planet and we'll need to find it before they can get a general alert out. If there are any ground-based threats, we'll neutralise them from the air so that we can deploy our soldiers in safety. It'll be a hard landing and there'll be no time for mercy."

"I'd prefer to be out there with the boys and girls, sir," said McLeod.

"I know, soldier. There are times you have to do what's best and I need you here more than I need you on the ground. Durham knows what he's doing with the comms pack."

"I have no doubts about Corporal Gax," said Red-Gulos.

"Nor I," said Duggan. "I'll speak to him now."

He used the internal comms to reach Corporal Gax. The Ghast confirmed he was in place by the front boarding ramp, along with the rest of the able-bodied. Duggan had spoken at length with his officers about their preferences between a foot assault and attempting to deploy some of the armour from the *Valpian*'s hold. In the end there'd been no genuine choice. The soldiers weren't familiar with the Dreamer armoured vehicles or artillery and they didn't want to attempt their use when they were under so much pressure. That meant Duggan would have to plant them as close as possible to the location of the missing crew.

The problem he tried to avoid thinking about was his uncertainty where McGlashan, Chainer and Breeze were detained. The details they had on the base were sketchy about most things except for the size. It was big and covered many square kilometres. There was a lot of ground to cover when the enemy could have a fleet already in place or somewhere close.

Since abandoning his crew wasn't an option, the only one left was to head in there and see what happened. As the minutes counted down, Duggan's grip on the controls tightened.

CHAPTER TWENTY-FOUR

ONCE AGAIN, the value of punishingly high processing brute force was made apparent when the *Valpian* entered normal space a mere thirty thousand kilometres from the surface of Invarol. Duggan blinked in surprise when he realised how close they were. Since he lacked the knowledge to fine-tune the lightspeed runs on the cruiser, he'd programmed in a command to arrive *as close as possible,* and this was what he ended up with. Given the monumental distances covered by even a short-duration trip at high lightspeed, it was incredible to think the *Valpian*'s AIs had been able to aim so close and get it right.

The planet Invarol wasn't what Duggan expected. He'd assumed they would find themselves somewhere high over a bleak, featureless sphere of grey rock, or, failing that, a planet encased in snow or one surrounded by swirling toxic gases.

In fact, the first impression of Invarol was of lush, verdant forests, covering millions of square kilometres. A jagged mountain range ran across the middle like a scar across an otherwise-beautiful face. There were oceans and deserts, with signs of ice at the two poles.

"It looks like the tales I heard of Old Earth," said McLeod. "Before it went to crap and they tried to fix it."

Duggan wasn't immune to the wonders of the scenery, but he couldn't spare any time to study it.

"We've come in on the wrong side," he said. "I'm taking us around to the Dantsvar facility. Sergeant Red-Gulos, I need to know if there are any hostiles."

"First sweep is a negative, sir," said the Ghast. "I am continuing my search. The air is clean and breathable, the surface conditions highly suitable for life."

The *Valpian* raced towards the planet's horizon as if the two were attached by an immensely strong elastic and it appeared as if the entire world rotated underneath them. There was little in the way of atmosphere so high up and the hull temperature remained low. The only thing which kept Duggan from going faster was a worry he might overshoot or simply miss what he was looking for.

"Sir? That's a city down there," said Red-Gulos. "A very big city – tens or hundreds of millions might live in it."

Duggan had a look. The sensors picked up few of the fine details at the speed they were going. There was enough to see tall, magnificent towers, each decorated in one of a thousand different colours.

"No grey," he said, scarcely believing his own eyes. The architecture looked incredible, even witnessed through the grainy high-speed focus of the sensors.

"There are more," said Red-Gulos. "Amongst the hills and amongst the forests. This side of the planet is home to dozens of cities."

"Aren't we meant to blow them up, sir?" asked McLeod. There was fear in his eyes.

"Do you want to?" asked Duggan.

McLeod didn't speak. He shook his head once.

"Let's stick with military targets for now," said Duggan. "The scope of our mission has changed and we need to make best use of our ammunition."

Neither McLeod or Red-Gulos offered an argument. They were soldiers and had little appetite to drop bombs on millions of unsuspecting civilians, enemy or not.

"There are aircraft in the sky," said Red-Gulos. "Small, non-military craft."

"Ignore them," Duggan replied. "We should be just about on top of the Dantsvar facility."

The forests petered out entirely and were replaced by arid plains which extended for over a thousand kilometres in each direction. It wasn't quite desert, being more of a dry, scrubby land with few trees and rivers.

"There it is!" said Duggan.

"I am scanning the facility," said Red-Gulos. "On the screen."

The base could have been lifted in its entirety from a human or Ghost world and dropped here on the plains. From high up, it was a rectangular grey slab of metal, laid flat on the ground. The majority of the buildings were clustered at the northern end. They were mostly high domes of a type Duggan had seen on one of the Ghasts' worlds. The remainder of the base was given over to dry docks and landing fields. There were vehicles in their hundreds, each heading to wherever it was they would go. Cranes and gantries sprung up from the metal as if they were the ugliest of flowers grown from the least fertile of earth.

When Duggan studied the feeds, he noticed there were huge yellow symbols painted here and there on the ground to indicate the function of each particular section of the base. One of these symbols caught his eye and he almost burst out in laughter at the convenience of it.

"The facility is twenty klicks wide by thirty long," said Red-Gulos, unaware what Duggan had seen. "There are four trenches, two of them occupied with craft larger than ours. The longest trench is eighteen thousand metres."

"What else?" asked Duggan.

"There are smaller craft parked towards the eastern perimeter. Two at twelve hundred metres length and one at fifteen hundred."

"What else?"

"The three smaller vessels are powering up their gravity drives, as well as one of the larger vessels in the nearest dock."

Red-Gulos had learned a lot about operating the comms, yet he wasn't able to interpret and deliver the information quick enough. A good comms man or woman could feed target data into the tactical system quicker than a warship's automated systems could manage it, since the comms officer could zero in on specifics. Without a comms officer onboard, the tactical system would update based on the broadest of sensor data and it could take precious additional seconds.

"There are ten surface-to-air clusters to the north, fully powered up and preparing to launch," said Duggan, watching as the *Valpian*'s AIs populated the threat on its tactical systems. "Six more to the south. I've identified a preferred landing site at the northern end and I'm taking us towards it. First, we're going to give these bastards something to think about."

"The northern clusters have launched, sir," said McLeod. "Four missiles per cluster. High yield from their size."

The *Valpian* was at a height of twenty thousand kilometres – close enough for the inbound missiles to strike them before McLeod was able to properly announce the launch. It mattered little and the warheads exploded against the cruiser's shields. The power gauges skittered left and right before they settled.

There were dozens of targets, each one automatically assigned a priority by the tactical system. The three smaller warships were given the highest priority. Duggan overrode the recommendation – it was the three thousand metre heavy cruiser powering up in the trench he was concerned about. It was on the ground but it wouldn't be there for long. He targeted and sent two hundred missiles towards it.

With rapid jabs of his frost-burned fingertips, he selected the smaller craft and sent them a hundred missiles each.

"The first heavy cruiser has got its energy shield up," said McLeod. "Zero direct strikes on its hull."

"The warship in the second trench has begun warming up its engines," said Red-Gulos. "It will be unable to lift off a short while."

Duggan fired a hundred missiles towards the second heavy cruiser. The *Valpian* was designed to launch in groups of fifty. Against smaller targets it was overkill, whilst against bigger opponents it was a simple and convenient number.

"Whoa look at that!" said McLeod. "Got them!"

Two of the smaller warships were gone – if they'd been equipped with energy shields it made no difference and both vessels were obliterated by the cascade of missiles. One of the warships made it a few kilometres off the airstrip before it was destroyed and pieces of its hull rained down onto the surface, smashing gantries and crushing hundreds of the workers.

"Damnit, we don't want to kill our own," said Duggan.

"We cannot back down, sir," said Red-Gulos.

"I know. It's maximum force or we lose," he replied.

The bridge lights dimmed and gauges jumped frantically. The first heavy cruiser fired three particle beams at the *Valpian*, none of which penetrated its energy shield. Duggan fired both of the *Valpian*'s particle beams in return. The weapons had zero travel time and he saw two huge circles of the enemy's hull light up in white heat. Without warning, a huge explosion ripped through the vessel, centred near to one of the particle beam strikes. The heavy cruiser was split into two parts, one of which was thrown from the docking trench, where it rolled onto its side.

"What the hell?" said McLeod in shock.

"We must have hit one of their ammunition stores," said Duggan. "It's destroyed, so stop looking at it. I need to know about the live targets."

Red-Gulos and McLeod were struggling with the overload of targets and information, so Duggan called up a view of the second heavy cruiser. It had suffered critical damage from dozens of plasma blasts. Its armour plating was ruptured and there were missile craters along its length. Duggan's instant feeling was that it was no longer a threat. He sent another fifty missiles towards it to make certain.

Only a few seconds had elapsed since the beginning of the engagement. The north and south batteries had some type of quick-load mechanism and they fired a constant stream of warheads towards the *Valpian*. The third of the smaller enemy vessels was still operation. At fifteen hundred metres long, it had enough potential to make it a genuine threat and it launched its own salvo of missiles.

"The light cruiser has reached an altitude of fifteen thousand klicks," said Red-Gulos.

"They're firing particle beams at us," said McLeod.

The *Valpian*'s energy shield continued to repel the incoming attacks. The main power gauge dropped to fifty percent and each additional strike pushed it further towards the point at which the shield would shut down.

"Those surface-to-air batteries are real high-powered stuff," said Duggan. "The northern batteries are too close to the buildings for me to risk firing at them."

"We can't let them continue for much longer," said Red-Gulos.

The southern batteries were not protected by their proximity to the populated sector of the base. Duggan sent them a gift of fifty missiles, which landed in a grid pattern amongst the six batteries. The emplacements were heavily fortified and mostly underground. It wasn't enough to prevent their complete and utter destruction by the armour-piercing explosives which dropped upon them. When the blast fires faded all that remained was a series of deep, ragged-edged craters. Secondary explosions followed, setting off yet more of the unspent missiles within the ruined batteries.

"That damned light cruiser is still climbing," said McLeod. "What are they playing at? Looks like they're trying to escape."

"They aren't," said Duggan. "They've probably guessed we're here for something and they're planning to get out of our reach so they can play hit and run."

"They're eighty thousand klicks up."

"Not far enough."

The *Valpian*'s two particle beams were recharged and they flashed on the tactical screen to show they were available. Duggan fired them at the light cruiser, along with a further two hundred missiles. The sensor feed showed the enemy vessel glowing white and orange with a ferocious heat that contrasted savagely with the infinite darkness of space.

"They're trying to activate their fission drives," said Red-Gulos.

"It's too late to change their mind and run," said Duggan grimly. The aliens on the fleeing warship were fellow soldiers, but he had no sympathy left to give them.

The smaller vessel's energy shield had already absorbed a large number of missile blasts. The following two hundred proved too much. Many of the *Valpian*'s warheads exploded a few hundred metres from the light cruiser's hull. Others got through the depleted shield and plunged into the softened outer armour.

The bridge screen went bright enough to make Duggan squint instinctively. The *Valpian*'s tactical system detected hundreds of new objects and assigned each a very low priority. Duggan watched the fiery wreckage for a fraction of a second before he tore his gaze away.

"This is a hard bastard of a warship," said McLeod as if he hardly believed the carnage.

"Ruthlessness and surprise," said Duggan, sending the *Valpian* at high speed towards the northern end of the landing field. It tore through the upper reaches of the atmosphere, until smoke poured away from the superheated nose and left a trail of grey vapour for a thousand kilometres behind. "And a hard bastard of a warship."

With only a few minutes gone by, the Dantsvar base looked completely changed. There were chunks of burning wreckage spread across many kilometres of the metal ground and fires burned in dozens of places. One enormous piece from the first heavy cruiser showed no signs of cooling down, as though a reaction was taking place within the two billion tonne irregular mass of broken engines. There was movement – smaller vehicles raced away in random directions, their drivers sent into a panic by the destruction around them.

"What about the northern batteries, sir?" asked McLeod.

"We have to ignore them," said Duggan. "Once we get low enough they shouldn't be able to target us."

As it happened, his chosen landing place was within three hundred metres of the ground-to-air emplacements. The buildings on the Dantsvar base covered an area of six square kilometres, so there was little hope of guessing where the prisoners might be held. Fortunately, the enemy had made the task of locating the missing crew much easier by painting the word *Detention* on the ground near to one low, flat-roofed building. The bad news was that the missile batteries were only a few metres from the prison's walls. In a way, it made sense to keep *disposable* personnel near to high priority targets like the ground-to-air emplacements.

"Corporal Gax, prepare to disembark," said Duggan.

"Understood."

At an altitude of one hundred kilometres, the missile batteries stopped firing. Duggan dropped the *Valpian* onto the surface as close to the prison building as he dared. He didn't particularly want to damage the landing skids, so he pulled up sharply at the very last moment. The landing wasn't perfect but it was as good as could be expected.

"Corporal Gax, you are cleared to disembark. Bring back our troops."

A light on Duggan's console indicated the forward ramp had disengaged. He accessed the underside sensors in order to watch his squad.

"Sir?" said McLeod. "There's bad news. Four of those missile batteries have started launching again."

"At us?" asked Duggan, realising how stupid the question was.

The tactical screen showed the furthest four of the batteries had begun firing their missiles high into the air. At a height of fifteen thousand kilometres, the warheads twisted in the air and shot downwards, striking the *Valpian*'s shields a few seconds later.

"What the hell are they doing?" asked McLeod. "They've got just as good a chance of killing themselves as us."

"It doesn't look like they care," said Duggan angrily. "I think we're too close for the remaining six emplacements to fire."

"Gax to bridge. We have detected missile fire."

The soldiers had already disembarked and they were spread out beneath the cruiser's hull, evidently reluctant to run out into plasma explosions. Duggan saw they had their space suits on, though they had eschewed the helmets in favour of over-ear communicators. The suit helmets were outstanding pieces of kit, but there were times you preferred to rely on your own eyes and ears. It was full daylight and there was no need for the encumbrance.

"Our energy shield extends over most of the building," said Duggan. "Get in there and get those prisoners! Do it quickly before our shield breaks."

"Yes, sir," said Gax.

The squad ran towards the prison entrance, their rifle barrels pointing ahead. Duggan found himself in a most unfamiliar and unwelcome position. He was reduced to a spectator with no way to influence events as they unfolded. While he drummed his fingers, missiles detonated off the *Valpian*'s energy shield and the status gauge crept slowly towards failure level. He bit his tongue to stop from swearing.

CHAPTER TWENTY-FIVE

FIVE MINUTES PASSED during which the squad entered the building, leaving two standing guard at the door. There was no need to force an entry and the metal double doors simply slid open to let the soldiers pass. It wasn't likely to be so easy when they got further inside.

Once he was sure there was going to be no quick abort on the rescue mission, Duggan raised the boarding ramp halfway up, in case any of the enemy thought they might take their chances at getting onboard. It was a remote chance, but one which was easy enough to prevent.

Duggan kept track of progress by listening in to the open comms channel. The men and women kept it tight and their talk was at a minimum.

"Twenty-five percent on this shield gauge," said McLeod. "They'll need to speed things up."

To Duggan's dismay, the prison was far larger than it appeared. His squad cleared the guards from the top floor and then discovered there were more floors below the ground. The building was in a state of lock-down and many of the doors were sealed. Fortunately, a single plasma grenade was sufficient to burn a hole through most of these barriers. As far as Duggan was aware, Bonner was out of what she called *subtle* explosives. If they came across any heavily reinforced doors, the only choice would be to make a really big bang.

The squad were busy searching the first underground floor when Duggan noticed the front boarding ramp was back in its down position. Then he saw something on the *Valpian*'s underside sensors. This time he made no effort to hold in his swearing and he unleashed a string of expletives. A figure stumbled away from the boarding ramp, her dark hair and features unmistakeable, a rifle held in one hand.

"Is that Lieutenant Ortiz?" asked McLeod.

"Yes," said Duggan through gritted teeth. He checked the live comms links in the area. "She's not carrying a communicator."

Kidd and Havon kept guard on the prison door. Duggan connected to Kidd's earpiece and told her to get Ortiz back onboard immediately. Kidd ran across and there was a series of angry gestures between the two.

"She's lost it, sir," said Kidd. "She's seen Havon and she's calling me a traitor. I think she believes we're still at war with the Ghasts. I can't make her listen to me – it's like she's forgotten what's happened and where we are."

At that moment, Ortiz raised her rifle threateningly. Kidd made a placating gesture and backed off. Duggan closed his eyes.

"Wait there. I'm coming," he said. "Keep her calm."

"Sir?" asked Red-Gulos.

"I have to deal with this," said Duggan. If he couldn't pacify Ortiz, the alternative was unthinkable.

He ran, fast and hard. The passages of the *Valpian* went by in a blur. Even so, he was sure he was going to be too late. He got through the airlock and to the top of the boarding ramp. It was hot outside and warm air filled the space, reminding him of childhood holidays on the coast near his home. There was a flash of exploding plasma against the *Valpian*'s shields, dispelling the memories when they were only half-formed.

Lieutenant Ortiz was on the ground. She looked agitated and kept her rifle aimed towards Kidd's chest. She was muttering, the words too quiet to make out.

"Lieutenant Ortiz!" barked Duggan. "What do you think you are doing?"

She looked up, her eyes vacant. Something flickered behind them in recognition of either Duggan's face or his voice. "Sir?" she said.

"I asked what you are doing, Lieutenant."

"I...I was dealing with..." She was lost and her face twisted in recognition of her own impairment.

"You will stand down and return to the ship."

Her rifle clattered onto the ground, forgotten. A few metres away, Kidd sighed in visible relief.

Ortiz walked obediently up the ramp and stopped in front of Duggan. "Sir?" she repeated.

"Rest. I'll get you home, Lieutenant," he whispered.

Her dark eyes cleared, if only a little. She smiled without speaking.

There was a commotion from the entrance to the building and the first of the soldiers emerged, their faces severe and filled with fury. Duggan's heart fell at the sight.

Glinter came next through the doors, and he carried something over his shoulder. It was the body of a woman, dead or alive, there was no way to see. Rasmussen came after. He had his right arm around the shoulders of another man and helped him through the door. Corporal Gax followed, helping a third prisoner. Duggan couldn't take his eyes off the body over Glinter's shoulder. He tensed the muscles in his jaw to try and keep his face strong.

Lieutenant Ortiz was still by his side. She had a puzzled look on her face as though everything was a mystery to her. Duggan beckoned Kidd across.

"Lieutenant Ortiz, this soldier will help you to your room. Go with her. We're leaving soon."

Glinter reached the boarding ramp.

"Is she alive?" Duggan asked, unsure what he would do if the answer was no.

The Ghost nodded once. "She's hurt. Corporal Weiss has given her a stabiliser."

"Hello, sir," said Chainer. He looked terrible, his face a mess of bruises. His hair hung loose over his face and it appeared as if someone had ripped patches of it from his scalp.

"We're in danger, Frank. I'll get us out of here."

Lieutenant Breeze came next, his eyes were swollen shut and his lips were blue. He stumbled past Duggan without giving any sign of recognition.

As the remainder of the soldiers marched onboard, Weiss appeared out of nowhere. "Their captors were in the process of questioning them," she said. "It wasn't gentle." Her face twisted into a look of hatred. "We killed the bastards."

"Will my crew live?"

"Lieutenants Chainer and Breeze will. I won't know about the commander until I examine her further."

Duggan could have wept at the uncertainty. "They're stubborn bastards. All of them. Did we lose anyone?"

"No. We faced guards, not trained soldiers."

Outside, another series of missile strikes from the ground battery lit up the already bright day.

"Sir, our shield gauge is at five percent," said McLeod over the comms.

"Why didn't you tell me sooner?" Duggan snarled. He took a deep breath. "My apologies. It would have made no difference."

McLeod sounded relieved when he answered. "Okay, sir. Sorry."

Duggan ran. He elbowed his way through the mass of soldiers in the airlock and dashed along the corridor. Tears formed in his eyes from emotions he couldn't identify. He wiped them away and raged in his own mind at the fears which might slow his reactions. There was only a single task to accomplish and that was to escape from this place before the cruiser was destroyed.

He threw himself into his seat, his eyes roving across the updates on his console. *Only one percent on the gauge.*

"Everyone is onboard, sir," said Red-Gulos. "The forward airlock is clear."

Duggan's left hand grabbed the control joystick and he wrenched it back. The gravity engines didn't howl, rather they emitted a sound which was so deep the vibrations were felt several kilometres away. The *Valpian* leapt away from the surface at an appallingly rapid speed, producing a series of deafening sonic booms.

At the same time as the warship hurtled into the sky, Duggan's hand flew across the weapons panel and he fired a wave of fifty missiles into the northern batteries. The emplacements were destroyed and their crews killed with them. The blasts took out a sizeable portion of the prison building. It was likely some of the people – the Estral – inside didn't deserve to die. *Add it to the pile of other things I'm guilty of,* Duggan thought.

"Last wave of theirs in the air," said McLeod.

Duggan stared ahead as he awaited the inevitable. The *Valpian* was at maximum velocity and several thousand kilometres above the planet. The incoming missiles were faster and they closed the gap.

From the corner of his eye, Duggan saw the shield gauge

recover by one single, solitary digit. *Two percent. It has to be enough.*

The missiles collided with the cruiser's energy shield. The gauge dropped immediately to zero and it began flashing at the same time as a warbling alarm went off on the bridge.

"Status?" he asked, hardly daring to believe.

"I'm not sure how to find out, sir," said McLeod.

Duggan looked for himself. "The hull is undamaged. There are no major alerts and we have attained a velocity in excess of two thousand three hundred klicks per second."

"Does that mean we made it?"

"Looks like it. I'm getting us to lightspeed as soon as possible. It'll be a random destination, somewhere far from here."

The fission drives seemed to take an age to reach critical mass, though Duggan was aware it was only his perception of time which was out of kilter. As the timer went below ten seconds, he became convinced something would go wrong – that a Class 1 Neutraliser would appear and shut them down, or the *Valpian's* engines would fail at the very last moment.

None of these things happened. The cruiser disappeared from local space and charged in defiance of physics towards the place Duggan had chosen. The last image he saw was a view of Invarol, zoomed in and sharpened by the *Valpian's* sensors. In that instant, he thought the planet one of the most beautiful things he'd ever seen.

There were several places other than the bridge Duggan would have preferred to be now that their escape was complete. However, it was important that he keep his seat for a period of time to ensure everything remained within its usual operating parameters. It was rare for anything to go wrong on a warship, but the transition to lightspeed was known to produce the occasional fault.

He sat uncomfortably, feeling worry, elation and anguish. His frost-burned hand stung and his forearm ached. The combination of emotions, pain and powerful drugs made him feel nauseous and his body craved the sleep he couldn't partake of for many hours yet.

"You owe me a drink," he said to Red-Gulos.

"I do not owe you a drink," countered the Ghast at once, his grey brow furrowed.

"You bet me we'd find the *Zansturm* at Invarol and we did not."

"I don't recall making any such bet." The Ghast looked absolutely baffled.

"It was a bet in spirit. An implied bet."

Red-Gulos' face lightened. "You are lying to me for the purposes of entertainment!"

"He catches on quickly does the sergeant," said McLeod.

"That he does," Duggan agreed with a chuckle. Sometimes the only escape was through humour.

The joke, poor as it was, only served to delay the inevitable and Duggan counted himself a coward for putting off what needed to be done. He located Corporal Weiss on the internal comms network.

"How are they?" he asked.

"We've only just got here. I'll need some time."

"How long?"

"Give me an hour."

She refused to be drawn further and, though he was desperate for even a hint of McGlashan's condition, Duggan left Weiss to get on with things.

The hour passed with extreme reluctance. After fifty-five minutes, he spoke to Weiss again.

"You'd better get down here, sir," she said.

Duggan did so, as fast as he was able.

CHAPTER TWENTY-SIX

THE INJURED WERE in the *Valpian*'s medical bay and looked after by Corporal Weiss. She wasn't able to use the Dreamers' medical kit, but she was well enough trained to make use of the beds. The bay was undersized considering how many troops the cruiser could hold. It was seven metres along each wall, dimly lit and with a tile effect to the floor and ceiling. The centre of the room was dominated by what Duggan could only think of as a *contraption*. In reality, it was a medical robot – tall, blue, vaguely cylindrical, with bumps and lumps. Spindly arms ending in needles and scalpels protruded from ten separate locations and there were twenty or so monitoring screens to keep track of a patient's wellbeing. It had a tiny gravity motor to allow for movement. When Duggan arrived, it was still.

The medical bay contained eight beds, each of which was situated in an alcove in the wall. The beds were furnished with meagre, easy-wipe mattresses and there were no sheets to be seen. It was cold in the room and smelled more like a mortuary than a hospital. It was a poor place to die and Duggan suppressed a shiver.

Four of the beds were occupied and Duggan walked from one to the next, starting with the closest. Ortiz was in the first bed. Her eyes were closed and her chest rose and fell slowly.

"She's sedated," said Weiss. "I'll keep her like this for as long as necessary."

Duggan couldn't think of anything to say, so he nodded and walked quickly to the next bed. There was a familiar figure on the mattress, with his head propped up by what appeared to be a folded spacesuit.

"You look like you've been through the mill twice and then back again, Frank."

"They were savage bastards, sir. So much for treating your prisoners with respect. They wanted the answers to lots of questions."

"We'll talk about it later."

The next patient was Lieutenant Breeze. His face was a mixture of blacks, blues and reds, with only a few areas where his skin was free of bruising. Much of the swelling had subsided, doubtless as a result of one of Weiss's quick-fix injections, and he had his eyes open. He wasn't a young man but had always been strong and indomitable. He looked older now.

"How are you doing, Bill?"

Lieutenant Breeze's gaze was surprisingly clear and when he spoke, he showed no signs he'd lost his mental faculties.

"I'm doing well. I lost a couple of teeth the Space Corps will need to replace for me. Corporal Weiss says one of my cheekbones was broken too. She's filled me with all sorts of accelerants and I swear I'm more likely to die from having too many injections in places a man should never have things injected. Strangely enough I reckon I could run a two hundred kilometre race and win it. The things they can do with medicine, eh?"

"Get some rest."

Commander McGlashan occupied the final bed. Duggan

wasn't sure if he'd unconsciously left her until last, or if chance alone had been responsible. Certainly, he was filled with dread and the thought of how she might be.

"Lucy?" he asked quietly.

"She can't hear you," said Weiss. "She's sedated as well."

McGlashan's face was unmarked and she was fully dressed. There was no way to see if she'd suffered any physical trauma. She was linked up to a portable medical box by a series of wires and there were four needles in her arm. Her eyes were sunken and ringed with grey.

"What happened?" asked Duggan.

"They injected her with something, sir," croaked Breeze from his bed. "I'm not sure what it was meant to do, but it knocked her out."

"Corporal?" asked Duggan.

"I think they gave her something designed to make her speak freely. Perhaps the drug works differently on humans or perhaps they gave her too much. There are traces of a compound in her body. I don't recognize it, but some of the guys in the Space Corps labs will have a name for it.

"Doesn't the med-box know?"

"It's a portable unit, designed to cope with battlefield injuries. It's not meant to replace an entire medical facility."

"What's it doing to her?"

"It's making a periodic flush of her blood and injecting large doses of synthetic adrenaline."

"Is that the answer to every damned injury? Ever-greater quantities of adrenaline?"

Weiss had heard the anger before and didn't take it personally. "Whatever compound they used on her, it's resistant to the drugs flush. If I had use of some better equipment I could fix this, I'm sure."

Duggan caught the underlying meaning in the words. "Do you mean she's dying?"

Most doctors would have hedged their bets. Weiss wasn't one to shy away from giving her honest assessment. "Yes, I think she's dying. Her organs are failing. I've been able to slow the process but not arrest it entirely."

The strength drained from Duggan's limbs and it became a struggle to remain standing. He didn't want the others to see his weakness and he took a deep, shuddering breath. It wasn't enough and he put out a hand to steady himself.

"Is there anything you can do?" he asked. He waved a hand towards the cylindrical medical robot. "Will this fix her?"

"I've had a look at it," said Weiss. "It works in a completely different way to anything I'm used to. I can likely get it to activate. As far as the treatment goes, you'd be taking a real gamble."

"Is there anything I can do to help? Perhaps one of the Ghosts will know how it functions. They are related to the Dreamers after all."

"I've already asked," she replied. "They know the basics of field medicine and nothing more."

"How long?" he asked, having put off the question for as long as possible.

"Twenty-four hours. Tops."

Duggan worked through the possibilities without having sufficient information to come up with the answer. *Can we reach a medical facility within twenty-four hours?* He'd lost track of how far they were from the Helius Blackstar, but it was definitely many more than twenty-four hours. If they reached the wormhole in time, they'd need to make a cautious approach to try and evade the enemy warships which they were certain to find in the area.

If they somehow managed to make it through to Confederation Space, the *MHL Gargantua* would have the facilities to cure almost anything. Unfortunately, he had no idea if the heavy lifter was going to be where they left it. In addition, the crew on the *Gargantua* weren't going to happily wait for a Dreamer warship to close in on them, so there'd be a time overhead involved with smoothing everything out. If the heavy lifter was gone, Atlantis was several days distant.

No matter how he tried to manipulate the numbers, the answer always came out wrong.

"If we do nothing, she'll die," he said, finally.

"Are you ordering me to try and work the enemy's medical robot?" asked Weiss. There was fear in her blue eyes, as though it was something she had no hope of figuring out.

He nodded slowly. "I need Commander McGlashan alive. We won't get through the wormhole without her."

"Very well," Weiss replied. "I'll see what I can do."

"What about Lieutenant Ortiz?"

"I can keep her stable."

"Don't try anything on her until we return to a Space Corps facility." He attempted a smile. "Unless you figure this robot out well enough that you can act with the utmost confidence."

Her shoulders sagged with the weight of the upcoming task. "I won't push it."

Duggan tried to summon up some humour. "When can I expect these other two layabouts to return to work?"

"Oi!" said Chainer. "I am recovering from near-fatal injuries!"

Breeze was unable to resist. "And caffeine withdrawal."

"As you can see, their physical injuries are merely superficial," said Weiss.

"It didn't feel superficial when they were knocking my teeth out," said Breeze mildly.

"How long?" repeated Duggan.

"I'd prefer they had at least three days to rest," said Weiss.

"Since we're effectively on a battlefield, I can begin preparations to discharge both of them in less than twelve hours."

"Bill, Frank, I need you," said Duggan. "Every step has been uphill since we got here. We're almost at the summit – I can feel it. I can't get us over the top without help."

Chainer coughed, as if to test how much he hurt. "I'll be ready, sir - as soon as Corporal Weiss tells me I can go. I could probably walk unaided by now. I feel stronger after just this single hour we've been here."

Weiss didn't pull punches. "It's an illusion, Lieutenant. You'll feel like total crap once the drugs wear off."

"You'll have to keep me topped up."

"Lieutenant Breeze?" asked Duggan.

"I'm keen to see what the *Valpian* can do, sir. I'll be there as soon as I'm able."

"Good."

Weiss turned her attention to Duggan's injuries. "Do you want me to take a look at your hand and your forearm?"

"No. Thank you. Save your efforts for my crew."

"Very well." Weiss stooped and pulled a tiny box from her medical pack. The box was red and about five centimetres square. A pale blue light flashed intermittently on top. "If the pain returns, press this to your bare flesh and it'll inject you with a few boosters."

Duggan looked at the box suspiciously. He reached out and took it, before he spun around to leave. His eyes caught sight of McGlashan as he did so and he had to walk quickly away to stop anyone seeing his face.

Outside the medical bay, he paused briefly. The clear air of the corridors was a welcome relief from the cold smell of decay. He closed his eyes and locked away all of the distractions that would slow him down. He had a duty to get everyone home and he couldn't fail them because his mind was elsewhere.

Red-Gulos and McLeod were at their seats on the bridge. McLeod was teaching the Ghast how to lie and the two of them seemed at ease. The people who were prone to excess stress generally didn't last too long in the Space Corps.

Duggan took his seat. "We're changing course. I'm entering the coordinates that will lead us to the Helius Blackstar."

"We're definitely going home?"

"As definitely as I can make it."

"Does that mean more fighting? I don't think I'm ready for a full-on engagement with an enemy warship," said McLeod.

"No offense, but I hope to send you back to quarters soon."

McLeod attempted to look hurt and failed miserably. "This seat has only just got warm, sir. I swear these Dreamers have discovered a way to ensure metal retains the cold. And now you want someone else to sit in it?"

"Your work in keeping the seat warm hasn't gone unnoticed," said Duggan. "I'll see you get recognition for it when we reach base."

"Are the rest of the crew going to be okay? And Lieutenant Ortiz?"

"I'm getting Lieutenants Breeze and Chainer back soon. That's enough to relieve you two of your duties. We'll need to wait and see what happens to Commander McGlashan and Lieutenant Ortiz."

"I wish them luck," said Red-Gulos.

"Me too," said Duggan. He updated the navigation console with details of their new destination. One of the *Valpian*'s AIs spent a few moments calculating the travel time. "Seventy-five hours."

He sat and waited. After a few hours, the pain returned to his hand and he was reluctantly forced to use the box Weiss had given him. He felt a sudden, sharp jab and the pain in his damaged flesh faded. His stomach informed him of hunger, so he attempted to get the alien replicators to produce something appetising. He failed and though he craved food, he couldn't bring himself to consume more than a bite or two of the grey paste.

A remote part of his brain wanted sleep, but he knew that if he lay down he would have no chance of drifting off. So, he sat and he waited some more. After eight interminable hours, he contacted the medical bay to see how Weiss was getting on. Her answer regarding Commander McGlashan was noncommittal. With regards to the other two members of the crew, she was more forthcoming.

"I discharged them fifteen minutes ago. Aren't they at the bridge yet?"

"No, not yet."

Duggan's first thought was that one or both of them had collapsed on the short journey between the medical bay and the bridge. He chastised himself for the negative thoughts. *More likely they've got lost or can't walk very fast.* Nevertheless, he stood, meaning to go looking for them. The sound of familiar voices stopped him in his tracks and Chainer stepped onto the bridge, closely followed by Breeze. They looked a mess, but they exchanged jokes as if nothing was amiss.

Both men were dressed in spacesuits and carried trays in one hand and their suit helmets in the other. Chainer's tray was piled high with burgers and perfectly-formed slices of pizza. Clear grease pooled on the surface of the cheese and Duggan's mouth fell open at the sight. Next to the food were two oversized metal cups, with round handles. A black liquid sloshed within. Lieutenant Breeze carried his own tray, similarly burdened with upliftingly calorific products. The smell of coffee and junk food filled the bridge.

"Hello, sir," said Chainer. "Nice looking bridge."

Red-Gulos stood without a word and let Chainer take his place.

"Engines, shields and various other facilities over there," said Duggan, pointing to the far-left pair of seats.

"Wow, look at the power we're outputting!" said Breeze through a mouthful of steak.

Duggan clapped Red-Gulos on the back. It was like hitting a huge side of frozen beef. "Your assistance has been very much appreciated, Sergeant. I'll make sure it gets mentioned in my report. I don't think I'll need you here anymore. There's no chance we'll be able to fool them again by pretending to be something we are not."

"No, sir. They won't fall for our lies next time."

McLeod was already sidling towards the door, evidently eager to get away from these imposed duties.

"Good work, soldier," said Duggan.

"No worries, sir."

Red-Gulos and McLeod left. Breeze and Chainer took their places. For the first time since they'd crashed on Nistrun, Duggan felt they were in with a real shot at escape. There was only one piece missing from the jigsaw and he couldn't stop himself from glancing regularly at the empty seat in front of the main weapons console.

CHAPTER TWENTY-SEVEN

THERE WERE any number of important things to discuss, yet Duggan was unable to prevent himself pursuing what was arguably the least important of all.

"How on earth did you get the replicators to produce steak, burgers and pizza?" he asked. "We've been unable to get anything better than paste."

"It's in the wrist, sir," said Chainer, taking a bite from his second slice of pizza. "We learned one or two things whilst in captivity."

"Show me how," said Duggan.

"We couldn't possibly do that, sir," said Breeze. "We're invalids. Corporal Weiss told us to move as little as possible for the next few days."

"I notice it didn't stop you diverting to the replicator on the way here."

"It was a very short diversion, sir."

"Show me what I need to do. I'll go to the machine and test it out."

"It's not as easy as that. There's a strange swipe-and-press action. I don't really know how to describe it any better."

Duggan gave up. He could tell they were playing games with him and he was tempted to wring their necks, except that he needed them alive.

"Very well," he said ominously. "You can't keep your secrets forever."

"Secrets?" asked Chainer innocently. "I have no time for secrets, sir. There's too much to learn about this new tech here for me to waste time with secrets."

"I've had a go at figuring it out," said Duggan. "It's not much more advanced than the Space Corps' latest gear. I can use most it, just a lot slower than I'd like."

"It's not bad stuff. Their comms transmissions travel faster than ours. Their sensors can't absorb data as quickly as ours, but they can interpret it more easily with this processing power at the backend."

"You're only seeing one of the *Valpian*'s cores," said Duggan. "There are three if you need them."

"Three?" asked Chainer. "We're fast enough already. It's no wonder the enemy keep getting the jump on us if they equip their warships with three cores like this first one. It explains how some of their vessels can pick up the anomalies of the stealth modules."

"The *Valpian* is special," said Duggan. "I'm convinced of it. The enemy have gone out of their way to recover it rather than simply blowing us out of the sky. Some of our capabilities are locked down, so I'm not quite sure what else we have installed."

"We've got three days to find out?" asked Breeze. The damage to his face looked particularly bad in the cool light on the bridge.

"Just short of three days, and I'm not convinced we'll be able to access everything without taking the entire ship to a Space

Corps lab. If we can get through the wormhole, that'll be enough."

"Not quite enough," said Breeze quietly.

"No. Not quite enough." Duggan sighed. "What happened to you? We got Frank's message which didn't answer every question."

"I tried to keep it succinct, sir. I knew you'd be in a hurry."

Duggan bit his tongue. "Tell me what happened."

Chainer opened his mouth, with an expression to indicate he intended to leave out no detail, however small. Breeze got in first.

"About fifty hours after you left for the base on Nistrun I managed to get a small amount of power running into the *Crimson*'s engines. Not enough for lift off, just sufficient to load up a few minor systems. Anyway, this big bastard of a battleship appeared, followed by this even bigger bastard of what we later found out was a Class 1 Neutraliser. We figured they wanted to destroy us so we got a couple of nukes off and Commander McGlashan tried to blow up the *Crimson* to stop them taking the stealth modules. The nukes didn't slow them much and the Neutraliser shut us down."

"We assume it picked us off the surface, sir," continued Chainer. "Next thing we knew, a small army of miserable-faced Dreamers cut their way through the forward hatch and detained us. We were eventually taken off the *Crimson*, but not before I'd overheard a few of their plans and made the recording which I'm glad to see you found."

Breeze took up the tale. "Then they carried us on a smaller warship to that base on Invarol. It was probably one of those vessels you destroyed when you rescued us."

Chainer touched his face gingerly. "We thought we were going on holiday when we first saw Invarol. Instead, there were fists and boots. They weren't very subtle and it was a bit hard to talk to them since our language modules didn't exactly do a good job."

"Did you tell them anything?" asked Duggan carefully. "Admiral Teron will need to know if the enemy has learned something which will affect how we act in the future. I will make it clear you had no choice other than to divulge the information."

"No secrets," said Breeze firmly.

"I told them a pack of lies," said Chainer, smiling at the memory. "They believed me for a while. Otherwise I think they might have killed me before you arrived."

"What about you, sir?" asked Breeze.

Duggan told them what had happened since Nistrun. As he spoke, he asked questions of his own to find out his crew's situation at various points over the last few days. There was little he hadn't already guessed.

"I feel we have accomplished much," said Duggan. "I am only sorry we had to destroy the *Crimson* and with it the data we took from their hub world."

"We've gained so much more," said Breeze. "I'm not just saying that to be optimistic. The *Valpian* is a wonder – I can see as much in the few minutes I've been able to check through these status screens. I don't even need to put on my suit helmet to interpret. Most of this is second nature."

"Gentlemen, we've been doing this for too long," said Duggan.

"I used to dream about comms consoles," said Chainer. "I probably still would if I ever got the chance to sleep."

Breeze laughed, not unkindly. "You need to get out more."

The three of them got to work. With the two experienced men alongside him, Duggan was able to unearth more of the *Valpian*'s intricacies. Red-Gulos and McLeod had naturally required a lot of hand-holding, which prevented Duggan from properly familiarising himself with the Dreamer systems.

They spent eight hours at it and by the end of the time, they were acting smoothly and in unison.

"I feel much more confident now," said Duggan. "I'm certain we'll need to fight our way through the wormhole and I need an experienced crew to manage it."

"When will you hear about Commander McGlashan?" asked Chainer. He was worried and not trying to hide it.

"I don't know," said Duggan. He stood. "I'm going to find out."

A few minutes later, he was in the medical room once more. There was only one significant change since his previous visit – the enormous medical robot had moved slightly towards McGlashan's bed. It hummed slightly and floated a few centimetres above the surface. Three of its thin, metal arms were extended, in order to push thick needles deep into McGlashan's chest. Several of the robot's displays listed information pertaining to the patient, though Duggan couldn't make sense of them.

Corporal Weiss was absent, so Duggan crouched next to McGlashan. Her cheeks were paler than he remembered and her eyes were just as grey. He placed the palm of his hand against her forehead. She felt as cold as the room itself.

"Lucy?" he whispered. "Don't die on me."

She didn't respond and he remained there for minutes or hours, until time itself lost meaning. He couldn't think what to do for the best. This was the one thing he couldn't plan his way out of. There was no illuminating spark of an idea waiting in the wings to make her live. The only thing he could do was sit and watch, hating every second of it. He felt utterly miserable.

Corporal Weiss arrived. She didn't offer a greeting and busied herself checking the medical robot. With a pensive look, she poked one of the screens.

"How is she doing?" asked Duggan.

Weiss didn't answer immediately and she studied several of

the readouts. "I don't know," she said eventually. "I've got this robot working, but I can't be certain what it's up to. I've used the translation modules in my suit helmet." She shrugged. "The enemy names for compounds are entirely different to ours. It means I'm left guessing most of the time."

"Is she still deteriorating?" said Duggan. "You thought she might have twenty-four hours. Sixteen have passed."

"I really don't know. In truth, I'm out of my depth. Show me a man or woman screaming in pain on a barren world somewhere you've never heard of and I'll know what to do. I'll know *exactly* what to do, which is why they sent me with you. I'm trained to fight and to save other soldiers so they can one day fight again."

Duggan saw that Weiss really did care beneath her hard shell. "Do what you can, Corporal."

"I will, sir." She hesitated. "If you can make the transit without Commander McGlashan, I'd recommend you prepare for that eventuality."

They weren't the words Duggan wanted to hear. He kept his head bowed for a few moments longer, before he headed for the exit.

It was time for his break and he headed for one of the replicators. He spent five minutes attempting to copy the gestures Lieutenant Chainer had finally agreed to show him. After the machine disgorged a dozen trays of mush, Duggan gave it a kick and went to look for a room. He passed a few of his squad members on the way and he forced himself to greet them in the manner they expected from their captain.

There was one room available in the officer's area of the *Valpian*. Duggan sat himself on the bed and watched one of the alien videos for a short time. It depicted rows of tanks with elaborately angular hulls scudding easily across the red rocks of an unknown planet. He switched it off. Either the *Valpian*'s databanks had been purposely loaded with only propaganda footage, or the Dreamers were even more warlike than he'd assumed.

Although he felt exhausted, Duggan was convinced he wouldn't sleep. He lay on his side and closed his eyes for a time, expecting the turmoil in his brain to keep him awake until he was driven from the bed. He cursed the human body for its inability to realise what was best for it. Before he knew it, he was asleep. Instead of wandering through terrible nightmares, Duggan's mind remained in a never-ending darkness which he found strangely soothing.

When he opened his eyes, he knew at once he'd overslept. He rolled out of bed, two hours late for his scheduled return to duty. Panic gripped him and he ran to the medical bay, convinced something bad had happened.

When he arrived, Commander McGlashan was exactly where he'd left her. The medical robot had decided to insert a fourth needle, this time into her arm. The metal appendages made it a struggle for Duggan to reach the bedside. He stroked her cheek in the hope there would be signs of warmth. There were none and he returned to the bridge, fully expecting to be admonished by Chainer or Breeze. They didn't bother.

"I hope you slept well, sir," said Breeze without irony. "You deserve it."

"I got you a steak," said Chainer, pointing to Duggan's seat. "It's probably gone cold now."

"Thank you, Lieutenant," said Duggan, picking up the tray. There was half a cow on it, covering a pile of potatoes. It was cold, but Duggan didn't care. "How have you been getting on?" he asked. Before leaving for his break, he'd asked Breeze to figure out a way to get the *Valpian* through the wormhole.

"I think I might have something," said Breeze.

Duggan fixed him with a stare. "Go on."

"Don't get too excited! It's only a theory."

"I'll take anything, Lieutenant. Even a half-cooked guess."

"If I'm correct it'll be good news for us, but distinctly bad news for humanity."

Duggan sighed. "That doesn't surprise me. What have you unearthed?"

"We know the Dreamers have been finding it difficult to get their ships reliably through the wormhole and we've theorised it's because their warships are not as solidly built as our own. We believe they rely on their energy shields for combat and therefore the hulls on their spacecraft are not designed strongly enough to withstand the stresses of the transit."

"We can't be sure any of it is true."

"Of course," Breeze acknowledged. "I believe the *Valpian* is built differently, sir."

"How so?"

"I've found some of the engine schematics. I don't understand everything, but I can see they've made them as solid as you'd find on a Space Corps vessel. In fact, their engines are denser than ours, so the *Valpian* can likely withstand moderately greater pressure than the *Crimson* could tolerate."

"There is plenty of interior space in comparison to the *Crimson*!"

"In percentage terms, there's actually little difference. The size of the *Valpian*'s rear hangar is where my theory falls flat. Anyway, I was kind of talking my way to the real reason, sir. The solidity of the *Valpian* is an indication they were aware of the problem. I think they've cracked it by other means."

Duggan took a guess. "The energy shield?"

"Exactly!" Breeze's eyes glowed as they often did when he got excited about something. "You told me the Dreamers' own particle beams couldn't penetrate the *Valpian*'s shields."

"I didn't know if that was anything new," said Duggan.

"The shields can't block everything, sir. If they had a sufficiently large power supply and enough processing speed to back it up, they could block most things for a short time. I believe the shields on the warships we've encountered so far are designed mainly to block explosives and are incapable of being put to other uses. I think the ones on the *Valpian* can do a whole lot more."

"We're carrying one of those Gallenium rocks," said Duggan. "It's under a hatch elsewhere on the ship."

"Why didn't you tell me? We've got more power than we know what to do with. That rock must be powering the shield."

Breeze was getting carried away with his ideas and Duggan attempted to bring him back on track.

"Will our shield get us through the wormhole?"

"I think so. Not on its own – I believe it will allow us to get close enough to the centre that when we activate our fission drives we'll jump directly through, rather than remaining in enemy space."

"Can you set it up for us?"

"I'm nearly there. It's nothing too technical - the ship has been designed to do most of the work."

Duggan ran his fingers through his hair. "We're not going to have an easy time of it. I'm sure the area will be swarming with enemy warships."

"We're fast. If we can get close enough to the wormhole, we'll jump through. Any missiles on our tail will be crushed at the proximity we're talking about."

"I hope you're right, Lieutenant. We need to get this ship home. Not only for us, but because it'll give the Space Corps and Ghast navies a ten or twenty year research boost. I'm convinced there's more to it than just a good shield as well. They've sent other ships through. Why are they so determined to get the *Valpian* back?"

"I'll keep looking," said Breeze. "If it's a weapons system, we might not find how to access it until the labs can brute force their way into the memory banks, and that will take time."

"Let me know if anything new turns up, Lieutenant."

Duggan tried to get himself comfortable and he readied himself for what he hoped would be the final obstacle to their escape. There were undoubtedly challenges ahead of them and they'd surely be difficult to overcome. If they escaped, the Space Corps would see the mission as a total success. For Duggan, it wasn't so straightforward and he could not envisage any sort of victory in which Commander McGlashan died to achieve it.

He sat, quietly brooding.

CHAPTER TWENTY-EIGHT

MORE THAN A DAY WENT BY, the hours wrung out and stretched until the passing of each one became a cause for minor celebration. Duggan visited McGlashan twice and on the third time found himself shooed away by Corporal Weiss who became impatient with his questions. During these visits, he was able to glean that the conditions of neither Lieutenant Ortiz nor Commander McGlashan had changed. Duggan felt guilty he was unable to do anything other than stare helplessly and with grim amusement he reflected how much McGlashan would admonish him for such stupidity.

He gathered the soldiers in the mess room and explained how they were going to attempt a transit to Confederation space. He expected feigned indifference, only to find human and Ghast alike professing relief at the idea. They'd had enough and needed hope for an end.

After he dismissed the squad, Duggan returned to the bridge. Lieutenant Chainer was nowhere to be found, whilst Lieutenant Breeze was poking around the *Valpian*'s weapons systems. It wasn't exactly his field, but like most experienced officers he'd spent time doing something of everything.

"Their missiles can be set to target either other vessels or incoming missiles," he said. "It's quite ingenious and allows them to carry extra warheads instead of loading up with shock drones or similar."

"I was aware of the facility but I couldn't get it to activate without taking excessive time," said Duggan. "In combat, it seemed better to rely on shields."

"It's another option, sir. Commander McGlashan should be able to make use of it. I notice the shields degrade when they absorb an impact and then slowly recharge. I don't know what will happen if we attempt to go through the wormhole with the shields nearly drained. The result is unlikely to be favourable."

"I'm intrigued by the particle beam," said Duggan. "When we were held in place by the *Antrajis* station, I got the feeling the enemy battleship didn't want to come into particle beam range."

"Maybe they preferred not to trade blows with a ship they wanted to recapture."

"You're probably right. Anyway, the particle beams I fired at the *Antrajis* hangar bay doors were powerful and they were very good against smaller vessels. They couldn't take out a five thousand metre battleship quickly. In fact, they were much less powerful than the ones onboard the Dreamer mothership. I'm probably hoping to find something that isn't there."

"We might find a Planet Breaker, buried away in the hull somewhere."

"I think we've already moved on from that particular weapon, Lieutenant. The Ghasts have incendiaries which can burn entire worlds without destroying the planet. The Space Corps will have the same thing in a year or two, I'm sure. We're back to the same situation we had with the Ghasts – trying to counter the enemy's technological advances while hoping our populated worlds remain hidden."

"Cat and mouse."

"They've got a few warships through the wormhole already. We're running out of time to come up with something."

"Even if the *Valpian* does have an unknown weapon or other capability, the Dreamers built it, so they can surely add it to more ships. They have the resources."

"They don't have the stealth modules. Imagine what the *Valpian* could do if we equipped it with those! We wouldn't need to creep around, hoping for the enemy to overlook us. The stealth tech is the best thing we've come up with in a century, yet it's only a defensive weapon." Duggan felt himself warming to his speech. "Think of what we could do to the bastards if we added the modules to this vessel. We'd have speed, firepower and surprise."

"It would feel like cheating," said Breeze, only half seriously.

Duggan laughed. "It *would* feel like cheating, but you know what? I could live with myself."

"Yes, me too."

They were lost in their thoughts for a moment.

"How long until we reach our destination?" asked Duggan.

Breeze didn't even bother to look at his console. "Eight hours."

"Where's Lieutenant Chainer?"

"Off somewhere, probably drinking coffee or sleeping. He's due back on duty any time now."

Duggan had slept a few hours previously and knew he wouldn't get another chance before they attempted the wormhole. It was bad timing on his part and he hoped he wouldn't be off his peak when the fighting started.

A sound made him turn – someone was coming up the steps leading to the bridge. The footsteps were slow and laboured. A figure appeared in the doorway and spoke, the words soft and quiet.

"Reporting for duty."

"Lucy?" said Duggan, jumping to his feet.

She looked terrible, her skin even paler than usual and her eyes sunken like those of a corpse. She swayed and reached out for the wall to steady herself.

Duggan got there and put his arm about her shoulder to stop her from falling.

"I'm fine," she wheezed. "Just a little weak."

"You should be in bed," said Duggan. "Lieutenant Breeze, speak to Corporal Weiss and find out why she let the commander out of the medical bay!"

McGlashan sagged. "I need to sit."

Duggan half-dragged her to one of the vacant chairs and she fell into it. "You need to rest," he said.

"Corporal Weiss told me we're going to attempt a transit soon. I figured you might need some help."

Duggan took a deep breath. "You're in no fit state to help, Commander."

"My mind is working perfectly," she said, her voice stronger than it had been moments before. "The walk here took it out of me. I'll be fine once I've had a chance to rest."

Corporal Weiss arrived, looking flustered. "Apologies, sir. I didn't know the commander was awake."

"Get her to the medical bay at once."

"Stop!" said McGlashan. "I can do this!"

Duggan studied her face and saw the trembling in her shoulders. "No. You can't."

McGlashan faced him and the anger was evident. "Yes, sir. I can." She took a deep, shuddering breath. "You can't make me sit this one out."

Duggan was rooted to the spot, as though a thousand pairs of eyes watched him carefully to see what his reaction would be. *She blames me*, he thought. *I can deal with that later. I have to do the best for everyone.*

He opened his mouth to give the order for McGlashan to be taken to the medical bay. He found himself speaking different words to those he intended. "Corporal Weiss, I want you to do whatever you can to keep the commander at her station."

"Yes, sir."

"Commander McGlashan? You can stay here and you have approximately eight hours to prove you're up to the task. If you suffer a relapse or if I think you're not physically capable of doing your duty, you go back to the medical bay without argument. Do you understand?"

Her eyes gleamed. "Yes, sir."

"Now damnit, get yourself up to speed with that weapons console. We'll need to be on top of our game if we're to come out of this one alive!"

Weiss hurried away to find supplies. Chainer chose this moment to return from his break. He took his seat without batting an eyelid and took a sip from his coffee.

"Hello, Commander."

"Hello, Lieutenant. Could you get me one of those? My mouth is a little dry."

Chainer sprang up. "Certainly, Commander! I'll be right back!"

"Since when did you start drinking coffee?" asked Breeze.

She shrugged in response and tried to smile. "Who's going to give me the lowdown on how this Dreamer stuff works?"

"I'll do it," said Duggan. He crouched next to her and began giving a crash course on the weapons console. McGlashan smelled strange and sweet – it wasn't entirely pleasant. It was an odour Duggan knew well. He remembered badly-injured soldiers whose breaths had carried the same scent shortly before they died. Duggan heard his voice crack and it was a struggle to resist the urge to wrap his arms around her.

McGlashan said little as he talked. She picked everything up as quickly as ever – she was an astoundingly astute learner. After an hour, she was operating the console smoothly enough and began to ask questions which Duggan couldn't answer easily.

Weiss showed up at some point in the training and plugged McGlashan into a medical box. It bleeped softly and soothingly. Duggan raised a questioning eyebrow and Weiss shrugged in response. The unspoken message was clear: *I have no idea why she's awake. She should probably be dead.*

It wasn't an alternative Duggan wished to contemplate. Therefore, he continued with his teaching, even though McGlashan was already as competent as he.

"I think I know what I'm doing, sir," she said, waving him away. "I've got another six hours to see if I can figure out any of the unknowns."

"What unknowns are these?" asked Chainer. "I only like unknowns when I find out what they are."

"We really need someone to check your brains," said Breeze. "They had a tenuous enough grasp on reality as it was. I dread to think what's happened to them since you took a beating."

Chainer did his best to look affronted and failed completely. "My brains work perfectly."

"We've got two locked down weapons systems and a secondary mode on the front particle beam," said McGlashan. "It's taking some time to figure out how to get access to them, if indeed we can."

"There's got to be a set of disruptors in there somewhere," said Breeze.

"Agreed."

They got on with it. Between them, they could operate the *Valpian* at an acceptable level. After that came the fine-tuning, which could make all the difference where an engagement was decided one way or another by split-second reactions. The fine-tuning came over years and months, rather than hours. Even so, Duggan was happy to have these extra few hours.

Every so often, he watched McGlashan from the corner of his eye. She was sitting in the seat to his left and occasionally closed her eyes as though she was exhausted beyond measure. Once, he noticed her entire body tremble violently and she gripped the edges of her seat to stop from falling. In other circumstances, he would have banned her from working on the bridge until she was able to demonstrate a substantial improvement in her condition. Here, he felt there was no choice other than to give her a chance. A part of him asked if he was treating her differently because of who she was. The question made him uncomfortable and he had no answer.

"Fifteen minutes until we enter local space," said Breeze.

"Is everyone clear on what's expected?"

Three voices responded. "Yes, sir."

"We're on the finest of edges," said Duggan. "If we fall to the wrong side, we'll lose everything we've fought for. All of this crap will have been for absolutely nothing. Those bases we destroyed and that fleet we wiped out won't matter a jot. If we get it right, we'll make a difference and there's nobody can ask more from us."

"Let's get on with it!" said Chainer, looking genuinely keen to throw himself into the fray.

Duggan found McGlashan looking at him with sad eyes. She was recovering from the drugs the enemy had injected her with – it didn't take a doctor to see it. The greyness under her eyes was fading and there was a hint of warmth in her skin.

"Are you ready?" he asked.

"Yes, sir. I won't let us down."

The remaining minutes flowed away like water. The *Valpian*'s three AI cores calculated the length of the journey to within a hundredth of a second. A few gauges flickered gently to indicate the switchover from fission to gravity engines and then they arrived.

CHAPTER TWENTY-NINE

"DO WE HAVE HOSTILE ACTIVITY?" asked Duggan, unable to wait for Chainer to confirm.

"Nothing close up, sir. It won't take me long to complete a wide area scan."

Duggan took the *Valpian* to fifty percent on its gravity engines, since he liked to be moving instead of waiting for the enemy to come to him. The warship responded eagerly as if it were ready for the challenge of what lay ahead.

Chainer called up the feeds from several of the warship's sensors and split them across the central bridge display. There was nothing but emptiness, seemingly an infinity of it, broken only by hints of distant stars. The forward sensor showed their goal – the Helius Blackstar blotted out everything and it was the absence of light which made it faintly visible against the rest of the darkness.

"Ten minutes away," said Breeze.

"No point in hanging around any longer," said Duggan. "We know what we're going to do."

"I've sighted two vessels away to starboard, sir. They're a million klicks away."

"Size? Speed?"

"Small and fast. Only a thousand metres long. I don't think they've detected us."

"Single-core models," said Breeze, already showing pride in the *Valpian*.

"Any others, Lieutenant?"

"Still scanning."

Duggan took the engines to one hundred percent. "I'm bringing us to maximum speed and aiming directly for our target."

"The two smaller vessels know we're here. They've changed course and are coming towards us. They have no hope of an interception before we get a shot at going through the wormhole. They've been joined by a third – this one is three times the volume of the others."

"They're going to be late to the party," said Duggan. "Eight minutes until we're at the Blackstar."

Breeze cleared his throat. "I've activated the energy shield manually, sir. All you have to do is aim for the middle of the wormhole and I'll launch us into it at the right time."

"We have a problem," said Chainer. "There's something much larger heading our way. This one's several klicks in length. It's been keeping close to the wormhole, which made it harder to spot. They're coming directly towards us."

Duggan knew what it was. "The *Zansturm*," he said. "Those bastards keep turning up where they aren't wanted."

"They must have guessed we'd end up here eventually," said Breeze.

"They will definitely intercept us, sir. We have to go by them to reach the wormhole."

"They've locked on," said McGlashan. "Missile launch

detected. A cool eight hundred coming straight at us. That's a good range they've got."

"They've given up trying to recapture the *Valpian*," said Chainer. "There's a fifth vessel here as well, sir. This one's a heavy cruiser by its size."

"I see them," said Breeze. "Well spotted, Lieutenant, they're eight million klicks away. They're warming up for a jump our way."

"This is hotter water than I expected," growled Duggan.

"Want me to return fire at the *Zansturm*, sir?" asked McGlashan. "I can answer with six hundred of our own."

Duggan didn't think it likely they could bring down the battleship's energy shield, but he didn't like to be attacked without giving a response of his own. "Yes, fire everything at the bastards."

"Our first wave is launched. They've fired again," said McGlashan. "At this rate we'll have five waves to contend with by the time we fly past them."

"They can have five of ours as well."

"We'll lose a big chunk of our shield, sir," said Breeze.

"Will we have enough to get through the wormhole?"

"I have no idea. If you want to play it safe, try and preserve as much of the shield as you can."

"In that case, Commander McGlashan, please use our own missiles to thin out their salvo."

"We can't get them all, sir."

"We can get some. Today isn't about fighting, it's about escaping. If we can get away, we'll have won."

"Our second wave of six hundred is away, looking to intercept the enemy inbound. If that's the fastest they can fire, our reload time is significantly shorter than theirs."

"What if we get out of here and they follow us through the wormhole?" asked Chainer suddenly.

"Our lightspeed jump will carry us away from the Blackstar," said Breeze. "If they're able to follow us they might well try it, but the odds of them emerging next to us are exceptionally remote."

"The heavy cruiser has jumped," said Chainer. "And there they are. They've overshot and are a hundred thousand klicks behind us."

"They're attempting to lock on," said McGlashan. "They've fired four hundred."

"We're not going to make it to the wormhole at this rate, let alone get through." said Breeze.

"I've hit the heavy cruiser with our rear particle beam," said McGlashan. "They've retaliated with one of their own."

"Negligible damage to our shield, sir."

"We're faster than them," said Chainer in satisfaction. "Not that it's going to make a difference."

The distance between the *Valpian* and the *Zansturm* decreased at nearly five thousand kilometres per second. Behind, the heavy cruiser gradually dropped away, though it continued to launch missiles in thick waves. McGlashan hit it with the particle beam for a second time and its nose glowed.

"Can we lightspeed jump past the *Zansturm* and then straight through the wormhole?" asked Duggan.

"We can do one jump past them. The trouble is, I don't know how long it'll take until we can fire up the fission drive again."

"The *Crimson* could manage two jumps with one damned core!"

"It was specifically set up to do so, sir. The *Valpian* could probably do the same, just not yet."

The first wave of the heavy cruiser's missiles struck the *Valpian*'s energy shield. Duggan's eye was drawn inexorably to the power gauge as it slid downwards. It was a long way from failure, but there was still a lot to deal with.

"There are two fission signatures across the wormhole from us," said Chainer. "Unidentified ship types."

Breeze laughed bitterly. "We chose a bad time to come."

"There was never going to be a good time, Lieutenant. Those two new ships rule out a short-range lightspeed jump. It's now or never – we've got to hope our shield holds out long enough to get through."

Duggan was beginning to feel like he was backed in a corner and armed only with fists, whilst his enemy closed in with guns and rocket launchers. The first of the *Zansturm*'s missiles met the interceptors from the *Valpian*. Many of the enemy missiles were destroyed, whilst others flew on. The heavy cruiser continued its pursuit and didn't show any signs of letting up with its bombardment, even when third and fourth particle beam strikes melted a vast chunk of its outer plating into a thick liquid.

"Our shield power gauge is at fifty percent of maximum, sir," said Breeze. "We're not going to make it. Do you want me to prepare a jump elsewhere within Dreamer space? We should have enough time before we're destroyed."

Duggan clenched his jaw tightly in frustration. To have come so far and be driven away like this was more than he could cope with. At that moment, McGlashan reminded him what made her such a valuable addition to his crew.

"I think I know what this secondary particle beam function is," she said.

Duggan was taken by surprise. "What?"

"I don't know a better way to put it, but I think it has a short-range overcharge. It can expel a much higher intensity beam."

"How short a range?"

"I don't know, sir. It wasn't available against the heavy cruiser at a hundred thousand klicks."

"Get ready to fire."

With that, Duggan swung the *Valpian* around in a tight circle. The forces exerted on the hull were immense and the metals creaked with the strain. A creeping nausea reached Duggan's stomach before the manoeuvre was complete. Then, he levelled the warship out, this time pointing it directly towards the incoming heavy cruiser.

"They're turning," said Chainer.

"Not quickly enough," said Duggan grimly. "Where's that particle beam?"

"Not available, sir."

"We're at fifty thousand klicks! I could hit them with a golf ball!"

The captain of the heavy cruiser had evidently been told to keep a certain distance from the *Valpian*. The enemy vessel twisted and turned as it attempted to increase the distance between them.

"Forty thousand klicks."

"They've launched missiles!"

"Thirty thousand."

From the corner of his eye, Duggan saw a large, square symbol illuminate orange on the weapons console next to him. McGlashan pressed it at once. The front beam turret made a soft thumping sound, unheard by those on the bridge. An invisible ray shot across the intervening space, linking the *Valpian* with the heavy cruiser for the tiniest fraction of a second.

"The heavy cruiser is....gone," said Chainer.

Duggan watched as a million chunks of overheated metal spread across his tactical display like the dying sparks of a firework. Some of the pieces were several hundred metres in length and Duggan had to change course rapidly in order to avoid the rapidly-expanding cloud of debris.

The death of the heavy cruiser didn't alter the state of the missiles it had launched. Hundreds of warheads smashed into the

Valpian's decaying shield, each punishing impact draining the cruiser's ability to repel further attacks.

"We're still in the shit, sir," said Breeze as another salvo, this time from the *Zansturm*, hit them.

"I'm launching interceptors as quickly as they'll reload," said McGlashan. "They're no more effective than a shock drone."

"Our shield is closing on twenty percent remaining. We'll die if we stay any longer. Sir, we need to get out of here!"

"Bring the fission drive online," said Duggan.

"Yes, sir. I'm selecting a random location, six hours away."

"That's not what I want, Lieutenant. I want you to get us close to the *Zansturm*."

Breeze stuttered for a moment. "That's a tiny jump, sir. Then they'll destroy us."

"No, they won't. We are going to destroy them."

"The front particle beam isn't ready to fire again, sir."

"It'll be ready."

The *Valpian*'s AIs prepared for this shortest of jumps.

"The *Zansturm* knows we're up to something, sir. They're preparing their own engines."

"Whoever they have in charge, he's a wily bastard," said Duggan in grudging admiration. "Do you think they know what we're up to?"

No one wanted to offer a guess. The *Valpian* performed its jump at the same time as the front particle beam overcharge light glowed. The cruiser arrived less than a hundred kilometres away from the enemy battleship – almost close enough for the naked eye to see. McGlashan activated the beam at the same time as the *Zansturm* went to lightspeed.

Duggan had often wondered what would happen if a spaceship were destroyed at the precise moment it went into lightspeed. On this day, he got a partial answer. The battleship disappeared in an immense cloud of energy. It reappeared, at least in part.

"Would you look at that!" said Chainer in wonder.

They saw the result – a trail of white-hot debris stretched for ten million kilometres in a straight line, heading directly away from the Helius Blackstar. The pieces, individually unable to sustain their presence in the chaos field that allowed lightspeed travel, re-entered normal space where they retained a fraction of the velocity they'd attained. Soon, they were so far away it wasn't worth the effort tracking them.

"That wasn't the entire ship," said Chainer confidently.

"They got away?" asked Duggan.

"Part of them got away, sir."

Duggan couldn't bring himself to feel upset that his foe might have escaped. The enemy captain had lost this engagement and Duggan bore him no ill-will.

"There are no further enemy vessels close enough to interfere with our transit, sir," said Chainer.

"Our shield isn't recovering very quickly," added Breeze. "Plus, it'll be a sort while until the fission drives will go for a second time."

"How long until the shields are at full strength?"

"Fifteen minutes if they continue at their current rate of recovery."

Duggan weighed up the options. There were five enemy vessels in the vicinity of the wormhole. The latest two arrivals were heavy cruisers and they were heading towards the *Valpian* at full speed. It felt to Duggan as if this was an opening he couldn't turn down. The enemy were flooding this area with their warships and this might be the last chance there was to return home.

The Helius Blackstar was four minutes away and the *Valpian* sped onwards, heading towards the fathomless depths.

CHAPTER THIRTY

"WE'LL HAVE forty percent of our shields remaining when we reach the outer edges of the wormhole's gravitational field," said Breeze. "We need to get to twenty thousand klicks and then I'll launch."

"The gravity increases exponentially, doesn't it?" asked Chainer nervously. "Can't we go at thirty thousand and have the same result?"

"Twenty thousand is when the ship's cores are programmed to fire," said Breeze. "I haven't had the time to do the calculations, so we'll need to rely on our enemy's mathematicians." He pondered for a moment longer. "In truth, this theoretical stuff is way beyond my grasp of numbers. That's why we'll leave it to the people who've devoted their lives to figuring it out."

Duggan kept a tight grip on the controls, his face impassive. Inside, his brain fought against the calm he tried to impose upon it. *The final moments. Success or failure.* He looked across at McGlashan and found her doing the same to him. He tried to smile and she did likewise. It was a start.

"The gravity is going to affect the hull soon," said Breeze. "I'm assuming the shield mitigates the effect partially or entirely."

"The power level is falling already," said Duggan.

The gauge wobbled and then moved downwards so slightly it was almost imperceptible.

"That's going to happen a lot faster the closer we get."

Chainer took a drink from his ever-present cup of coffee. "We're at a distance of one hundred thousand klicks."

"The shield is dropping – faster now."

"Ninety thousand."

Duggan opened an internal comms channel, realising he'd left his warning far, far too late. "Ladies and gentlemen, prepare yourselves for transit."

"Thirty percent on the shield."

"Seventy thousand."

"Look at how fast we're going!" said Breeze.

Two thousand eight hundred klicks per second.

The shield's energy reserves fell. Where it had begun slowly, it started tumbling at an ever-increasing rate. Duggan fancied he could hear the walls flex under the strain and dismissed it as the workings of his overactive mind.

"Sixty thousand."

"It's going to be tight."

Three thousand four hundred klicks per second.

"Forty thousand."

"We're not going to make it."

"Too late to pull out."

Five thousand klicks per second! Catch us if you can!

"Twenty thousand."

"Shield at zero. Launching."

The *Valpian* went through.

Duggan blinked, his mind suddenly empty. His consciousness fought hard to remind him who he was and the memories came rushing back. The sensation was familiar – he remembered it from the first transit through the wormhole. The feeling of dislocation was milder this time, as though his body was already adapting.

"*Did we make it?*"

He was unsure if he'd spoken the words or merely thought them. He tried again.

"Did we make it?"

"Give me a second," said Chainer thickly.

Duggan looked at the others in turn. McGlashan looked ill and she retched twice. She gave her head a shake and Duggan was relieved to see her visibly recover. Breeze was asleep, as though his brain coped with the inexplicable by shutting down temporarily.

"I need you at your stations!" Duggan said loudly.

"Impatient bastard," muttered Chainer.

Duggan pretended he hadn't heard. "I need a short-range scan, Lieutenant. The enemy are known to be active on both sides of the wormhole."

"I'm on it, sir."

"Then, I want you to send a signal to the Juniper. In fact, send it to every allied spacecraft you can find and let them know we are not to be fired upon. Alert them to the fact this is a prize of war and we wish to return it intact for study."

Breeze woke up and got to work at once, like he'd voluntarily taken a nap and was once more raring to go. "Since Lieutenant Chainer is busy, I can advise you we are two hours away from the wormhole, sir." He grinned. "We made it."

Duggan grinned as well and he felt the weight of a thousand burdens fall away from his shoulders.

"We've got nothing nearby, sir," said Chainer. "In fact, we've come out near to where we left the *MHL Gargantua*. It seems like months ago."

"Have you sent a comms broadcast? We're getting out of here as soon as possible and I don't want to arrive to a warm welcome from our own side."

"I've sent the message, sir. It should get disseminated to our fleet in the coming seconds."

"Very well. Lieutenant Breeze, set a course for Atlantis. This time, we're going to have that holiday."

"Oh crap," said Chainer. The tone of his voice was filled with angry resignation. "The *Excoliar* is half a million klicks to our rear."

"This will damn well not happen again!" said Duggan. "Lieutenant Breeze, give me those fission engines!"

"They're in preparation, sir. The enemy vessel has jumped towards us."

"Now two hundred thousand klicks."

"What I would give to destroy them!" Duggan raged. "Can we fire an overcharged beam at them on their next jump?"

"I'll give it a try, sir," said McGlashan.

Duggan saw the anguish in her face. "I won't let them take you again."

"It's not your choice to make, sir."

The *Excoliar* disappeared for a second time. When it reappeared, it was only a few hundred kilometres away. McGlashan tried to launch missiles and fire the particle beams, to no avail. The lights on the bridge went out, leaving them in darkness.

"Get your suit helmets on," said Duggan. He reached for his torch and flicked the switch.

"No need for that, sir," said Chainer.

The lights came on once more.

"What the hell?"

"Don't get your hopes up. When they did this to the *Crimson*, I discovered I could tap into some residual power. There's not enough to do much useful, but at least we'll be able to see. It's how I was able to make that recording and tweak a few bits of the *Crimson*'s comms systems."

"Can we fire our weapons?"

"We couldn't on the *Crimson*."

"What *can* we do, then?"

"Internal comms. I can probably get you a low-resolution feed from one of the sensors."

"What about a distress signal?"

"I can send one, but it'll be slow and I don't know how far it'll travel."

Duggan was furious. He could hardly believe after what they'd been through, escape was snatched away just when it seemed as if they'd finished the mission.

"Send a distress signal. They need to know the *Excoliar* is here."

"Done." Chainer leaned back and put his hands behind his head.

"What are you doing?" asked Duggan.

"We're stuck, sir. We have to wait to see if they destroy us or send over troops to storm the ship."

"Get me a sensor feed. At least I can look at our enemy while they decide our fate."

An image appeared on the main screen, grainy and out of focus. There was insufficient power to clean the picture up, but Duggan could see enough. The *Excoliar* hadn't changed, nor had he expected it to.

He watched it for a time. A wait of a few seconds was enough to tell him the enemy didn't plan to destroy them. A minute became five and Duggan ordered his troops to suit up and prepare to repel boarders. The *Excoliar* took no further offensive action – it simply remained in place, eight hundred kilometres away from the *Valpian*.

"What are they playing at?" he muttered.

Five minutes became ten and ten minutes became thirty. Duggan couldn't take his eyes away from the screen. The others sat quietly, like the fight was beaten out of them.

"That's a shuttle," said Chainer. "Two shuttles."

"I see four," said Breeze. "Big ones."

"There's a hull-cutter coming after them."

Duggan spoke over the comms. "Sergeant Red-Gulos. Take the men towards the hangar bay with as many explosives as you can carry."

"How many do we face?" asked the Ghast.

The shuttles were big and Duggan tried to guess how many they could carry. "A thousand. Possibly more."

"This is the end of us."

"Yes, Sergeant, this is the end." Duggan picked up his helmet and prepared to leave the bridge. "Let us make it hard for them."

Red-Gulos laughed in response and left the channel in order to ready the squad.

"Get your guns," said Duggan to his crew.

"Yes, it'll feel good to shoot a couple of them," said Breeze.

"You'll shoot fifty, Lieutenant. Don't pretend you can't aim."

"I suppose I'll have a go as well," said Chainer.

"Don't leave me behind," said McGlashan. It was clearly an effort for her to stand and she struggled out of her chair. "I don't like losing, sir."

"Nor me," Duggan said, reaching out for her. She tumbled into his arms and he gave her a hug, noticing how weak and frail she was. "Remember, you've only lost when you can't squeeze the trigger anymore."

"Yeah. Let's get them."

This was the moment Duggan had dreaded all of his life. The moment when every chance at success was taken from him, leaving defeat as the only option. The taste was bitter.

He wasn't sure what made him turn. A change in the intensity of the light perhaps. The sensor feed became even more blurred, as though the residual power which Lieutenant Chainer described was fading rapidly away. The view was still clear enough for him to see the dwindling fires of plasma on the front sphere of the *Excoliar*, the light stark against the blackness of its metal hull.

"Look!" he said.

The others turned in time to see more explosions against the Neutraliser's armour.

"Six! Eight! Twelve!" said Breeze in breathless excitement as he counted them.

"Four more on the central part of the superstructure!" said Chainer.

Duggan rushed across to the central console in order to get a closer look. "They're going to run!" he said. "They've *got* to run!"

The *Excoliar*'s captain was reluctant to give up his catch and he kept the vessel where it was. There was no way to see if the Dreamer vessel was firing weapons of its own. Whatever action it took wasn't enough to prevent another series of detonations against the front sphere.

"Go on!" shouted Breeze. "Piss off!"

The *Excoliar* fled. One moment it was there, the next it vanished, abandoning those on the shuttles to certain death. Without the tools to keep a track of its whereabouts, Duggan had no way of knowing if it had gone to lightspeed or simply performed a short-range hop to take it away from the missiles raining down upon it.

The lights on the command console came on again.

"Get in your seats!" roared Duggan. "Lieutenant Breeze, get us away! Anywhere!"

"Hold!" said Chainer excitedly. "I'm detecting at least ten allied vessels close by, including three Ghast battleships! And I've got an inbound comms message, sir! It's the ES *Maximilian*!"

"Patch it through."

"Captain Duggan?"

"Fleet Admiral Teron."

"We have driven off the enemy vessel, whatever the hell it was. I see you've returned with something of great value."

"Yes, sir, you could say that."

"You don't need to hang around. I'm sending you some coordinates which are in a neutral area of space. We'll need to strip that warship down for tracking beacons before we let it anywhere close to one of our worlds."

"The *Valpian*, sir. It's called the *Valpian*. We've received the coordinates."

"Get on your way, Captain Duggan. I look forward to reading your report."

"It'll be a good one, sir. I promise."

"Things have changed since you left. Good and bad. I'll fill you in when I can."

"We're going to lightspeed in a few seconds. Goodbye, sir."

"Goodbye, John. And welcome home."

"It's good to be back."

The *Valpian*'s fission engines unleashed their energy, pouring it out into the void. The warship disappeared from local space, leaving the fleet of allied vessels far behind. Duggan leaned back, his elation tinged with the faintest sorrow. He had no idea what his future held and for this short time, it didn't matter.

LOOK out for more books in the Survival Wars series, coming soon!

FOLLOW ANTHONY JAMES on Facebook at facebook.com/anthonyjamesauthor

THE SURVIVAL WARS SERIES

1. Crimson Tempest
2. Bane of Worlds
3. Chains of Duty
4. Fires of Oblivion
5. Terminus Gate
6. Guns of the Valpian

Printed in Great Britain
by Amazon